T0284070

"A poignant story of the love between [...] *Amber's Way* is written with tendern[...] Readers who have battled an illness [...] resonate with the cast of endearing characters."

ALICE J. WISLER, award-winning author of *Rain Song* and *Life at Daniel's Place*

"What an amazing and touching story. It captures the essence of a brave little girl and all of the family and friends that surrounded her. Instead of sadness I felt the author captured the beauty of life and how one young child could capture the hearts of so many. A must-read."

PATRICIA TALLUNGAN, President, Children's Neuroblastoma Cancer Foundation, Bloomingdale, Illinois

"My heart was captivated by the delightful personalities and relationships in *Amber's Way*. This remarkable work by author Gloria Galloway had me laughing and then crying as the story portrays the cancer journey of a courageous young girl whose indomitable spirit is an inspiration to everyone who knows her. Unforgettable and highly recommended."

LANA McARA, award winning author of *Shaken but Not Stirred*

"*Amber's Way* is an achingly beautiful story. The profound bond between mother and daughter is palpable. Readers will love the whimsy that Jane Doe brings to the tale. The author's storytelling had me crying, then laughing and wanting to hold my loved ones tight."

JESSICA NOBRIGA, Senior Advisor with Better Place Forests

"*Amber's Way* had me experiencing a rollercoaster of emotions, from laughter to tears, unfolding the poignant tale of a brave young girl navigating the challenges of cancer. The author did a superb job, and it is readily apparent she did her homework. This wonderful book has my wholehearted recommendation."

DEE WALTERS, Author of *Healing the Broken Heart*

Amber's Way

GLORIA GALLOWAY

SelectBooks, Inc.

New York

This edition published by SelectBooks, Inc.
For information address SelectBooks, Inc., New York, New York.

First Edition
ISBN 978-1-59079-556-9

Library of Congress Cataloging-in-Publication Data

Names: Galloway, Gloria Michelle, author.
Title: Amber's way / by Gloria Galloway.
Description: First edition. | New York : SelectBooks, 2024. | Audience:
    Ages 12-14. | Audience: Grades 7-9. | Summary: When four-year-old Amber
    is diagnosed with cancer, she and her mother remain undaunted and create
    joyful lives during her eight-year remission from the illness.
Identifiers: LCCN 2023022029 (print) | LCCN 2023022030 (ebook) | ISBN
    9781590795569 (paperback) | ISBN 9781590795576 (ebook)
Subjects: CYAC: Cancer--Fiction. | Mothers and daughters--Fiction. | Family
    life--Fiction. | BISAC: YOUNG ADULT FICTION / Health & Daily Living /
    Diseases, Illnesses & Injuries | YOUNG ADULT FICTION / Family / General
    (see also headings under Social Themes) | LCGFT: Novels.
Classification: LCC PZ7.1.G3494 Am 2024 (print) | LCC PZ7.1.G3494 (ebook)
    | DDC [Fic]--dc23
LC record available at https://lccn.loc.gov/2023022029
LC ebook record available at https://lccn.loc.gov/2023022030

Book design by Janice Benight

Manufactured in the United States of America
10 9 8 7 6 5 4 3 2 1

To my husband Bob. Forever in my heart.

You always believed in me . . . I did it!

PROLOGUE

Five-year-old Amber Langston lay on her back squinting at the clouds above the thick forest of trees that surrounded her. The funniest cloud looked like the big monkey she saw at the zoo. He had very long toes. They were crooked and folded, one over the other like crossed fingers behind someone's back. Amber knew what that meant; he was up to some monkey business! She laughed and wiggled her own toes, imagining what it would be like to walk on clouds and float across the sky.

She wasn't used to the quiet of Placerville and the house near the woods. Right now she heard only the sound of the wind moving through the trees. There were no bells and buzzers and no one woke her up to take her blood or give her medicine. There were no bright lights all night long, just a little night-light in her bedroom. Best of all, there were no whispers everywhere about her cancer. Now she heard birdsongs floating in the air.

She got up to go back to hostess her tea party with Mr. Fluffle, her beloved teddy, and his family.

She unfolded her napkin and dabbed at Mr. Fluffle's chin before she poured him another cup of herbal tea. Mrs. Fluffle sat across from her husband on the picnic blanket with her arms wrapped around their baby named Junior. Since he showed no interest in the chocolate chip cookie on his plate, she broke off a large piece of the cookie and popped it into her mouth.

"Yummy, Junior. You don't know what you're missing!"

Her mother's voice called from the patio, "Everything all right, honey?"

"Uh-huh. We're just finishing our tea."

"Okay. Holler if you need anything."

Amber was wearing the t-shirt her Auntie Lexi gave her on the magical day when Dr. Beth told her she no longer had cancer. It pictured a warrior fairy with her own likeness. She was happy it still fit. She gained a lot of weight after she left the hospital. She was glad she didn't have to listen to the whispers around the bed about how skinny she was. All of that was over. Now she could enjoy tea parties and trips to the beautiful forest.

The days in the cabin were lazy. She and her mom were still resting a lot. Momma was on the porch swing, dozing again. Today she said they would explore what was beyond the bend in the dirt road. So she was sure Momma wouldn't be mad if she just took a short walk with Junior while she finished her nap.

Amber tiptoed into the kitchen to make a peanut butter sandwich. She wrapped it in a baggie along with two cookies and dropped them into one of her mother's cloth satchel bags. She added two juice boxes and a small blanket for sitting on the ground.

Amber tucked Junior under her arm and quietly walked through the tall grasses next to the cabin. She headed for the dirt road she knew would lead them to the forest. She soon spied a clearing ahead, ablaze with beautiful flowers.

She wasn't sure if it would be okay to pick flowers for her mother, but maybe on their way back she would find some to bring to her.

The grasses were up to her shoulders. It was like being in another world. Butterflies and bees filled the air with their wispy, buzzing sounds as they played musical chairs from flower to flower. Amber watched them fly up and away. She followed them, squeezing Junior's hand so he wouldn't be left behind.

"Don't worry, Baby. You're safe with me. That's what my nurses told me when I was in the hospital—that I was safe in their care. You see? They were right, and they taught me how to do the same for you."

She waded through thicker stalks of spring growth with the fragrance of pollen filling the air. She whispered again to Junior, "I'm all better now. I really am. Come on, let's pick some flowers for my mother and your mommy, too." Soon she spotted what she was looking for: white fairy-lanterns. After picking a handful, she got out the blanket and sat down with Junior to have a drink.

She held the juice box next to his embroidered mouth. "We need to keep up our strength." Junior seemed tired and sleepy, so she didn't force it on him. Instead she saved enough juice for their walk back.

"Are you all right, Baby? You seem a little out of sorts. That's what my momma tells me when I get quiet and moody. Maybe we should rest."

Amber lay down beside Junior, and they were soon asleep. When they woke, she was surprised to see the sun was setting. Dusk was creeping in, and a light rain began to fall. She picked up the blanket and wrapped it around her shoulders.

"You must be cold, Baby. I'll tuck you in under my shirt, and that way we'll both stay warm." Still, she shivered and trembled from the cold. She turned to head back to where she was quite certain the road was. "I think it's this way, down this hill, because we walked uphill to get here. Right, Baby?"

As the evening deepened, she became a little worried that she was headed in the wrong direction, although she was still convinced they should be walking downhill to find their way back.

Every few steps down the hill she stopped to listen. Standing as still as she could, she shouted, "Is anybody there?" But only the rainfall answered, spattering against the leaves.

Amber wondered what her father would do. He had been a brave warrior in a place called Iraq where he took care of wounded soldiers.

It was her turn to be brave, but how could she take care of Junior and herself? She looked around for a sheltering tree. They were all so tall, and their branches were too high. As Amber walked on, scanning the landscape for refuge, she noticed some of the smaller evergreens had cascading branches that surrounded their trunks like big, hooped skirts.

"Come on, Baby. We're going to crawl under here." When she pushed away the piney branches she found the ground was surprisingly dry. It was damp only in a few spots. Layers of dried needles cushioned them. Despite the sheltering branches, she couldn't stop shivering. After she took off her wet clothes and wrapped the thin blanket around them, she decided to spread her clothing on the branches so anyone passing by would see them.

"Don't worry. We'll just wait here until the rain stops."

Amber closed her eyes and listened to the wind and rain. For the first time she was no longer sure they'd find their way back. She kept reminding herself to be strong and whispered *be brave, be brave* under her breath. She took out the peanut butter sandwich she'd packed and offered nibbles to Junior.

"You'll stay warmer with a little food in your belly," she told him, but he had already dozed off, and she, too, felt sleepy.

She was startled awake by the sound of a dog barking. Frightened, she moved deeper under the tree. Then she heard voices calling her name.

The branches suddenly parted as she and Junior were scooped up by strong arms that wrapped them in a big warm blanket.

"Amber?"

She nodded, too tired to speak.

The man shouted over his shoulder, "I've got her!"

"Hi Amber. I'm Deputy Scott, and this furry little guy is Pip. We're both very happy to see you."

Studying her face, he inquired, "Are you hurt, Amber?"

She was too distracted by the sound of a radio nearby to answer him. A woman's voice was repeating that she had been found. The rescuer went to Pip and gave him a treat. She patted Pip's head and praised him again and again. "That's my good boy. You found her. Good dog! Good job!"

The deputy asked again if she was hurt.

She shook her head. Her teeth chattered loudly as she replied, "No. But I'm so cold."

"We'll soon fix that. So this must be Junior. Is he doing okay?"

Surprised by his concern for her teddy, Amber held Junior up for inspection.

Deputy Scott peered at him and nodded. "Your mom told me about your bear family. Junior's mom and dad are going to be happy to see you, too. There's an ambulance nearby. The medics are going to give you a quick checkup."

Amber was sitting in the ambulance, sipping a cup of hot cocoa when a car pulled up. Her mother pushed open the door and rushed toward her. She took her in her arms and held her tight.

Amber felt the shudders of her mom's sobbing and patted her back. She never wanted to make her mother this sad again.

"I'm sorry, Momma. I didn't mean to worry you. I thought about what Daddy would do, and it helped. Sometimes stories about him make me feel like I really know him. I sort of think he was with me."

Her rescuers walked over to the ambulance.

"Momma, this is Deputy Scott. And this is Pip. He found me! And that's Pip's mommy."

Deputy Scott shook hands with her mom and introduced them to Kathy. He said she was Pip's handler.

"I have to say, Mrs. Langston, that your little girl has some savvy outdoors skills. She took cover under the shelter of a Weeping Cypress and was protected from the rain. And she hung her clothing on the branches where they could be easily spotted."

"Thank you! Thank you so much for bringing my baby back safe!"

Amber piped up, "You have to thank Pip too, Momma."

The dog wagged his tail as her mom knelt down and hugged him. "Thank you, Pip. What a smart dog you are."

One of the paramedics closed the ambulance doors and approached them. "Amber seems just fine Mrs. Langston.

But you are welcome to have her checked out further if you have any concerns."

"I don't know what to say other than thank you. I am so grateful to all of you."

Amber gave Pip a final hug before they got into the police car, and her mother wrapped her in a warm coat. As they headed down the road, Amber climbed on her lap.

"I'm all right, Momma."

"I'm so glad you were found unharmed. But you have to promise me you'll never wander off like that again."

Swallowing hard to get the words past the lump in her throat, Amber whispered, "I promise."

They were silent for a few moments before Amber said, "Now I have my own vacation story to tell . . ."

"A vacation story?"

"Yes. When our teacher asks us to tell what we did on our vacation, all I could ever think of were hospital stories."

"Honey, that's all behind you now. No more hospitals."

"I was scared of the woods, Momma. I tried to be brave, but I was really scared."

"Baby, you can be scared and still be brave. Your daddy was in a very scary place. Remember his medal I showed you? He got that for his bravery."

"My daddy was a *hero*."

"Yes, baby. He was a hero."

* * *

Jessica was surprised by how quickly Amber bounced back from her frightening experience. Before allowing herself to be tucked into bed, she announced what she wanted to wear on her first day of kindergarten. Her sulk lasted only a few seconds when Jessica nixed her fairy costume idea.

After Amber fell asleep, Jessica sat in the chair next to her daughter's bed. Although her body screamed for relief, she couldn't bring herself to leave her side. She thought about what had happened when she let her guard down. How close she came to losing her again.

It was some time before she took off her shoes and lifted Amber's covers to climb in beside her. Her daughter's soft breaths lulled her to sleep.

PART I

Beginnings

1

Stanford, California 2004

The irritating ringtone of her Nokia woke Jessica from a sound sleep. She tried to ignore it. When she finally glanced at her watch it was 1:00 a.m. She'd gone to sleep with her head on the open pages of the California Bar prep book. She felt as if her brain was fried from the pressure of trying to write one passing answer. A vague memory of her dream came back to her. *Standing in front of a jury for closing arguments, in the nude . . .*

She snatched up her phone and barked, "This better be life or death important!"

"Brian?"

"Do I sound like a Brian to you? Wrong number!"

"No, wait! Don't hang up. Please?"

She hesitated, oddly aware of welcoming the distraction of some random stranger calling her. He had a Tom Hanks quality to his voice. Really, who could hang up on Tom?

She was wide awake now, and the thought of returning to the workbook was fleeting. Leaving the law books on the desk, she moved to her bed and propped up her pillows. "Do you always call Brian at one in the morning?" she asked in a teasing voice.

"I'm sorry I woke you."

"It's okay, but why not just hang up and call Brian?"

He laughed.

She muttered, "Right, dumb question."

"What's your name?"

"I don't give out personal information to strangers on the phone."

"So, let's get to know each other. I'll start. Daniel S. Langston Junior, E-2, 999999999."

"Is that supposed to be your name, rank, and serial number? You're in the military?"

"Yep. The United States Army. The E-2 stands for Private Second Class, and the nines, well, my serial number's classified."

"Private Langs . . ."

"Call me Danny. Now it's your turn."

Says who? she thought as she asked, "Are you at boot camp?"

"Nope, I graduated boot camp. I'm in my first week of advanced training in Houston, Texas. What color is your hair?"

Thinking it over, she decided her hair color was hardly a state secret. "Some would call it strawberry blond. Are you an only child?"

"Strawberry, my favorite fruit. And no, I have two sisters. Chloe is the oldest. Ginny's in the middle, and I'm the youngest. You?"

"I have my sister, Lexi . . . sort of. I mean, we grew up together in the foster system." Why was she telling this stranger intimate details of her life? The only plausible explanation was sleep-deprivation. She seldom spoke of her private life. It was just that—private.

A voice in her head answered: *because you're bored, lonely, and vulnerable, and he's a nice voice at the end of a telephone line who you're never going to meet.* Lost in her thoughts, she didn't catch what he said next.

"I'm sorry. What did you say?"

"The foster system. That must have been rough."

"It wasn't bad. Lexi and I were lucky. We were in one home until we aged out. We had a roof over our heads, food in our bellies, and clothes on our backs. Howard Grayson, the man who fostered us, was on disability from a job injury. Vera, his wife, was a house frau. We had no illusions about being a real family. The Grayson's took us in because the state paid on our behalf, and they needed the money. But they weren't unkind. Lexi and I became our own version of family. We aren't sisters by blood. We're far more than that. We're sisters of the heart—the best kind."

Remembering those early years brought a lump to her throat. She swallowed hard and sought to lighten the mood. "So, the baby of the family, huh? Did you always want to be in the military?"

"Nope, my first choice was to become a doctor, maybe a gynecologist."

She laughed as he joined in.

"A close second was astronaut. Right up until I discovered there were no toilets on those rocket ships."

"Really?"

"Yeah, really. I was totally disillusioned. Alan Shepard peed his pants the first time out. I'm not kidding. Look it up. The flight was supposed to last fifteen minutes. They didn't think about how long he'd be suited up on the launch pad. And then there was the infamous floating turd incident in 1969."

"You sure know your spaceship history."

"Trauma sticks in your mind. So, what was your teen passion?"

"Reaching puberty."

His laughter filled her ear, and she laughed in response. "I was a late bloomer. At twelve, a group of us thought we were oh so worldly, hanging out in our grunge clothes. We were Kurt Cobain wannabes We decided to latch onto a cause, and Lexi had the bright idea of taking up the banner for women's rights."

"Remember the late '60s when female protestors burned their bras for women's liberation? They used what was called *a freedom trash can*. We even had our own can. We labeled it, 'Equal Pay for Equal Work.' The girls were really into it, enthusiastically waving their bras in the air. That was lucky for me because nobody noticed when I wadded mine up and threw it into the flames."

"You sound like you were quite advanced for your age back then. Are you interested now in meeting a healthy, mature, well-built, fun-loving guy?"

"You'll never know and FYI, your response seems to be from a typical horny male."

"I beg to differ. I am anything but typical. True, I'm a young American male with a healthy set of gonads, but that doesn't define me. My heart is the only organ in my body that'll determine my partner for life. I can promise you that."

"Really? I don't think you owe me any promises. Now I wonder what you consider the best attribute of a woman?" She expected a flippant response—such as big boobs, long legs, thick hair reaching to her knees. His answer surprised her.

"A woman who believes in fairytale endings. What about you?"

"Oh, I can't top that."

He turned serious. "Tell me your name, what's your number?"

"My number should show up on your cell phone."

"I won't get the use of my cell for another week. I'm using an old push-button phone in one of the admin offices on base, and it's a piece of crap. Half the keys stick, including the star key. I'm out on a limb here. I can't sit here all night trying to figure out the number I dialed, I have to get back before I'm missed. Please, I don't want to lose you."

"I'm sorry, Danny . . ."

"Wait! What if I was meant to call this number? What if you're hanging up on our future?"

Jessica hesitated. "I won't pretend I'm not tempted, but I'm a cautious person. How can I be sure you're not a scammer? The internet is full of horror stories."

"I made the news once. How about that?"

"I guess that depends on exactly how you made the news."

"I saved a five-year-old in our neighbor's backyard pool. Bobby snuck out, and his mom found him floating face down. She started screaming and I pulled him out, but he wasn't breathing, so I did mouth-to-mouth resuscitation while she called 911. You can look it up. It's in *The Outlook*, a Portland-based newspaper. We lived in Troutdale. The Stafford family, Bobby Stafford. It happened on March 17, 1997."

"Please look it up."

"I'm sorry, Danny. It's just not in me to form a relationship based on a telephone conversation." Jessica disconnected the call and turned off the bedside light. She yanked the pillow from behind her and gave it a good punch, then lay down and closed her eyes. Her resolve stretched into long minutes before she turned the light back on and picked up her phone. She glared at it, daring it to ring. How difficult could it be for him to figure out the number he dialed? *Impossible,* that's how hard.

His last words played again in her mind. Was he right? Did she hang up on her future? His claim was ridiculous, and with or without him, she had a future planned. If he had dialed the right number, neither of them would know the other existed.

She looked at her mirrored closet door and remembered her eight-year-old self. In one hand she had her favorite doll, resplendent in wedding finery. She recalled that Lexi's dolls were forever in on-again, off-again relationships. Hers were soulmates, and they lived happily ever after.

She smiled, remembering their thrift store toys, always ragged around the edges. Vera often gave her scraps of material and the use of the sewing machine. At an early age, she became skilled at designing and making clothes. Her favorite designs were wedding gowns for her dolls.

Despite her resolve she was curious and brought up the news article on her phone. It read *Local boy, Danny Langston, saves a life.*

Okay, so he hadn't made up his story. Did that mean she owed him a chance? Was he right? Had she hung up on her soulmate? If only she had Dr. Ruth on speed dial . . . wait, she had her own version of the famous therapist. A far better advisor and confidant.

A very irritated Lexi answered after five rings. "This better be good."

Jessica explained her predicament. Lexi remained silent, while Jess pictured her scowl.

"First of all," Lexi asked, "did he send up a red flag on your scam-dar?"

"Not really. He seemed genuine. And he saved his neighbor's five-year-old from drowning when he was fifteen. I read the newspaper article."

"Yeah? Well, Ted Bundy saved some lives, too, when he worked the suicide hot line. Look, it's obvious that man charmed his way past your defenses. So, here's my advice: Put that incredible brain of yours on pause and lead with your heart."

"But—." The phone went dead. So much for solidarity.

Danny answered her callback on the first ring.

"Hi. I'm Jessica Novack, JDW, 362436. Those post-nominal letters after my name: JDW, they stand for Juris Doctorate Wannabe, and the last numbers are my measurements, but not really, because those are classified. You asked what I would want in a partner. Let's see . . . someone who will look at me fifty years later with the same sparkle in his eyes as he did on our wedding day. And why aren't you back in the barracks?"

"I was waiting for your call."

"You're that sure of yourself?"

"No, I don't have some oversized ego. I waited, hoping you'd call back, and you did. For me this is an affirmation of my initial impression of you and me—that somehow, despite what might seem like obstacles, we belong together. I can't explain it, but I feel it. Do you know what I mean?"

The earnestness in his voice was reassuring, but she still felt hesitant. "You haven't met me in person," Jessica answered, "so I'm not sure about your reasoning, but I think the word for it is serendipity."

"Yes, exactly. You believe in happy accidents, right?"

He didn't wait for her to answer. "And another thing, I can promise you the look in my eyes will be the same each and every day for the rest of our lives."

"You can see into the future, too?"

He laughed and then answered, "Theoretically, I'm going with yes."

A week later, Danny began calling her whenever he was free to use his cell. They exchanged childhood stories, their likes, dislikes, and favorites of all types: food, music, movies, and hobbies. For instance, he was a fan of bacon cheeseburgers and fries, a typical meat and potatoes guy. She learned, too, that his sisters and his mother were significant influences. They taught him to respect and admire women. He also took cues from his father, who helped his son grow into a considerate and compassionate man—skills he'd need as a combat medic. It was no shock that his favorite movie was *Top Gun* while she favored romantic comedies like the hit movie she'd just seen, *13 Going on 30* with Jennifer Garner.

As a couple, Jessica thought they broke along typical male/female lines.

* * *

On the tenth week of Danny's training he had a rare weekend pass. As Jessica raced across the Bay Bridge toward the San Francisco airport she wished she had asked him for a photo of himself. She had no idea how she would spot him among the hundreds of travelers.

The passenger window on her '96 VW Golf no longer fully rolled up and was letting in exhaust fumes and the cold ocean breezes. Why hadn't she repaired it ages ago? She wanted to impress Danny, not seem like the typical clueless female. She dodged around a big rig in the middle lane, earning a honk and a finger wave she was pretty sure wasn't a thumbs up.

At least she was on time. She parked with four minutes to spare before Danny's flight landed. Airport security prevented her from greeting him at the gate, so she waited at the foot of the escalators. She knew to look for a man in civies rather than a guy in uniform—all fine but a bit of a disappointment. She would have loved to see him in his uniform.

Various men headed in her direction, many about the right age to be her soldier. A few threw her the full figure gaze and one winked, but they kept on walking. Then she saw him: The ear-to-ear grin, his impossibly handsome features . . . and oh those dimples. He would stand out in any crowd. His toned physique turned heads, although he didn't notice. Clearly, he had eyes only for her.

Danny's duffel bag hit the floor as he wrapped his arms around her, lifting her to her toes. He reluctantly set her down as departing and arriving passengers swirled around them. Hefting his bag once more, he grasped her hand and led her through the crowd to a nearby empty bench.

They didn't speak as they took each other in.

His hand came up to cup her face. "Hi."

Her hand came up to cover his. "Hi."

When they stood beside her car, Jessica glanced at Danny's long legs and winced. "Sorry, I should have rented a car. I wasn't thinking."

"No worries. I'm limber enough these days." He laughed and pulled the lever, shoving the seat to the end of its track, then pulled the second lever to recline the seat so his head would clear. His dimples flashed. "Like I said—limber. My first car when I turned sixteen was a used 1993 Geo Metro. I was at my full height then and felt like a sardine in that tin can of a car."

Jessica suspected it was a little white lie to make her feel better. "A Geo Metro, huh? Then this must feel like old times."

He winked and slid into the passenger seat.

She started the engine, but before she could pull out, Danny reached for her hand. "So, what do you think?"

"About what?"

He pointed at himself, twirling his finger in front of his face. "Do I pass muster?"

Jessica pretended to give it some thought. "Not at all what I imagined," she said, pausing a few seconds for dramatic effect but soon felt sorry when he looked crestfallen. "But everything I hoped for," she hastened to add. Tilting her head, she tucked her hair behind her right ear.

"And me?"

"A vision straight out of my best dream ever. What I love most about you . . . well, there's nothing I don't love about you."

His fingers came up to curl around her chin. She had pictured this moment many times, though never with a car console separating them. Everything faded around her as his thumb traced the outline of her mouth.

He kissed her forehead, and soon the tip of her nose before his mouth settled on hers. His lips were soft, exploratory. Her toes curled in her suddenly too tight shoes. Just as he deepened the kiss, a car alarm blasted nearby.

Even that barely unglued them. Danny finally pulled back and asked, "How about we save this for more comfortable surroundings?"

"Yes, let's."

2

The Fairmont Hotel sat in the middle of San Francisco's Nob Hill District. Jessica's second embarrassing moment came when she pulled the car up to valet parking. Luckily, the attendant looked like he was fresh out of high school and wouldn't care about her ancient mode of transportation. While Danny peeled himself from the car, she discreetly slipped the kid a twenty and was rewarded with a big, toothy grin.

Danny saw to the business of checking in as Jessica admired the grand entrance with its marble floors, columns, and the beautifully ornate ceiling. The lobby was filled with people milling about, but her sister was easy to spot. The pink streak in her hair stood out in any crowd. With all the horror stories on the internet, Jessica had to admit she was glad Lexi insisted on this precaution.

Jessica's nerves surfaced when the valet opened the door onto a large two-bedroom suite.

Danny tipped the man and turned to take her in his arms when the door closed behind him. He lifted her chin and studied her face before he kissed her. She was surprised when he stepped back. It was not what she expected, especially after what happened in the parking garage.

"Jess, you're strung tight as a guy wire. I won't bite. You have my word on it. I don't have plans to ravish you. At least not right now. I want us to know each other, one-on-one. I'm sure of my feelings, and I want you to feel the same." He pulled at his top buttons. "I'm going to shower to get the flight off. Why don't you call your sister? She's got to be bored in that lobby all by herself."

Jessica's gasp of surprise made him smile. "Yeah, Lexi and I had words about your complete lack of common sense. Running off to meet a man you've never laid eyes on. Your sister is one fierce lady. Tell her for me those are some cool boots, and if you still harbor any doubts, I'd be more than happy to put her up in a hotel nearby."

Jessica waited until she heard the water running before she called Lexi.

Lexi answered on the first ring. "I have just one word for you. *Hottie* and *wow*. Okay, two words, but do I need to come up with my mace can?"

"Why didn't you tell me you'd talked to him?"

"Sis, how long have you known me? Did you really think I'd let you run off to meet some guy who for all you know is a serial killer? Take a good look at the internet."

Jessica hated admitting Lexi was right. "Remember the old song by Martha and the Vandellas, 'Love Makes Me Do Foolish things'?" Anyway, Danny said to tell you he likes your boots. He also said that if either of us still has doubts, he'll foot the bill for a hotel room for you."

"Tempting, but no. I'll be heading on home."

"Do you want to drive my car back? I can call down to the lobby."

"No way am I asking valet service to bring that sorry thing around front. It's an embarrassment to the grandeur of this famous hotel. I'll take BART like I planned. Public transit versus your VW Golf? No contest!"

"She might not be pretty, but she's never let me down."

"Yeah, whatever. I'll let you get back to private hottie."

Danny came out of the bedroom dressed in slacks and a blue polo shirt. The word *yummy* came to mind, followed closely by Brad Pitt in *Fight Club* ripped. Jessica found her voice with difficulty. "Are you not allowed to wear your uniform off base?"

He tucked his dog tags inside his shirt before answering. "We *can* wear our uniforms on domestic flights, but we're generally discouraged from doing that." He shrugged. "It stems from the fear of being targeted."

Jessica felt a shiver go up her spine. She'd always known servicemen stationed in war zones faced danger, but here at home?

They sought out the concierge for recommendations on nearby attractions. He handed them some brochures. They'd nearly reached the revolving door when he called Danny back. They spoke for a few minutes and shook hands.

"What was that about?"

Danny smiled. "Franz just wanted to thank me for my service."

Jessica wondered how he knew Danny was a serviceman. She took a good look at him and realized his military bearing was unmistakable. His close-cropped hair, his posture, even his walk screamed soldier.

One brochure touted the Fountain of the Tortoises in the center of Huntington Park. They picked up sandwiches from a local market and headed there first.

The benches facing the fountain were all occupied. An elderly couple rose from one nearby. The woman waved them

over, calling out, "We're just leaving, you can take our seat."
She eyed them as they drew closer. "Newlyweds?"

Danny took Jessica's hand and tucked it under his arm.
"Sadly, no."

"Nearly weds, then."

At Jessica's look of surprise, the woman added, "We were
young and in love once. I know the signs."

The couple walked away holding hands and Danny
leaned over and whispered in her ear, "Picturing us in fifty
or so years?"

She blushed. "Yes."

They ate their lunch and engaged in people-watching,
discovering they shared that affinity. A jogger with a golden
retriever paused to run in place while his dog sniffed and then
anointed the fountain.

Danny smiled and asked. "Do you like dogs?"

"I love dogs."

"Large or small?"

"As cute as they are; I can't picture you with a chihuahua.
What about a border collie or a golden?"

"I could get behind that."

Jessica thought the fountain was even more beautiful up
close. The base was fashioned from pink and white marble
with four bronze youths standing on dolphins. Each seemed
to be reaching out to a tortoise above.

Danny frowned as he looked up at the fountain. "Okay,
the dolphins and turtles seem appropriate, but what's with
the cherubs?"

Jessica laughed, "Well, it *is* a replica of a four-hundred-
year-old fountain in Rome."

"Rome. Okay, sure, that explains it. So, the last time we talked, you were deciding what law specialty you were going to pursue. Are you leaning toward anything?"

"Yes, family law."

"Divorce?" he asked. "That'll keep me in line."

"That's the first thing that comes to mind regarding family law. Divorce, sure. But there's much more to it."

"Like what?"

"There's surrogacy, in-vitro fertilization, adoptions, child welfare. It doesn't take a shrink to figure out my specialty stems from growing up in foster care. Who better to help kids navigate the system?"

Danny nodded. "Exactly. You care and it shows. Kids will respond to that. You're going to be so damn good at it, Jess."

His support meant the world to her. "I think so too."

"Do you plan to go into private practice?"

Jessica nodded. "That's my long-term goal, but I interned last summer for a large firm in Sacramento—Marsden, Walker, Hall, and Associates. Amanda Marsden wants me to join them. I'm close to accepting their offer, but I need a few more details. That said, I'm sure this firm will give me the experience I'll need to go into private practice when I'm ready. What about you? Career military?"

"No. Enlisting was a means to help cover tuition for medical school. I plan to go into pediatrics."

She smiled. "What, not gynecology? You'd have women lining up by the hundreds to have an appointment with you."

A toddler suddenly came into their line of sight, making a run for the fountain before her mother scooped her up.

"How many kids do you figure we'll have?"

Jessica didn't have to think twice about that one. "Lots," she answered.

"I guess you'll do."

"*Oh, really?*"

* * *

.A visit to Grace Cathedral was next. It was described as one of the largest Episcopalian churches in the country. It was also famous for the unique mural collection. They were mostly biblical, along with several murals depicting San Francisco's history, including one of the 1906 earthquake. The stained-glass windows were a surprise. There were portraits of Adam and Eve alongside ones of Albert Einstein and Robert Frost. The views of the city were spectacular from the top of the South Tower. They held hands and wandered the labyrinths, both inside and out.

Back on California Street, they window shopped until Danny noticed the slight faltering as she walked. The man missed nothing.

"You're tuckered out, right? Much as I admire your game spirit, I think we'd better head back to the hotel."

In their room, Danny urged her to rest. "Jess, why don't you stretch out on one the beds? It's a while before we'll have to dress for dinner."

Jessica gave in and did as he suggested. She looked at him over her feet, "You're not tired? You're not going to join me?"

"You're asking a soldier in training if he needs rest? A typical day for me starts at 5:00 a.m. with a physical fitness test. That's a three-mile run in twenty-eight minutes, *plus* a minimum of three pull-ups and fifty crunches in two minutes. So, I'm good. You get some shut-eye, I'll see you in a couple of hours."

Jessica was too tired to protest. She succumbed to sleep minutes after he left the room but woke hours later to the feel of Danny's warm breath against her cheek. She circled his neck with her arms, lifting her face for a kiss.

Danny obliged but then pulled back. "Keep that up, and we'll never make it to dinner."

"Would that be a bad thing?"

"You're killing me." Reluctantly, he disengaged her arms. "Come on. Our dinner reservations are for six-thirty. That gives us just enough time to shower and dress."

In the elevator, Jessica peppered him with questions. "Are the reservations for dinner here in the Fairmont? How did you manage that on such short notice?"

"Not here, but it's a short walk. Franz made the arrangements. His way of thanking me for my service. The sous-chef is his cousin."

"A sous-chef where?"

Danny only smiled.

The man was infuriating. "At least tell me how fancy it is so I know if I've dressed right."

"Best word to describe it is *swanky*."

* * *

Jessica had a pretty good idea where they were headed when they stood at the entrance to the Mark Hopkins Hotel. Her suspicions were confirmed when Danny pushed the button for the nineteenth floor.

"Danny . . . Top of the Mark?

"Yep, sometimes being a serviceman has its perks."

Swanky was more than the right word, and she was so glad Lexi had talked her into wearing her elegant black dress. Although she favored vintage-style clothing, her sister convinced her that this was a night for fireworks, not nostalgia. The lacy black V-neck sheath fell to her knees, but the shorter lining ended at mid-thigh.

Danny gave a soft whistle when she removed her coat. "Nice!"

Warmth suffused her body from head to toe. She never thought of herself as unattractive but viewed Lexi as the dynamic one in their duo. Attraction aside, she felt special in Danny's eyes.

They were seated at a window table with breathtaking views of the Golden Gate Bridge and San Francisco after dark.

Their waiter placed two long menus in front of them, then added a third book-sized menu to the table explaining it was the martini list. He told them the Mark featured over one hundred varieties of the martini.

Luckily, Danny cut to the chase, "What do you recommend?"

"The most popular drink for the ladies is the Golden Gate martini, a chocolate lover's favorite. For the gentlemen it's the restaurant's namesake. It's a straight up, straightforward blend of Ketel One, vermouth, and two olives."

Jessica nodded and Danny ordered for them, "That's one Golden Gate and one Top of the Mark."

The views were spectacular. As promised, her drink was a chocolate lover's dream. Their dinner was beautifully presented and cooked to perfection, but it all paled compared to her feelings about the man seated across from her. She was enthralled with him. And it was clear he felt the same. They held each other's gaze throughout the meal.

How did she get so lucky? Just from a phone call . . . the wrong number, of all things.

* * *

After dinner, they moved to the lounge bar where a pianist played, and a few couples swayed on the dance floor.

Their waiter, Henry, took their drink orders, and when he left, Danny placed his hand over hers. "How am I doing so far? Enjoying yourself?"

"I'll sum it up in one sentence. I'm glad you dialed the wrong number."

Before he could reply, Henry was back with their drinks. He set them on the table and turned to Danny. "May I ask if you're a serviceman?"

Danny ran his fingers through his short-cropped hair and nodded. "Private in the Army."

Henry extended his hand. "Thank you for your service."

Danny shook his hand, and Henry nodded toward the bank of windows. "The Top of the Mark is known for the great views of the city and fine dining, but it's also filled with wartime history. Where you're sitting now is known as the weeper's corner. During World War II, the wives of the servicemen would stand here and watch as their husbands' ships sailed out of the bay headed for war zones in the Pacific."

Jessica turned to look, but the city lights blurred the port. Still, she imagined those women and the heartbreak of watching their men sail off to an uncertain fate. She felt a sudden chill at the thought of Danny being deployed to global hotspots. She quickly pushed those thoughts aside. This was a night for celebration.

Henry pointed out a display case holding various bottles with papers attached to them.

"Before you leave, you'll want to take a look at this. It holds another time-honored tradition here at the Mark. It dates back to WWII when American servicemen brought their dates here for their final drink before leaving their homeland. They would purchase a bottle of liquor and leave it with the bartender so he could offer a free drink to the next member of the military who sat at the bar. The soldiers and sailors would write notes to wrap around their bottle saying who they were and why they bought the bottle. Besides telling their stories, some left small mementos and photos."

"Thanks for sharing the hotel's great history. We'll check out the display."

They sipped their drinks and listened to the music. When Henry came back, Danny glanced at Jessica, who shook her head. He pulled out his wallet, "Just the tab, Henry. Thanks."

Jessica felt tears threaten as they stood looking at the browned and curled notes around the bottles. "I can't help wondering how many made it back."

They stopped by the piano where Danny stuffed some bills in the tip jar.

As if by design, the next song on the pianist's playlist was "I'm in the Mood for Love."

Danny took her hand and led her to the dance floor. "He's playing our song."

Feeling shy, Jessica hesitated, but when he drew her close, she wrapped her arms around his neck and gave into his embrace and the sultry tune.

Danny's lips grazed her ear, and he whispered softly, "You feel good."

Jessica closed her eyes and whispered back, "You do, too."

"Danny?"

"Hmm?"

"You said you wanted me to be sure of my feelings. I'm sure."

He stopped abruptly and took her hand. He led her off the dance floor and headed toward the elevators.

Back at the suite, he slipped off her coat and draped it over the sofa. Then he took her in his arms and kissed her. He paused only long enough to remove the combs from her hair, tossing them next to her coat. He tucked her hair behind her ear and nuzzled her neck, whispering, "You take my breath away. I've heard that in songs and read it in books, but the words never had more meaning for me. I'm in love with you, Jess."

"I've told myself it's too soon," Jessica whispered. "It's crazy, but I can't fight it. I don't want to fight it. I love you, too."

She stepped back and kicked off her heels. Standing in her stocking feet, she reached behind and struggled for the zipper but gave up and put her arms around his neck, "Your room or mine?"

She felt his smile against her forehead. "Mine's closer."

✳ ✳ ✳

Jessica woke up feeling euphoric. Faint traces of Danny's aftershave lingered, but the man himself was missing. Her disappointment quickly gave way when she heard him answer the door. Room service, she hoped. She grabbed a hotel robe and twisted her hair into a top knot.

Danny was dressed in a sleeveless t-shirt and jeans. Tight jeans. She focused on the cup of coffee he poured for her. Caffeine—she told herself that was what her body craved.

"Hey sleepyhead. You're just in time. Wasn't sure what you liked, so I kinda winged it." He lifted the lids on several plates to reveal bacon, sausage, eggs, and toast piled high. Another plate held four different varieties of fruit.

Jessica groaned. "I guess the one thing we've never talked about is our morning eating habits. I usually grab a piece of fruit on the way out the door. It's a no muss, no fuss kind of breakfast."

She watched in amazement as Danny piled his plate high with something from every serving dish. She glanced down at her meager fare. Fruit, two slices of bacon, and a single triangle of wheat toast. She stabbed a strawberry and pointed it at him.

"What?" A forkful of dripping pancake was halfway to his mouth.

"How do you do that? How can you eat that much and look that fit?"

He ducked his head and flashed the dimples. "Great metabolism."

"Not fair."

"Yeah, I get that a lot. Especially from my sisters. So, what would you like to do today?

"Check out time is 11:00 a.m. I don't think we'll have time for much."

"Not so. Our room service waiter said the front desk will hold our bags till we're ready for them. My flight doesn't leave till 5:00. We have plenty of time. So, what's your pleasure?"

He flashed his dimples and Jessica slapped his arm playfully.

"Okay. Other than me, what's your pleasure?"

"How do you feel about flea markets?"

"I don't know any guy who doesn't like used car parts and tools they have no use for."

"For real? Or are you just humoring me?"

"Lady, I'd enjoy watching grass grow with you. I'm kind of partial to bluegrass music. But I'm old school: I prefer vinyl. Some of my best finds came from flea markets. There's one particular album I'd like to get my hands on, *Texas Flood* by Stevie Ray Vaughn, circa 1983. You can help me look."

"What got you into bluegrass and record collecting?"

"My dad. He still has the record player from his college dorm room. It's his prize possession. He got me into bluegrass music as well. I have fond memories of recording mixed tapes together. We took them everywhere, even on our fishing excursions. We never caught anything worth keeping. Likely because the fish weren't into our music. Didn't bother us at all. Dad hated cleaning fish, and I hated hooking worms."

"Well, if you're sure, I'd love to help you look for that album."

An hour later they were strolling along Ninth Avenue with the booths lined along every bit of open roadway.

They held hands as they wandered through the vendor stalls. Danny encouraged her at every turn and seemed to take pleasure in her delight at the wares to be found.

They laughed when they came upon a booth selling old used car parts but moved on without stopping.

The next one offered vintage clothing, and one mannequin stopped Jessica in her tracks. It displayed a cream silk blouse with a tatted lace bodice. The hand beaded detail was exquisite.

"I just put that out this morning," the woman behind the counter commented. "Vintage 1900s. It would look lovely on you. Would you like to try it on?" Without waiting for an answer, she began undoing the buttons.

Danny gently nudged her. "You heard the lady."

She modeled it for him. The look in his eyes and his low whistle made the decision for her.

They left the booth with her new treasure tucked under her arm. "Okay, I've got my find. Now it's your turn. Rather than wandering around aimlessly, why don't we ask someone if there's a record booth?"

A passerby heard her and stopped. "You won't find a vendor like that here, but there's an old record store called Off the Charts Music a couple of blocks past 10th street. Head toward Golden Gate Park; you can't miss it."

The shop was enormous. Danny's eyes lit up when they walked through the doors. Posters hung from the rafters and soft rock played over the store's sound system.

"Smell that? There's no denying the scent of old records— laminated cardboard and plastic wrap. Brings back memories."

Jessica wrinkled her nose, "Yes, I definitely smell it. Carboard and plastic wrap with just a hint of fast food." She found it oddly inviting.

Danny headed straight for the blue grass section and began flipping through the albums. A store employee wandered over. Jessica estimated him to be in his mid-sixties. His clothing and ponytail gave off a definite hippie vibe. She liked his peace sign T shirt.

"Need help finding something?"

"*Texas Flood . . .*"

"Stevie Ray Vaughn. *Sweet.* I haven't seen that one around. Might have better luck finding it through a collector."

"Yeah, I might. But I'd miss the thrill of the hunt."

"I hear ya, man."

Jessica wasn't surprised by his peace sign gesture before turning away to help another customer.

They continued to browse but came away empty-handed. After stopping to treat themselves to ice cream, they headed back to the hotel.

Back at the hotel, they stood in the lobby as they waited for the car to be brought around. Time had flown by so quickly. Jessica fought back tears as Danny put his arm around her shoulders.

As if sensing her thoughts, he tried to reassure her. "It's only eight weeks. I'll be back before you know it. Now smile for me. I want to take the memory of your beautiful smile for my dreams..."

* * *

Jessica pulled into the curbside drop-off outside his terminal. She got out and came around the car as he pulled his duffel out of the back seat. She meant to be brave; she was determined not to cry. Right up until he crushed her in his arms, raining kisses all over her face. Who was she kidding? The waterworks came full force.

"Don't cry, Jess. Ah, God. Don't cry. It'll be all right, I promise."

She nodded but only clung harder.

Danny finally stepped back and held her at arm's length. "This isn't over, not by a long shot. I love you, and I'll be back."

"I love you too."

He was almost at the doors when he dropped his bag and rushed back to her for one more embrace. Then he was gone just as quickly.

She watched until he disappeared at the top of the escalator.

*   *   *

Four weeks later, Jessica's phone woke her from a sound sleep. She swore softly and thought it better not be a telemarketer.

"Sorry I woke you."

Her heart leapt at the sound of Danny's voice.

"Are you decent?"

"Danny, I am *not* sending half-dressed pictures out on the World Wide Web."

"Good to hear. But I'm drawing a crowd out here in the hallway. Throw something on and open the door, would ya?"

Jessica was glad her go-to sleepwear consisted of shorts and a t-shirt. She flew across the room to the door and flung it open. She would have jumped into his arms if he hadn't been holding a giant bouquet of roses.

Paying no mind to the neighbors who'd gathered, she snatched the flowers and tossed them on the sofa. Grabbing his arm, she pulled him inside and slammed the door. Then she leapt into his arms, raining kisses all over his face.

It was a long time before she took a breath and found her voice.

"What . . . how—? Did you go AWOL?"

"Nope. The Sarge okayed it."

"Really? So, he's an old softy after all?"

"He doesn't have a sentimental bone in his body. First, he put me on latrine duty for the next four weeks. Then he kicked me out of his office."

"Then how did you manage to—?"

"I strongly suspect the Missus Sarge had a hand in it. Don't get too excited, it's a one-day pass. I'm expected back in time for my 5:00 a.m. roll call."

Another thought occurred to her. "How did you know where . . .? Oh, from Lexi, of course."

Reaching over the back of the sofa, she retrieved the bouquet. "I'd better find a vase for these. They're beautiful, Danny."

In the small kitchen, she dug under the sink for her one and only flower vase. When she turned to grab the scissors from the knife block she found herself staring open-mouthed at Danny who was kneeling in front of her refrigerator. He held a small velvet jewelry box in his hand.

"Will you marry me?"

At that moment she knew he was everything she'd imagined him to be. She looked into his eyes and knew she'd found home. Her answer came easily. "Oh, yes."

She expected a whoop of joy. Instead, he stood and slipped the ring on her finger. Then he bent his head and kissed the palm of her hand. The simple gesture took her breath away.

Later, lying in bed with her head on his chest, Jessica held up her hand and admired the ring on her finger. It was a stunning vintage piece. Yellow gold, in the design of a starburst.

Danny kissed her forehead. "It belonged to my grandmother Rose. My dad's mother. She passed away last year and willed it to me."

"Oh, Danny. I'm so sorry."

"Yeah, me too. But she lived a full and wonderful life and went peacefully in her sleep with all her faculties intact. That was important to her. She couldn't bear the thought of losing her memories. I'm pretty sure she's smiling down on me right now. She would have loved you."

"I wish I'd had the chance to meet her."

After a few moments, Danny's good humor was back. "So, how do you feel about short engagements?"

"How short?"

"Four weeks?"

"I've always wanted to be a June bride." She realized he'd been holding his breath when he let it out in a rush. "You know, never in my wildest imaginings, did I see myself being proposed to between my fridge and the kitchen sink."

"I'll bet you never dreamed you'd meet your future husband on a phone line either. Jess, nothing about our court-ship has been conventional. Think of how much fun we're going to have telling our kids and our grandkids that story."

3

In early May Jessica was at a table in the Stanford law library surrounded by reference books. The July Bar exam loomed, and she was getting in as much study time as she could cram into the remaining eight weeks. Lexi's voice interrupted her thoughts.

"Pack up your stuff. We need to get going."

Jessica sighed and threw down her pencil. "Where is it I'm supposed to be going?"

"That wedding dress shop on Channing Avenue called Mementos I've been telling you about. Your wedding is only a month away. Remember? The shop specializes in authentic vintage gowns. You're going to love it, I promise. The owner is looking forward to our appointment."

Jessica resigned herself to the interruption, knowing it was useless to argue with her sister.

"Fine." She slammed her books into her backpack, then into the trunk of Lexi's car. "Let's get this done as fast as possible. But you know, the wedding isn't a Ritz-Carlton affair. It will be in his parents' backyard. I could just wear that white suit and get a silk blouse off the rack to go with it."

"Are you kidding? Really? Not while there's breath in my body! You're talking about your high school graduation suit? Lucky for you the grad gown covered it up. Never mind all those wedding dresses I watched you make for your dolls."

"Lexi, it's vintage. You know I love things with history."

"Honey, it was ugly then, and it's ugly now."

Mementos Bridal was sandwiched between a barbershop and a bookstore on Channing Avenue, just a few miles from the campus. Jessica was hooked the second she gazed through the storefront window. A mannequin wearing a sequined 1920s Gatsby flapper dress stood in front of a panel with a Great Gatsby movie poster pinned to it. The display evoked memories of the Jazz Age and the Roaring Twenties. She loved the Fitzgerald novel, and she loved the dresses of that era even more. Sadly, they weren't designed with her figure in mind.

The bell chimed when they opened the door. A woman looked up from behind a large glass display. She smiled and nodded.

"Lexi, I'm so glad to have you back. And you must be Jessica. I'm Lois Hughes. I understand you're looking for a vintage wedding dress. You've come to the right place. Just let me finish up here and then we'll have a look-see."

Lois Hughes was *a mix* of the quintessential grandmother with sparkling eyes and reading glasses hanging from a lanyard around her neck. She dressed her pleasantly plump figure in style—no house dresses for this lady. Her perfectly tailored slacks were topped by a foam green silk blouse accented by a paisley scarf. Jessica knew she was in good hands.

After closing her jewelry display cabinet, Lois led them to a far corner of the shop. The wall was flanked by mirrors, and a tall dress rack stood in front. She offered them tea and scones.

Jessica remembered the lone apple she'd eaten for breakfast and answered for herself and Lexi, "We'd love some, thank you."

"I'll be right back."

"Now that's service," Lexi whispered.

The three of them discussed dresses while sipping tea and enjoying the delicious scones. Jessica expected to be led back to pick through a rack of dresses, so she was surprised when Lois remained seated.

"I do things a little differently than you're probably used to in department stores. My stock is very fragile. The dresses are not vintage style, but actual period pieces. Your sister told me stories of you as young children and how you used to pour over wedding dress patterns and fabric."

Jessica shot Lexi the evil eye before turning self-consciously back to Lois. "I liked making wedding dresses for my dolls. Just silly kid stuff, you know?"

Lois leaned forward. "Not at all. Every bride-to-be I've ever met has planned her wedding from a very young age. So, let's talk about what you have in mind. Full length or tea length gown?"

"Tea length. The ceremony is going to be in my future in-laws' backyard."

"What about material—lace or satin? I'm thinking taffeta or tulle aren't contenders. A-line or full skirt with a petticoat? And what kind of neckline would you prefer?"

"Definitely no taffeta or tulle. I'm leaning toward straight or A-line, but I'm not opposed to a full skirt. I don't like anything up high on my neck. I love the flapper dresses like the one in the shop window, but they don't suit my figure."

Lois nodded and rose. "It's so much easier when a client knows her body. I do have some dresses I think you might like."

Lexi reached for another scone, then drew her hand back. "Better not, I'm the maid of honor, and it won't take much to size out of the black leather skirt I've set aside for the ceremony."

Jessica knew her sister was only kidding, but Lexi's whole body oozed attitude, from the pink streak in her hair to the black lace up platform boots she favored. She wouldn't put it past her to defy tradition by strolling down the aisle in black leather. She flashed her sister the look.

Lexi ducked her head. "Just kidding. Lois helped me narrow my choices."

"You've already shopped for dresses?" Why didn't you tell me? I want to see."

"Uh-uh. You first."

Lois returned with three dresses, but she needn't have bothered. One look at the ivory swing dress had her gasping in delight. Beautiful lace overlaid the gown, forming a classic V-neckline and extending to the long sleeves. She stepped up to take a closer look. She ran her fingers across the fabric almost reverently and smiled at Lexi.

Lois led her to a large screened-off area, showed her how the dress zipped on the side and how to hook up the accompanying petticoat. "I'll go wait with your sister for the grand reveal, though do call out if you need help."

As perfect as it appeared on the rack, Jessica was enthralled with her image in the mirror. The skirt belled out beautifully at the bottom, making her waist look tiny. She clapped her hands over her mouth and twirled around. Once, twice. She shimmied and would have added another twirl if Lexi hadn't called out impatiently.

"Hey, I'm dying out here. How about sharing the moment?"

Jessica stepped out, and both women smiled and nodded.

She saw the tears well in her sister's eyes and knew this was the one.

Jessica fingered the bow on the satin belt around her waist. She looked at Lexi. "It's perfect, isn't it?"

"Oh, yeah," Lexi agreed.

Lois nodded and opened a small box she had on her lap. "I've got the perfect veil for that dress."

"I was just going to put a sprig of baby's breath in my hair . . ."

"This will change your mind." Lois stood and attached the piece before Jessica could say more. Lexi came up beside her, gave her a brilliant smile, and turned her to face the mirror.

Jessica ran her fingers over the netting, her voice barely above a whisper. "You're right, it's perfect."

Lois fussed a little more with the placement and then stepped back. "It's a blusher veil, a simpler version of the birdcage. I like to think of it as the peek-a-boo look."

* * *

A June bride. Cliché or not, it was Jessica's favorite time of year. After a brief stop at the Portland airport hotel, they were on the road to Troutdale, Danny's hometown. Her mother-in-law had insisted on hosting the rehearsal dinner. Jessica would have protested, but Danny assured her Ellen was happy to do this for them. Plus, it was being catered, further easing her mind.

The Langston home, just outside Troutdale, was on the western edge of the Columbia River Highway, a twelve-mile drive from Portland.

Jessica tried to tamp down her nerves on the drive. Danny reached over and put his hand over hers. "It's okay. My parents already love you. The rest of the family will, too. I promise."

"That reminds me. I want to apologize to them."

Danny searched her face before returning his gaze to the road. "What are you apologizing for?"

"That they were forced to make the trip to the bay area to meet me."

"Jess, you were in the middle of prepping for the Bar. They completely understood. Besides, with Dad's busy schedule and the grandkids, they don't get much time to themselves. It was a romantic getaway for them."

Jessica leaned over and kissed his cheek. "Thanks."

"Get a room." This came from Lexi in the back seat.

A large archway marked the city's entrance. It read: Troutdale, Gateway to the Gorge.

Lexi laughed and said, "Troutdale, huh. Wonder how it got its name?"

Jessica spoke up before Danny could comment. "Oh, I read up on that . . ."

"Of course, you did," Lexi mumbled.

Ignoring her sister, Jessica explained, "The town's name came from a former sea captain named John Harlow. He was a prominent businessman—"

Lexi interrupted again. "Aren't they always?"

"Do you want to know how the town was named or not?" Lexi held up her hands in surrender. "A prominent businessman built a country home by the Sandy River. Apparently, he had trout ponds on his farm. Ergo, Troutdale. Cool, huh?"

Danny stopped the car, ending the discussion.

Jessica's eyes widened in delight at the site of Danny's childhood home. A Folk Victorian farmhouse.

"Close your mouth, Sis. You're embarrassing yourself," Lexi quipped before stepping out of the car.

Danny laughed as he led them up the wide steps, "You two wear a man out. It's like watching a tennis match, the way you volley barbs back and forth."

Jessica smiled at her sister. They might not see eye to eye on all things, but they did when it counted.

Danny's sister, Ginny, met them at the door. Jessica knew this only because he'd mentioned she was in the family way. He hadn't used the word enormous, though. Her petite frame probably had a lot to do with that. But she was also eight months along.

Ginny favored her mom. Her round, heart-shaped face was fresh-scrubbed, and her long brown hair was done-up in a messy, relaxed braid. Jessica sensed a great friendship coming up.

Ginny was all smiles. She looked at them and then at her stomach. "Sorry, not much of a hugger these days. Come in. Mom's busy badgering the caterers. She said to bring you back; she wants to say hi. Fair warning, she'll likely boot you out right after. Join us in the library. We're all holed up in there trying to stay out of her way. When she's on a tear, it's best to keep clear."

They found Ellen out on the back patio directing the table setup. Jessica thought again how youthful she appeared. She was sixty-one. If not for the beautiful silver hair, her age would be difficult to pinpoint. As she came around the table Jessica admired the heels she wore. She could spot a pair of Jimmy Choo's a mile off. Ellen's slim ankles peered out under chic cropped pants. Comfort *and* style, Jessica thought.

Ellen set a napkin on the back of a chair and pulled her in for a long affectionate hug and then stepped back to search her face. "Jess, it's so good to see you again. I wanted to thank you for that lovely dinner. With a name like The Stinking Rose, I was a bit suspicious, but the food and atmosphere were everything you promised. I still can't believe Daniel talked me into trying garlic ice cream. I meant to send you a thank-you card, but time got away from me."

Ellen surprised Lexi when she hugged her just as fiercely. "Lexi, I've heard so much about you."

Before Lexi could respond, Ellen waved them away, "Now, go join the others in the library. Shouldn't be more than another thirty minutes until dinner."

Daniel Sr. stood when they entered the library. His eyes lit up at the sight of his son. Seeing them side-by-side, the resemblance really stood out to Jessica. They were nearly the same height and had the same brown eyes. Gentle was the word that came to mind. A thick silver mane told her Danny would not go prematurely bald. The deep bond between father and son came across in Danny's many conversations about his family. Here was proof.

Daniel came forward. Jessica put out her hand, but he took her in his arms instead. "It's so good to see you again. Welcome to the family."

To Lexi's relief, Daniel simply took her hand and said, "Lexi, it's so nice to finally meet you."

Chloe, the eldest, was tall like her brother and father and a little more reserved. No hug, but she offered Jessica her hand and a peck on the cheek. "It's nice to meet you, Jessica. Danny's told us so much about you."

Danny's older sister was gorgeous. While his mother and Ginny would best be described as wholesome and pretty, Chloe's features were fine-boned and elegant. Danny had mentioned she favored her grandmother, Rose. Jessica ran her thumb over her engagement ring and wished again that she could have had the opportunity to meet her.

Chloe's husband Warren was GQ handsome. He was in real estate and had been top agent the last three years running.

Jessica knew her sister would have something to say about that.

As they walked further into the room, Lexi whispered, "He can give me an estimate of my property any time."

And there it was. Jessica only smiled.

Ginny introduced her husband Bill, a Prince Harry redhead with twinkling eyes that, according to Danny, bespoke a mischievous nature. Jessica sympathized with his pale skin and abundance of freckles. Although her freckles were less pronounced, she suffered the same aversion to sunlight.

Last, but certainly not least, came Brian, the best man whom Danny described as the perennial frat boy. The full beard and shoulder-length hair added to that image. He was tall and barrel-chested. Jessica soon found herself lifted off her feet in a bear hug, a fate poor Lexi suffered as well.

Mercifully, dinner was called soon after, and they all headed for the backyard.

Ellen had outdone herself. The table was decorated beautifully with a gold table runner, and each place setting had a folded napkin in the shape of a swan. The showstopper, though, was the table canopy strung with twinkling lights and bountiful garlands decorated in an array of fresh flowers.

Jessica was overwhelmed. Her knees were shaking as Danny led her to the chairs decorated with gold sashes. A small plaque hung from the seat backs. One read Husband-to-Be, the other read Bride-in-Waiting.

Danny pulled out her chair and kissed her on the cheek before sitting beside her. Jessica leaned over and whispered in his ear, "You're right, your mother is a natural at this."

The Columbia River Pearl Oyster House catered the dinner. As Jessica read the small menu cards, she was in awe at the sheer bounty of the five-course meal. It started with grilled scallops wrapped in prosciutto. Ellen chose spinach and lemon soup for the second course to keep it on the lighter side. Jessica nearly laughed at that. Caesar salad was next, followed by oysters on the half-shell.

She eyed the oysters with bewilderment. Luckily Danny took pity on her and showed her how to use the tiny fork to move the oyster around, then slurp it from the wide end.

When she still looked uncertain, he pretended to kiss her cheek and whispered, "Just suck it down, don't bite it. The texture is off-putting for some."

No one was going to call her a wuss. She gamely did as he instructed and then bit into it. She resisted the urge to spit it out. Claiming she was too full to eat another bite, she urged her remaining oysters on Danny.

The final course was a raspberry mousse, and for Jessica it was the perfect antidote to raw oysters. She finished hers and half of Danny's as well.

Daniel clinked his glass with a fork and cleared his throat. "I'm not much for speeches. I hope you won't mind if I don't stand up. I'm more comfortable seated."

Jessica nodded. Danny called out, "Wouldn't have it any other way, Dad."

His father cleared his throat again. "I taught my son how to ride his first bike and how to toss his first football. He's an ace at wheelies. Since he's in the Army and not the NFL,

I'd say I wasn't quite as successful at teaching sports." He reached for Ellen's hand. "As for navigating the roads of a good union . . . I can only hope we set a good example."

That had everybody teary-eyed.

Brian lightened the mood, "I can best describe Danny as a scrawny kid. I was always a sucker for the underdog, so I appointed myself his protector. Look at him now. He can take me down with one arm tied behind his back. As for his taste in women, I'd say he knows how to pick 'em!"

Loud laughter rang out. Danny grabbed Brian by the shoulder and playfully ground his fist into his chin.

The stories grew funnier and bawdier as the night progressed. There was little doubt that the free-flowing champagne added to the hilarity.

* * *

Jessica and Lexi took a taxi back to their hotel. When they'd changed into their pjs, they laid down on the beds facing each other.

Lexi yawned and smiled at Jessica. "That's a good family you're joining, Sis."

"Yeah, I lucked out. They are great. I'm glad I answered that phone. Danny's the best thing that ever happened to me. Speaking of which, Brian couldn't take his eyes off you all night."

Lexi choked back a laugh and got the hiccups, a frequent nuisance brought on by drinking too much. She held her breath, but to no avail.

Laughing, Jessica handed her sister a glass of water, and refilled it twice before the hiccups subsided. Lexi threw herself back on the bed and covered her face. "Brian? Seriously? Forget it. I am so not into younger men."

"I'm pretty sure he's our age."

"Let me put it another way. I am so not into men who never grew up."

Lexi had little patience when it came to men and relationships. Jessica would give him one day before he'd be shark bait in her sister's hands.

"Yeah, he is kinda like a big kid. So, what was with you and Chloe sneaking off together?"

"Nothing sneaky about it. I noticed her eyes crossing when you and Danny's mom started talking architecture. We retreated before sheer boredom set in."

"It refers to an architectural style. The homes are kind of plain, but the trim is really decora—"

Lexi plugged her ears. "Read my lips. I. Don't. Care."

"Okay, fine, but I still want to know what you talked about."

"Oh, this and that."

Her refusal to elaborate spoke volumes. "Lexi, what did—"

"Basically, she asked if you were as goody two-shoes as you seemed. I told her you are. Annoyingly so."

"Thanks a lot, but that revelation didn't take a half-hour. What else?"

"She talked about how it was being Danny's sister growing up. I talked about how it was being your sister. You know, the usual . . . if you break his heart, you'll have to answer to her. If he breaks your heart, he'll answer to me."

"Well, neither of you will have to worry about that."

"Yeah, I got that. By the way, what's in the box Ginny gave you?"

Jessica laughed. "She put together an album of family recipes. Before you say anything, I didn't have the heart to tell her the only culinary chops I possess are whether I'll be eating toaster waffles or toaster strudel for breakfast."

The alcohol she'd consumed soon put Lexi into a deep sleep. Jessica slept fitfully; her mind filled with thoughts of her coming wedding day. She finally gave up around seven. Piling the pillows behind her back, she reached for her journal, the one she started the morning after *the call*. She smiled as she read her entry from that day.

Thumbing through pages of musings, she paused at the last one. Her vows.

The first line made her smile and imagining Danny's reaction prompted a giggle. She stopped mid-laugh, but it was too late.

Lexi opened one eye and scowled at her. "Give me one good reason why I shouldn't kill you."

"It's my wedding day?"

"Give me another."

"You won't get to wear that gorgeous maid of honor dress. Go back to sleep, I promise I'll be quiet."

"Yeah, like that's going to happen. At least put the coffee on. Are there any donuts left?"

"There's one. You go ahead. I don't think I'll be able to keep anything down."

They sat at the small table in the hotel room. Jessica drank tea while Lexi enjoyed every crumb of the chocolate fudge donut.

4

The ceremony was a small, intimate affair. Jessica felt tears threaten when Ellen handed her the bouquet she'd fashioned from the flowers in her garden. Ellen wrapped the bouquet with a vintage handkerchief that had been beautifully embroidered by Danny's grandmother, Rose.

Breaking with tradition, Lexi and Jessica walked up the aisle arm in arm. Lexi carried a smaller bouquet of the same flowers and was resplendent in the flapper dress from the Mementos display window.

Danny's nephews were ring bearers. Ginny's son Bill Jr., aged six, carried Danny's ring while Chloe's eight-year-old son Michael, carried Jessica's.

Danny had asked to choose the music for the wedding. It was a small ask and one less thing she had to worry about. She was surprised when the traditional "Here Comes the Bride" came over the speakers. She was certain he would pick "The Band Played On" given his obsession with strawberry curls.

Danny's eyes shined as she came to the end of the aisle and handed Lexi her bouquet. She remembered back to their first conversation when he said she could be hanging up on their future. She did see her future in his eyes, and more. She saw the promise of forever.

The music ended as the minister gazed at them, smiling in the midst of their enchantment with one another. He raised his arms and then lowered them to indicate everyone should be seated.

"Welcome all to this wonderful ceremony as Danny and Jessica pledge their lives to one another. But first I would like to share with all of you a few comments on the union these two young people are about to embark upon."

"A happy and successful marriage is not something that simply happens. Falling in love is the easy part. The foundations of a fulfilling and long-lasting marriage are constructed in a series of small steps. They include cultivating good humor, accommodation, and a willingness from each partner to be flexible. These are the cornerstones to a successful partnership, and they involve sacrifice, work, resilience, compassion, and forgiveness, with an emphasis on forgiveness. Jessica and Danny, you each will make mistakes; you each will annoy one another and even hurt one another on occasion. This is what we humans do."

"The antidote is always the same: compassion and forgiveness. It is the wise spouse who never lets the sun set with anger in the air. Be kind and open to one another. Compromise when you can and yes, sometimes when it might feel more like a sacrifice to do so. One-upmanship, keeping score, or demanding accountability regarding the minutiae of day-to-day life is energy wasted and love denied. Cultivate openness and generosity in each day of your lives going forward and in doing so, you indeed will live the dream of happily ever after. With this guidance offered, we will now hear your vows."

Jessica began with a catch in her voice as she held back tears, "Danny, I'm so glad I didn't hang up on our future. I do believe in fairytale endings, thanks to you. I love you. On

this, our wedding day, I pledge to you the rest of my life." She slipped the simple gold band onto his finger and then raised his hand, touching the ring with her lips.

She watched him struggle with his emotions. He swallowed hard, then smiled. "Well, technically speaking, you did hang up on me."

They heard surprised laughter behind them. When it died down, Danny continued, "I'll be forever grateful that you called me back. I made a promise to you then, and I make that same promise now. The look in my eyes will remain the same every day of our married lives. I love you, and I pledge to *you* the rest of my life." He slipped the ring on her finger, then lifted her hand to his lips and sealed their union by kissing her ring finger, the palm of her hand, and finally her lips.

The minister chuckled, "Well, the kiss usually comes after I pronounce the couple man and wife, but I'll make an exception this once. Danny, Jessica . . . I now pronounce you man and wife."

The women of the Langston family might have had a hand in picking the music for the processional, but the music blasting out of the speakers for the walk back down the aisle was all Danny: "Signed, Sealed, Delivered."

Only her husband could get away with doing the funky chicken to a Stevie Wonder song. Jessica was quick to get into the groove of it. Their guests joined in the fun. Every wedding has its funny moments and Jessica knew this video would be shared and laughed over for years to come.

The festivities were soon under way. The food was sumptuous, catered once again by the seafood restaurant. Jessica suspected someone had a word with the caterer about the oysters since they hadn't made a second appearance. Despite that, she had little appetite. Every fiber of her being was attuned to the man seated beside her—her husband.

The meal ended and the toasts began. Traditionally, the father of the groom would be the first to raise his glass. But Brian rose and, clearly tipsy, grasped the chairback to steady himself.

"Hi everyone. For those of you who don't know me, I'm Brian. I have the honor of being the groom's best friend. I'm here to toast this deliriously happy couple and to toast myself as well. Why would I toast myself, you ask? Well, I also have the great distinction of being the hero in this love story. After all, Danny was trying to call me when he made the wrong call and got the right connection. We've known each other since first grade when I took him under my wing. I felt sorry for the dude. He was the object of some serious bullying. My advice, maybe not the best, was to tell him the next time he got goosed he should turn the other cheek. Yeah, you get the picture. He didn't get goosed anymore, but he was the butt of a lot of jokes after that." The room erupted with laughter.

He waited for the room to quiet again before continuing. "Let's raise our glasses to the happy couple and wish them many years of wedded bliss!"

Lexi was next. "Thanks, Brian, you're going to be a hard act to follow."

Laughter rippled again.

Lexi took a big swig of her champagne before setting the glass back on the table. "I've known Jess since I was four years old. We're not blood sisters. Jess, being the more poetic one, came up with a name for that. We're sisters of the heart. I say that's the best kind."

Danny clapped, and the rest of the room followed suit.

Lexi cleared her throat. "We've always had each other's back. Always. We might fight, like sisters are prone to do, but just let anyone else hurt her, and they'll answer to me." She pointed a finger at Danny. "You'd do well to remember that, Mr. Langston."

Danny held up his hands in self-defense.

"In all seriousness, I know my sister could not have made a better match. If you look up *soulmates* in the dictionary the definition will read Jess and Danny."

Lexi raised her glass high, with a teary smile, but it was empty. Brian poured some of his bubbly into it. "So, here's to the bride and groom!"

Danny pulled Jess to her feet, leading her to the dance floor. The music began, and there it was: a Guy Lombardo version of "The Band Played On," the 1895 song about a suitor named Casey and the girl he married with the strawberry curls.

Jessica whispered against his ear, "You might need serious therapy."

Danny whispered, "Why's that?"

"You have an obsession with strawberry curls."

"And proud of it. I can picture our little girl—my dimples, your eyes, my sense of humor, and your beautiful strawberry curls."

"What if our firstborn is a boy?"

"Hey, Kenny G rocks the do, and I'd expect no less of our son."

"Okay, Okay. You win. I don't stand a chance in a war of words with you. But Kenny is *not* on our list of boy's names."

When the song ended Brian began chanting "garter toss, garter toss!" Jessica was grateful that Danny chose to remove the garter with his hands and not his teeth. Exposing her leg was embarrassing enough. Brian made certain he caught it, of course. She figured it had more to do with the win than for the good luck it was said to bring.

Next came the bouquet toss. Jessica knew Lexi would avoid the catch at all costs, so she pretended to turn her back before whipping back around and pitching it directly at her sister. Lexi was startled into catching the bouquet. She sent her a murderous look, but Jessica only smiled.

Near midnight, as the festivities continued unabated, Danny pulled Jessica aside. "What say we ditch out?"

The music was loud and the dancing frenetic. Jessica glanced at the crowded dance floor and saw Lexi and Brian. They appeared to be doing little more than holding each other up. Who would have thought . . .?

When she nodded, Danny grabbed her hand and led her toward the front door where their luggage waited. As expected, there was also a long string of cans tied to the back bumper of the car.

While Jessica was contemplating what they were going to do about the noise makers, a Yellow Cab pulled up alongside the curb. Danny opened the door and bowed at the waist. "Your chariot awaits."

At her look of surprise, he added, "It had nothing to do with the racket and everything to do with avoiding a DUI, or worse."

The driver loaded the luggage, and they were on their way.

Jessica glanced back at their car which blocked the driveway. "Wait. What about the keys, how will they move the car?"

"I slipped Dad the keys and told him the plan."

The cabbie glanced at them in the rearview. "Newlyweds. Congratulations. Where's the honeymoon?"

"The Big Island of Hawaii," they answered in unison, then laughed.

The cabbie grinned. "Nice."

Danny's attempt to carry her over the threshold of the hotel doorway nearly landed them both on the floor. While he retrieved their suitcases from the hallway, Jessica moved the curtain aside and peeked out the window.

"So much for the view. A dark and dingy parking lot."

Danny came up behind her, wrapped his arms around her waist and nuzzled her neck, "They'll get no complaints from me."

Their flight out of Portland the following morning was delayed, pushing back their arrival at Kona International to seven in the evening. By the time they checked in at their hotel it was nearly nine o'clock.

They ordered a meal from room service and had little energy for anything more than falling into bed.

Jessica woke early that next morning as the first rays of sunlight seeped into the room. Trying hard not to wake Danny, she slipped from the bed and tiptoed across the room to the balcony doors. She stood admiring the breathtaking view as the sun's first rays illuminated the horizon on the Big Island's Kohala Coast.

Before she turned to go inside, Danny's arms slipped around her waist. Resting his chin on her shoulder he said, "You should try for a little more sleep. It's going to be a big day."

"And miss this? A sunrise in paradise?"

Jessica shivered. He grabbed the bedspread, wrapping it around the two of them as the sun rose. The brochure in their room called this the blue hour, the moment the sky changes colors in the morning light. This was worth rising at daybreak.

"Danny, it's just as I'd imagined. I've never seen anything more beautiful."

"Umm, you're right. Except there's one thing more beautiful."

He gently turned her around and swept her into his arms, carrying her to the bed.

She wrapped her arms around his neck. Oh, yes, another thing worth waking up for.

Danny was hell-bent on cramming as much adventure into their honeymoon as he could manage.

The second day on the island had Jessica clinging for dear life to the zip line of the Kohala tour. She wondered why she'd let her husband choose the excursions in Hawaii. Lucky for her, the guide told her she could descend at her own pace.

They started out on side-by-side lines until Danny yelled, *"Come on, let's do this!"* and kicked it into high gear. The big show-off.

Jessica clung for dear life to the zip line. Did she forget to mention she was afraid of heights?

After the first line, Jessica's determination kicked in. She picked up the pace. Half an hour later, Danny slowed down so they could enjoy the views of the Kohala forests and the beautiful waterfalls together. This was their honeymoon, after all. They went through eight lines in all. It was clear Danny needed to learn a thing or two about accommodation, consideration, and collaboration.

Back in the off-road vehicle, Jessica gave Danny a much-deserved punch in the arm. "Tell me again why I let you have free rein over our tour activities. I'm scared to ask what's on the agenda for tomorrow."

"Aww. Admit it, we're on an adventure of a lifetime."

"In case you hadn't noticed, I was the one screaming in terror. I think I forgot to mention I'm scared of heights." What she would not admit was that she had never felt more alive. Some things were best left unsaid. Especially where it concerned her crazy adventurous husband.

Her favorite part of the excursion was swimming in the cool water below a private waterfall. Next, she and Danny along with the other six members of their tour group had a picnic lunch on a cliffside overlooking spectacular views of the Pololu Valley, carved into the Kohala volcano.

In their group of eight, Danny and Jessica were the only newlyweds. A toast to their happiness was raised with soda-filled paper cups.

That night in their hotel room, Jessica stood by the open slider gazing out at the night and listening to the crashing waves illuminated by the slender slice of moonlight. She just couldn't get enough of the view.

She was propped up in bed when Danny joined her fresh from his shower. He kissed her shoulder and asked, "Happy?"

"Very much so." When he began to pull back, she put up a hand and stayed him. "Thank you."

"For?"

"For today. For our wedding. For loving me."

She was soon breathless from his intoxicating kisses. After a few minutes, he pulled back. His fingers smoothed back her hair. "You must be tired, it been a long day."

"Yes, it has been a long day, but I'm not *too* tired."

* * *

Danny let her pick the activities for the next day. She chose terra firma. They rose early after learning it was Kamehameha Day, celebrating one of the island's greatest rulers, King Kamehameha who united all the Hawaiian Islands. The quaint little town of Hawi in North Kohala was his birthplace.

A twenty-five-foot-long lei was draped over the king's statue to start the celebration. An opening blessing was followed by hula dancers. And a floral parade the likes of which Jessica had never seen.

The parade featured the usual floats and marching bands. But Jessica caught her breath at the sight of the king and queen followed by elegant riders on horseback. Eight in all, a nearby native explained the princesses represented the eight Hawaiian Islands. They were dressed in beautiful riding gowns with colorful leis. The horses sported leis as well.

Danny poked her in the arm and flashed his dimples, "As Lexi would say, 'Close your mouth; you're embarrassing yourself.'"

"Ha ha."

After the parade they wandered the streets. Jessica happily browsed the booths displaying traditional arts and crafts. She filled her satchel with trinkets.

Most of the stores and shops on the street were closed. While Danny went to get them shaved ice, Jessica looked at the window display of an art gallery. One small painting caught her attention. It could have been taken from the balcony of their hotel room. She looked at the description card and discovered it was the Kohala Coast at sunrise.

Danny handed her the cup of shaved ice and asked, "Find something?"

"Right there, see? It could be the view from our balcony window."

"You're right. Hey, I spotted a bookstore around the corner that's open. Want to take a look?"

The following day, Jessica wasn't sure what scared her more—flying in a helicopter or soaring above a live volcano. Of course, Danny was having the time of his life as he shouted to be heard over the pulsing thwop-thwop of the chopper blades. He pointed excitedly out the plexiglass windows as Jessica nodded, giving a thumbs-up before turning away and closing her eyes. One glimpse of the glowing hot lava and the thought of falling into it was enough for her.

A towheaded teenager sitting directly across from her must have noticed the abject terror in her eyes because he grinned. He was at that gangly age, not quite at his full growth. His hands rested on his knobby knees. His t-shirt read, *Helicopters Don't Fly They Beat the Air into Submission.* He imitated a zipper closing over his mouth and winked, signaling her secret was safe with him.

Jessica laughed, knowing she was busted.

That afternoon, Danny suggested a walking tour of Hawaii's biggest attraction—he wanted to see lava up close.

"How about a hiking tour? It includes a ten to twelve-hour long hike."

His dimples flashed. "Just kidding."

Thank God.

Later, seated at a beach bar, and relaxing after their morning chopper tour, they shared a ridiculously large Mai Tai in a pineapple.

"Did you see the sign, Jess?" He pointed to a note card propped against a couple of glasses on the bar top and then read it aloud: "Ask the Kimo to demonstrate his award-winning flairtending moves! What do you think?"

She nodded. "We can't miss that."

Danny motioned to the bartender. His name tag read Kimo, so Danny smiled and waggled the card.

Kimo grinned, and a bottle and shaker were soon flying. He did a frontal flip with the bottle, then a side flip, then did one behind his back. Other patrons soon gathered for the show.

He did a trick he called the rainbow flip, tossing the bottle from one hand to the other high over his head and catching it with the shaker. The bottles and shakers flew faster and faster, and soon higher, and higher still. Cheers and shrill whistles filled the air, and Kimo's tip jar was soon stuffed.

When Kimo finally took a break, he pointed one of the bottles at Danny, "Want to give it a try? I'll teach you some basic moves."

Danny was up and around the bar in a flash.

Kimo showed him the three basic grips: the bartender's grip, the juggler's grip, the reverse grip. His final and extra trick was a frontal flip.

"You still want to give it a try?" he asked.

"Oh yeah. Gotta impress the new wife."

"All right, you're up, chief. Do me proud."

Danny executed the rainbow flip first and it went reasonably well. Not quite as high, or as fast, but it landed in the shaker. He was instantly cocky with his success, and then flipped a bottle high above his head and tried to chase it with the shaker, only to have it come down on the bar top. A collective gasp rose then died quickly as the bottle bounced off the counter. It was apparently made of rubber.

Jessica learned something remarkable about her husband early-on. He made friends easily. Wherever they went they often found themselves surrounded by people. Lexi would undoubtedly attribute it to his astrology sign—Sagittarius. If she remembered it right, the ninth sign of the zodiac was described as being a risk-taker with a gregarious social nature and a compassionate personality. It fit Danny to a T. Maybe there was something to reading the stars.

Soon after they took seats at a nearby table, a native Hawaiian couple joined them. They introduced themselves as Adam and Leila Kamaka.

The couple immediately seemed like friends they'd known for years, although when Adam mentioned his recent return from a tour in Iraq, Jessica froze.

She'd been trying her hardest not to think about Danny's deployment. He was scheduled to fly out two days after their return. While her husband was stoked to get a firsthand account of the war, Jessica didn't think she could bear to listen. Though the bar was little more than an open air enclosure with a thatched roof, she felt confined.

She managed to smile at Leila and asked "How about a walk on the beach?"

"Great idea." Leila stood, retrieving her beach bag.

Jessica grabbed her hat and began slathering on more sunblock. They walked to the edge of the surf, both enjoying the waves that teased their feet before receding. "I'd give anything to have your naturally tanned skin," Jessica remarked.

Leila laughed, "I'd give anything to have your hair. Red, with hints of gold; it's beautiful."

"Unfortunately, this skin has two hues: white or burnt orange."

A little further down the beach, Leila spread out a blanket in the sand, just out of reach of the waves.

"So, how did you and Danny meet?" she asked as they stretched out in the sun.

Jessica chuckled. "A chance in a million. He dialed the wrong number."

"I'm sorry, what?"

She'd told the tale many times, but never tired of the story. "So, Danny was calling his friend, Brian, and got me by mistake. He begged me not to hang up, then talked his way past my defenses and, I guess you could say, he talked his way into my heart. What about you and Adam?"

"It was an arranged marriage. But not what you're thinking. We grew up next door to each other from the age of four. He was my best friend. We were practically inseparable. At age six, we made a pact. He even gave me a ring. It was one of those bread-wrapper ties."

"That's so sweet. But Leila, how did you bear it when Adam was deployed to Iraq?"

A shadow fell across Leila's sober face. She took a moment before she answered.

"There were days when I devoured the news. At other times, I couldn't bring myself to turn on the television or pick up a newspaper. When I knew he was on a mission, I too often convinced myself something had happened. Then I'd hear from him, and it would ease my heart for a little while. I won't lie to you. It was the hardest thing I've ever gone through."

She reached over for Jessica's hand. "But he came back. Jess, look at me . . . he came back."

After a while, they made their way slowly toward the bar. The men met them halfway.

Adam put his arm around Leila's waist. "We should get going. My mom's expecting us."

Leila explained, "Adam's father Akoni is celebrating his eighty-fifth birthday. It will be a big get-together. We promised to help."

Jessica brushed the sand from her feet and slipped her sandals back on. "That's all right. We need to get back to the hotel, we've got early dinner reservations."

Leila looked at Adam.

He nodded. "Danny, you and Jessica should join us. You'll get to see an authentic Hawaiian luau, something you'll never forget."

Danny put his hand on Adam's shoulder. "Thanks man, but we wouldn't want to be the extra last-minute guests. No sense adding to your mom's burden."

"There isn't anything she loves more than a big gathering. Adding a couple of place settings is no problem. We could literally feed the whole population of Hilo with the spreads my mother puts on."

Danny glanced over at Jessica's eager face and said, "Okay, count us in."

The Kamaka family lived on two acres of land just minutes above downtown Hilo. On the drive over, Leila described some of the more unique Hawaiian customs.

"Our most distinctive Hawaiian tradition is the *Honi Ihu* greeting. It can be startling if you're not prepared for it. It will begin with a hug and a kiss on the cheek but also involves touching noses."

Adam laughingly added, "That's both sexes by the way."

Danny, up front in the seat beside him, chuckled, "Good to know."

Leila explained, "The root of the custom derives from the exchange of breath. It has a deep spiritual significance for our people. It isn't practiced much today, but *our* family beliefs are steeped in tradition."

Adam glanced at his wife in the rearview. "Best tell them about Aunty and Uncle."

"Oh, right. It's common practice in Hawaii to call our elders *aunty* and *uncle*. The easiest way to explain it is to compare it to calling someone sir or ma'am. It's considered respectful but friendly as well."

Danny turned in his seat to look at Leila. "So, if I've got that right, I should use the term aunty for your mom, grand-mother, and your aunt."

Leila smiled and nodded.

"Okay, got it."

Jessica smiled as they drove up a paved palm lined road. Only in Hawaii could a home be this close to a populated city and yet have the feel of a private sanctuary.

Both Jessica and Danny were grateful for the aunty and uncle custom. They'd surely have been banned from the party if they tried to remember the names of the fifty or so guests.

They dined on traditional Hawaiian dishes including the famous pork dish, the Kalua Pig. It was like pulled pork, but with a pungent wood smoke flavor. It was cooked in an underground oven. Jessica had heard of Poi but didn't real-ize it was actually a thick paste. Poi was made from taro root and reminded Jessica of yams. It had a sticky pudding-like consistency. Lomi Lomi Salmon, and Poke, the Hawaiian version of Japanese sashimi, was served as well. The dishes were all delicious. She'd never tasted anything like them. The banquet was topped off perfectly with freshly grown pineapple and passion fruit.

When the meal concluded, a group of local musicians tuned up their guitars and ukuleles. Leila and several women went to the large patio for a hula. After a couple of numbers, the dancers urged guests to join them. Leila wouldn't take no for an answer, so Jessica found herself drawn forward. Each of the women were given flower leis, but Leila reached into a bag behind one of the musicians and pulled out one made up of seashells.

She placed it around Jessica's neck. "Aloha." She followed it with a kiss to the cheek and whispered, "It's a traditional gift of friendship."

Jessica hugged Leila, "It's beautiful. Thank you."

After some pathetic hip sways, Jessica concentrated on the hand movements. She felt she was semi-competent at that.

Danny soon joined in. The man wasn't just a pretty face; he had rhythm and the moves to go with it.

As the evening wound down and most of the guests departed, Adam's father beckoned Danny and Jessica to come sit with him.

Akoni wasn't a big man; he was slender with ropey muscles and work-roughened hands. "Thank you for coming. I hope you've enjoyed yourselves."

Jessica answered for both of them. "Happy birthday, Uncle. We had a wonderful time. It's been the highlight of our trip here to the islands."

Adam's mother, Nalani came to sit beside her husband. "I understand you are newlyweds. *Ho `o maika`i. Noho me ka hau'oli.* That means, Congratulations. Live happily ever after."

Danny took Jessica's hand, "Thank you."

In the quiet of the evening, Adam's parents recounted stories of their lives. The one of how they met was especially poignant since it happened on Sunday, December 7, 1941, the day of the attack on Pearl Harbor.

There was a faraway look in Akoni's eyes as he talked about that day.

"My family lived in Pearl City then. It was a peninsula that jutted out into Pearl Harbor, parallel to Ford Island where the Navy air station was based. At nearly eight in the morning, a tremendous explosion rattled the windows. I remember running outside to the sight of a string of airplanes diving toward the anchored ships in the harbor. I could see the Rising Sun emblem on the side of the planes. I knew then that the Japanese had attacked us."

Akoni brought his glass to his lips, but it was empty. Danny quickly refilled it with a pitcher from a nearby table. Akoni took a long, deep drink before continuing.

"I was an ensign in the Navy. It was by sheer chance I wasn't on base that day. Many ran into the hills and hid in caves. I was lucky to catch a boat to Ford Island. I saw sunken Navy ships in flames on both sides of the island. It was a terrible sight."

"So much destruction, so much loss of life . . . but one rescue attempt stands out in my mind. On the ships that had rolled over, Navy yard workers frantically cut large holes through the hulls of the ships. They managed to save quite a few sailors. I joined those working to repair planes. We worked like mad men. Our fury was spurred on by the dead and the dying that surrounded us. I don't think that rage ever truly left any of us. We did all that we could to get our planes airborne; shifts were twelve hours on and twelve hours off."

He looked down at his right hand, flexing and unflexing his fingers. An old scar was visible between his thumb and wrist. "The slip of a power shear sent me to the base hospital. Little more than a flesh wound, but my lieutenant ordered me to stand down."

Nalani took her husband's hand and held it. "It could hardly be called a scratch. It took ten stitches to close it as I remember."

He gave his wife a loving look. "That was how we met— the one good thing from that dreadful day."

* * *

Later that night, Jessica stood on the balcony of their hotel room. It was their last night on the island.

Danny came into the room fresh from his shower, a towel slung low on his hips and one folded into a turban on his head.

"Quick! Where's my phone? I've got to get a picture of this."

"Ha ha, very funny." He sat on the edge of the bed and patted the bedspread. Come here, I've got a proposition for you."

"Oh? What kind of proposition?"

He turned serious. "How 'bout we make a baby?"

"What, right now? You know I'm on the pill. There's little chance of that happening." She reached for the towel around his waist. "Still . . . I don't mind getting in practice."

Against all odds, a tiny seed was planted that night.

5

Mid-September found Danny nearly three months into his tour in Iraq, and Jessica decided it was time to confirm her suspicions. She made an appointment with a gynecologist at the Palo Alto VA Medical Center, just a short drive from Stanford.

Thankfully, traffic was light because her thoughts were a jumbled mess. How was it possible? She was on the pill. Danny would be thrilled, but he would be on the other side of the world when their baby was born. Was she ready for motherhood? She was thrilled and terrified at the same time.

Dr. Curtis Stevenson's exam room was white on white—walls, cabinets, sink, and window blinds. She hated these exams and tried to distract herself by tracking the small cracks in the ceiling tiles above her head.

Dr. Stevenson completed his exam and lowered the paper blanket draped over her knees. "Okay, you can sit up now."

She shifted to the side of the table and watched as he rolled his stool over to the computer stand near the windows. Despite the receding hairline, he appeared to be in his mid-thirties. His defiance was a thick and burly mustache. He had kind blue eyes. He glanced over at her and asked, "When was your last menses?"

"Mid-May. So, I'm pregnant, right?"

"Yes, I'd say your about two and a half months along."

"But I've been on the pill for years."

"Well, birth control pills are certainly effective, but they're not foolproof. In some instances, it can be as simple as failing to take them at the same time each day."

"Wow . . . I'm really going to have a baby." Her angst disappeared in a flash. It didn't matter that her life was going to be thrown into utter turmoil. She was going to be a mother. She stiffened her spine and made a silent vow to the tiny being nestled in her belly—*I'm going to be the best mom ever, I promise.*

Addressing Dr. Stevenson she asked, "Is it too soon for an ultrasound to find out if my baby is a boy, or a girl?" She knew Danny would insist on knowing.

"Ultrasounds to determine gender are generally done at nineteen weeks. Right now, I'm going to write out a prescription for prenatal vitamins."

* * *

Jessica drove home from the doctor's office at a leisurely pace. Now that her pregnancy was confirmed, a deep calmness washed over her. She had told no one of her suspicions, including Lexi, who was on night duty these days. Jess glanced at her dashboard clock; Lexi was likely awake. Eager to share the news, she turned onto her sister's street.

Lexi answered the door still dressed in her nightwear: a t-shirt that came to her knees and wooly socks. She turned away without a greeting. Her sister had obviously not had her caffeine fix.

With the coffee started, Lexi took two cups out of the cupboard.

Jessica held up her hand, "None for me, thanks."

"Have you had lunch? I've got leftover pepperoni pizza."

"Maybe some fruit. I'm trying to cut back on salt." She peeked in the fridge when Lexi pulled out the pizza box and a handful of grapes. "Got any juice?"

Lexi leaned against the counter and crossed her arms over her chest. "No coffee, cutting back on salt and eating fruit. Scrounging for juice? You're preggers!"

"Wow, that was a quick diagnosis," Jessica observed with a wide smile.

Lexi practically flew across the kitchen. She grabbed Jessica's arms and danced her around in circles.

"Careful, or you'll shake the baby loose."

"I'm going to be an auntie! Holy shi—I mean holy moly. Gotta watch my language. Danny will be over the moon. You didn't tell me you stopped taking birth control."

"I didn't. My doctor said birth control pills aren't one hundred percent effective. Plus, they're supposed to be taken at the same time every day. Who knew?"

"I did." Lexi searched her face. "How are you feeling about this?"

"Scared out of my mind. Danny may as well be on the moon. He's nearly that far away. But I made this baby a promise, I'm going to be the best mom ever."

"Absolutely, you will be. And I'm going to be the best auntie ever."

* * *

Jessica couldn't wait to tell Danny he was going to be a father, and although they were in frequent contact, for obvious reasons there was no set schedule. About six the next evening the opportunity arrived when she heard the sound of Skype notes.

As Danny's face came into view, Jessica thought Skype was the world's greatest invention ever. She touched her fingers to the screen, "Hi there. You're up early." It was five in the morning Baghdad time.

"I wanted to get on the horn first thing." He touched his own fingers to the screen. "You're a sight for sore eyes."

"You, too. I was hoping you'd call. I've got news. I visited the doctor yesterday."

His smile quickly turned to concern.

"Sorry, what I meant to say was that I visited our *family* doctor yesterday. In other words, I'm preggers."

He nearly tipped the table over when he jumped up and whooped with joy. "Hear that, boys? I'm going to have a baby!"

A couple of the guys grumbled half-heartedly about his using up all the comm time, but the rest of them were fist pumping and grinning. Good news was rare in Iraq, and the news of a new life called for a celebration.

Danny sat back down and adjusted the screen. "Do something for me? Hold the screen up to your belly. I want to talk to my daughter."

"Who said it's a girl? And darling, our baby is the size of a kidney bean right now." Nonetheless, she did as he asked.

Several heads appeared behind him. They disappeared when Danny barked, "Stand down. This isn't some skin show."

Danny put his face close to the screen. "Little one, this is your daddy speaking. I'm not going to be there for the big day, but when I get home, I'll always be there for you. That's a promise. You take care of yourself. And do your dad a favor? Go easy on your mom. Okay?"

* * *

By mid-October Jessica had settled into her condo in the capital city of Sacramento. Amanda had made good on her offer, and she was now a full associate at the firm of Marsden, Walker, and Hall. She loved her two-bedroom condo, a ten-minute drive from the office.

On a quiet Saturday afternoon, Jessica sat in a rocker in her second bedroom watching her father-in-law put the crib together. He was doing a fair job of it, considering he hadn't glanced at the assembly instructions.

Ellen was busy folding dozens of darling "onesies" and placing the infant bodysuits in the dresser—all gifts from grandma and the aunties. Ellen hummed as she worked.

Danny's parents had surprised her with a weekend visit. They arrived bearing gifts and offers of help. She was so grateful for their presence. They brought Danny home for her, particularly Danny's father: the timbre of his voice; the way he cocked his head as he puzzled over an idea or a project. These were traits he shared with his son.

Lexi walked in carrying a tray with mugs of steaming coffee and a glass of orange juice for her. While they took a break, Jessica reached into her satchel. She pulled out a couple of folded sheets of paper. She unfurled and flattened out the first. Her grin was huge as she held it up for them to see.

"It's a girl!" she announced.

There were hugs and joy all around.

Unfolding the second sheet she added, "And I passed the bar!"

"Wonderful," Daniel added. "Let's keep the good news coming."

"Absolutely," Lexi chimed in.

"We have another gift for you, Jess" Daniel announced. "It's something Danny sent from Hawaii. He asked us to bring it to you and stipulated it should be on a special occasion. I can't think of a better time." He handed her a box wrapped in brightly colored paper.

Jessica peeled back the paper and lifted the box cover. Inside was a small rectangular object secured with bubble wrap. It was the painting she'd admired through the gallery window the day of their Hawaiian holiday. She hugged it against her chest as she wiped away a few tears and held it out for her in-laws to see.

Ellen ran her fingers over the intricately carved frame. "Danny wrote that it was the view from the balcony window of your hotel."

"Yes, it was breathtaking. I couldn't get enough of it."

When her in-laws left for the hotel, Jessica sat in the rocker in the nursery and talked to Amber who was now the size of a tomato. Danny approved wholeheartedly of the name but insisted on waiting for the sonogram results before picking an alternate boy's name. Her husband was a stubborn man.

"Your father is going to be insufferable when he learns he was right all along. But he's a keeper. You'll see. He'll probably spoil you rotten, and he already has plans to have you fitted for a chastity belt as soon as you reach puberty. Just humor him. He'll grow out of it, I promise."

Jessica felt the slightest flutter in her belly. "Amber, was that you?"

Almost like providence, she heard the chime of her laptop and reached into her satchel.

Danny wasted no time in asking, "So, was I right?"

"Hello to you, too. And you'll soon find out. Your parents were just here. Daniel put the crib together for me. They also gave me that painting from our honeymoon. I should have known you were up to something when you didn't insist on going back to the gallery to purchase it."

"I love doing the unexpected. Now don't keep me waiting any longer. Was I right?"

"I bought one of those gender reveal confetti poppers. Are you ready? Watch closely . . ."

She pointed it at the ceiling and twisted the bottom to activate the spring-loaded mechanism. Pink foil rained down all over her and the keyboard.

Danny whooped and hollered, "It's a girl!"

Jessica heard cheers in the background. She set the computer on her lap for Danny's customary chat.

"Hey Amber. It's your daddy again. You and I, we're going to have to teach Mommy that she should never doubt a *father's* intuition."

Jessica rolled her eyes. Then the flutter came again. She placed the laptop back so that Danny's face came into view. "Danny, our daughter just moved!"

"Of course, she did, she agrees with me."

The baby books she devoured from the start confirmed that unborn babies could hear, but it wasn't until they reached six to seven months that they could hear sounds or voices outside the body. She didn't have the heart to tell Danny. He was so giddy with excitement.

"One more thing before we sign off . . . I passed the bar!"

* * *

During her communications with Danny over the following weeks, Jessica began to see a change in him. He appeared drawn and weary before he masked it behind his customary good cheer. She started to worry.

Then a ray of hope loomed on the horizon. Rumors started circulating among the enlisted men of plans to shorten the twelve-month tour lengths. Her chats with Danny once again were light and informative.

Two weeks later, Jessica gripped the sides of her laptop as Danny explained the official statement just handed down.

His voice was heavy with disappointment. "Word is tours will *eventually* be shortened, but they've added the caveat that it will only happen when the insurgency comes down and it's determined the Iraqi army is *properly* trained to fight."

Jessica knew what that meant: for now, shortening tours was off the table.

Tamping down her disappointment, Jessica tried to lift his spirits. "Any change in government regulations moves at a snail's pace. We both know that. It's okay. We'll get through it. You'll be home before you know it, and Amber will be here to greet you."

Danny held his hand up to the screen. She did the same. The move conjured up memories of the feel of skin against skin. Danny lowered his hand and asked in earnest, "How's our little girl doing? Giving you much trouble?"

"I think our sweet Amber is trying to figure out what she wants to be when she grows up. From the constant pounding to my midsection, I'd say she's narrowed it down to two possibilities. A ballerina or an Olympic sprinter."

"That's my girl!" His laugh gladdened her heart. "I can't wait to—"

He cut out mid-sentence. Apparently internet service was spotty that night.

Jessica put up a brave front for Danny's sake, but she spent many sleepless nights over the next weeks. Worry was her constant companion. Leila's words again played in her head as she tried her best to focus on anything but the news coming out of Iraq. Regardless of her feelings, the weeks slogged by relentlessly.

She climbed the stairs and stood in the nursery admiring the mural of rainbows and unicorns on the wall behind the crib. It was pure joy and fantasy—a wall of make-believe. This room was where she retreated when the days bore down on her. She felt so alone much of the time and often dealt with evening nausea. Her doctor reassured her that this was a normal part of pregnancy, and that she should do her best to eat small amounts of healthy foods throughout the day— homemade soups, dry toast and tea, and fresh fruit too, but nothing tasted right.

Jessica knew she had to try more diligently to eat normally. Thanksgiving was just a few weeks away, and she and Lexi would be joining the Langston clan for the holiday. She shuddered at the thought of all that rich food but certainly did not want to worry Danny's family about her poor appetite.

Thanks to her sister, she was forewarned to take along an extra suitcase. A surprise baby shower was apparently in the works.

During their most recent call, Jessica showed Danny the dozen booties his mom had sent. He had laughed, saying "I'll bet my mother's note preached that a baby can't have enough booties. Am I right?"

"Of course, you're right. You know your mother well."

Near dinner time, Jessica boxed a gift for Ellen that she planned to give to her on Thanksgiving. The gift was a vintage Lennox aluminum serving platter, beautifully embossed with a turkey and harvest vegetables. Danny's mother shared her love of things with a long tradition.

She decided to do one more quick wrap before heating the leftover lasagna. Pasta and red sauce had never been one of her favorites, but oddly enough, these days it helped settle her stomach.

She heard a knock on the door and set aside her ribbons. When she looked through the peephole and saw Danny's parents, she glanced back to make sure her gift for Ellen was hidden.

"Ellen, Daniel. What a surprise. I was just wrapping up a gift for you, Ellen, but you're going to have to . . ."

The words died on her lips when she saw the abject sorrow in Ellen's hollow eyes.

Daniel caught her before she collapsed on the floor.

When Jessica came to she was lying on the sofa. Throw pillows elevated her legs. Danny's mother hovered over her. She tried to sit up, but Ellen urged her to remain lying down.

Daniel had his medical bag open. He checked her pulse and listened to her heart. The baby's too. "Your vital signs are good. Amber's heartbeat is strong. Are you feeling any pain?"

Jessica shook her head and sat up. "The Army made the notification to you?"

Daniel put the stethoscope back in his bag. He pulled an armchair closer to the sofa and sat down heavily. Leaning forward, he clasped his hands together, clenching and unclenching them as he replied. "Danny put in a request that we be notified first. Given your condition, he thought it best."

Jessica tried to absorb what he was saying. "How . . . when?"

They heard a loud knock and looked toward the door. Ellen rose. "That's Lexi, I'm sure. We called her when we pulled into the driveway."

Lexi sat beside her on the sofa and took her hand. Jessica turned again to Danny's father. "Tell me."

Daniel's voice was gentle. "It happened early this morning, around five o'clock. We took the first flight out . . ." He hesitated and seemed unable to continue.

"Please, it can't be worse than what I'm imagining."

"His helicopter was downed by rocket-propelled grenades. We were told it was a massive explosion. There would have been no time for fear . . . or suffering." Daniel took a handkerchief from his pants pocket and wiped the tears from his face.

It was her undoing. Jessica whimpered before violent sobs racked her whole body. Daniel stood and took her in his arms. She wanted to run, to hide, to be alone with her grief. But she recognized his pain and stayed in the circle of his arms. What little strength they had combined to keep them upright. She reached out to Ellen, holding her hand as well.

Daniel and Ellen spent the night in Jessica's bedroom. She slept on a roll-away in the nursery. Lexi refused to leave her side. She slipped in beside Jessica, much the way she had when they were children. and the rumble of thunder sounded outside the window.

* * *

Danny's funeral was held at Arlington National Cemetery with full military honors. Jessica stood between Lexi and Ellen. Daniel held his wife's hand. Ginny and Chloe and their families filled the rest of the front row. Behind them, Brian sat among a number of college and high school friends.

Jessica gazed out at the sea of headstones and watched the hearse slowly make its way to the gravesite. It was only a few days before Thanksgiving. She didn't believe there was anything to give thanks for.

Jessica fought with every ounce of her being to stay in control. A slight wind carried the smell of newly mowed grass. She breathed in deeply, idly wondering how many gardeners it took to keep the grounds so beautifully manicured.

The back of the hearse opened, and she concentrated on the white-gloved hands of the honor guard holding the brass rails of the coffin. She thought of the few teeth and bones nestled inside, which were all that remained of her husband.

Although the cemetery representative had gone over the step-by-step details of the ceremony, she remembered none of it and was relying on mimicking those around her.

During Taps and the three-gun salute, she escaped into the shapes of the clouds above, watching two float and move together to form the shape of a heart. The separation between them could only represent some unknown finite time until she and Danny would be together again. It was a thought she clung to for months and on into years.

The Langston family minister made the trip to Arlington to officiate at Danny's funeral. Reverend Joshua Kimbrel. Jessica remembered him from her wedding. He'd seen to the family's spiritual needs for years, and Jessica was grateful for his presence. She knew Danny's family would find comfort in his words.

Reverend Kimbrel's features were tight and drawn in sorrow. He shared stories culled from family memories and Jessica's own reminiscences.

She tried to listen, but her thoughts wandered to her own special memories—one was how Danny convinced her over the phone to trust in him. To trust in *them*.

She thought of the dimples that flashed often. She remembered how he was blessed with a happy soul, and would show his love with grand gestures, like the day he proposed. She recalled his tender expressions of love, his sealing the ring on her finger with his lips on their wedding day and the look of unadulterated joy on his face when he learned he was going to be a father.

Her loss came back tenfold when the fact hit home that he would never see their little girl. *Oh God*.

A fist tightened in her chest, and she gripped Lexi's hand. She had to keep it together just a little longer.

Reverend Kimbrel held out his hands and lifted them. "Please rise for the final prayer."

"Heavenly Father, I ask for your blessings to be bestowed on Danny's family. I pray for peace for all who are gathered here today mourning the loss of a husband, a son, a brother, a comrade, and a friend. Eternal God, we praise you for the great company of all those who have finished their course in faith and now rest from their labor. We praise you for those dear to us whom we name in our hearts."

Soon after the sermon ended, the honor guard came forward once again. The flag folding began. Jessica closed her eyes but startled at the sound of the snapping fabric. When the folding was complete, the flag bearer stood before a stunned Daniel. The soldier's voice was solemn and strong as he intoned, "On behalf of the President of the United States, the United States Army, and a grateful nation, please accept this flag as a symbol of our appreciation for your loved one's honorable and faithful service."

Jessica knew she made the right decision to have the flag presented to Danny's father. His eyes glistened with tears as he looked over at her and nodded his thanks. She knew it was what Danny would have wanted.

* * *

After the ceremony, Lexi drove the rental car back to the hotel. She was worried about her sister. Jessica hadn't cried during the service, and she was silent on the drive.

Back in their room, they changed into comfortable clothes, and Lexi pulled the drapes against the afternoon sun. Though the room boasted two queen beds, she laid down beside Jessica, wanting to be within reach if her sister needed her.

They lay facing each other, but still there were no tears from Jessica.

Lexi was the first to break the silence. "That service was exceptional. So steeped in tradition. I think Danny's family took comfort in that. It was kind of you to have the flag presented to his father."

"Did you know that the flag gets folded thirteen times? It's meant to represent the original thirteen colonies. And the tricorn shape is made to appear like the hat worn by the patriots of the American Revolution." Jessica delivered her response in a monotone voice, worrying Lexi even more.

"No, I *didn't* know that."

"And did you know that Taps has lyrics? At one time it was known as "Butterfield's Lullaby." I guess the words went through more than one version. This is the current version, Jessica whispered:

> *Day is done,*
> *Gone the sun, from the lake, from the hill,*
> *   from the sky,*
> *All is well, safely rest,*
> *God is nigh."*

Lexi knew her sister all too well. Jessica had done her homework so she would know what to expect. Lexi pictured her at her laptop pouring over every detail of military funerals. This was her way. It was why she passed the bar with flying colors, and why she was a great lawyer. She always did her due diligence. It was her coping mechanism.

Lexi reached over and switched off the light. "Try to get some sleep. It's hours yet before we need to leave for the airport."

Lexi dozed off, awakening later in a bed that shook from the force of her sister's sobbing.

PART II

A New Life

6

Five weeks after the funeral a soldier, who had served with Danny in Iraq, sat in Jessica's living room fidgeting with the brim of his baseball cap while she got him a cup of coffee.

Reverend Kimbrel put Ted McNerney in contact with her. Tall and broad-shouldered, his youthful face had a smattering of freckles across the bridge of his nose. He looked more like a high school linebacker than a veteran of a foreign war. He seemed vaguely familiar. Then she realized why she recognized him.

She handed him the mug and set a coaster on the edge of the coffee table. "I remember you. It was the day I told Danny he was going to be a father. Your head popped up behind him on the screen. Am I right?"

Ted squirmed a little in his seat and nodded. "Yes. Me, Zach, and Cody. We meant no disrespect."

Jessica laughed and waved her hand in the air. The gesture seemed to put him at ease. He managed a smile. When she sat down, he was sober again.

"I'm real sorry about Danny."

Jessica didn't meet his gaze immediately. Instead she fidgeted with a loose thread on the sleeve of her blouse.

Seeing her discomfort, Ted took a sip of his coffee and raised the cup. "Missed this the most. The nearest Starbucks was my first stop when I hit stateside."

Jessica looked up. "Thank you for coming, Ted."

"I contacted Reverend Kimbrel because I wanted to pay my respects and maybe talk some about Danny and what went on over there."

"Please continue. I'd like to hear about that."

Ted smiled again as he seemed to be reflecting on his memories.

"He sure was a talker, Danny was. It was hotter than blue blazes, and we all missed home. Danny's stories helped us cope. My favorite one's gotta be how you two met. He liked calling it *the wrong number, but the right connection*. Did you know he was bragging he was going to be a daddy even before you called with the news? And it was going to be a girl. Didn't matter that we pointed out there was a fifty-fifty chance it would be a boy."

He raised his cup and took several gulps before resting it in the palm of his hand. He stared at it for several beats. When he looked up, his gaze was sorrowful.

Jessica swallowed hard and whispered, "Were you there when it happened?"

"He saved my life. Danny saved my life. Three men down, one with a life-threatening wound. It turned into a soup sandwich . . . sorry. Military jargon for it turned bad without warning."

"I was applying a tourniquet when bullets started flying all around us. Danny returned fire. We radioed for an air strike, and it gave us the time we needed to load the wounded into the HEMTT. That's a heavy expanded mobility tactical truck. I'm going to have to get used to civilian talk again."

"We got word that a helicopter would be landing five clicks—about three miles south of us. We knew the soldier with the bleeder would have a better chance if he was airlifted out, so we headed that way."

Ted set the coffee cup back on the coaster and declined Jessica's offer of a refill. "When decision time came for helicopter or truck, Danny reminded me I owed him one. He stepped into the bird and sent me a jaunty salute. Then he laughed. That Danny laugh, you know?"

Jessica offered a weak smile and nodded.

Ted worked his fist through the inside of his cap, adding "That's how I'll always picture him."

After Ted left, Jessica retrieved the picture album from her nightstand. She had avoided it until now. She flipped the pages and stopped at the one she took on their honeymoon. It showed Danny about to step into the helicopter that flew over the volcano. And there it was—the jaunty salute. Oh yes, she remembered that *Danny laugh.*

* * *

The first pain came at nine in the morning on a cold, blustery Tuesday in March. It felt more like indigestion than the beginnings of labor. Jessica chalked it up to the breakfast burrito. Should have stuck with her pre-pregnancy diet. Fresh fruit seldom led to indigestion.

She reached for the antacid in the cupboard beside the sink, then thought better of it, just in case. She noted the time, also just in case.

Back at the kitchen table she booted up her laptop. She studied the trial brief she had worked on long into the night. As far as dissolution of marriages went, this one was straightforward. Judith and Anthony Samuelson: married eleven years, separated for three. Their union produced two children, Anthony Samuelson, Jr., aged nine and Kayla Samuelson, aged seven.

A parenting plan and a child support agreement were in place. Property and assets would be split straight down the middle. If they were this agreeable about their divorce, why couldn't they put that effort into making the marriage work? Not her call. She wished all her cases were this neat and simple. Divorce usually leaned heavily toward the ugly side.

Jessica reached across the table for her satchel and felt the next tug. She looked at her watch. Fifteen minutes, give or take. Okay, then. She called Amanda Marsden.

"You're in labor? And on the phone with me?"

"Just started, and I wanted to update you on the Samuelson case. I'm going to email you the file and law brief. The brief is done, just needs a glance over."

"Jessica, go have your baby. The next words I want to hear from you are, *She's a beauty*!"

The time between contractions grew shorter. When they started closing in on the magic number eight, Jessica put in a call to Lexi. Luckily, Amber decided to make her debut appearance into the world on her auntie's day off.

The phone rang four times before Lexi answered, "Okay, now what are you craving? It's my day off, you know. Trying to get some *me* time in."

"I'm in labor."

Lexi was suddenly all business. "How far apart?"

"My water just broke!" She gasped. "Hurry!"

Jessica didn't want to know how many traffic laws Lexi broke, but what seemed like only minutes later, Lexi was helping her into the car and then rushing back inside to retrieve her purse, keys, and the overnight bag prepped and waiting in the entry closet.

Jessica hollered, "Oh my God, I forgot to call Dr. Olmstead."

"Done. On his way."

The contractions were coming closer and harder as Lexi coached her from the driver's seat. "Okay, remember your breathing exercises: hee-hee-hoo, pant-pant-blow."

Jessica let her know what she thought of that advice between contractions, "I'm going to kill you. Just wait. You're done for!"

Lexi just laughed.

Despite the rush to the hospital, Amber took her own sweet time popping into the world. Jessica endured two more hours of feeling as if her lower body was tying itself in knots just before tearing itself apart.

Lexi never left her side, and Jessica was grateful for her presence. Not that there weren't moments when she wanted to throw something possibly lethal at her sister's head. The platitudes, "think positive thoughts" or "concentrate on why you're here" and "remember the end game," drove Jessica crazy.

"A sports analogy, *really*?" Jessica shot back.

Amber Langston made her grand entrance at five minutes past three in the afternoon on Tuesday, March 25, 2005. She weighed in at six pounds, seven ounces. According to Lexi, March 25th was the day of dynamism, meaning those born on that particular day were highly dynamic and among the most active and energetic people. Lord help her.

Jessica knew her daughter's lungs were fully developed because she came out screaming. She knew her daughter was a fighter when they laid Amber on her chest and she waved her fists.

Jessica kissed the top of her daughter's head. "Hi Sweetie." She felt unbridled joy and love that was unconditional and fiercely protective.

Lexi leaned over the bed and kissed Jessica's forehead. "Kinda wonderful, huh?"

"Oh, yeah."

"So, I'm forgiven?"

Jessica reached for her sister's hand. "Couldn't have done it without you. Thanks, Sis."

Later that evening, while Jessica nursed Amber, her thoughts turned to Danny. The glorious feeling of her daughter in her arms came with a dark cloud of sorrow over her joy because he would never experience this profound wonder.

To dispel her melancholy, Jessica shared memories of him with her daughter, a practice she would continue for years to come. "I bet you didn't know that your daddy had a superpower. Don't laugh, I'm serious. His power was the art of persuasion. He could have made big bucks as a telemarketer. You know why? Because he talked me into loving him over a phone line. Know something else? If science had made a breakthrough, and men could give birth, your daddy would have been first in line."

* * *

Jessica found a surprise upon her return from the hospital. Ellen and Daniel were waiting inside. Lexi confessed she made the arrangements.

Daniel held a teddy bear large enough to need its own crib. A further surprise came in the form of a rocker-recliner. It bore a suspicious resemblance to one she'd admired in a Macy's ad. She shot her sister an accusing look.

Lexi held up her hands. "Don't look at me."

Ellen nodded, "We thought Momma deserved a gift, too. Now, give me that precious little one. You go up and have yourself a nice nap. You must be exhausted. A hospital is not a restful environment."

Jessica wasn't fooled. Ellen wanted to get her hands on her granddaughter. But there was no way she was going look a gift horse in the mouth. She had nursed Amber just before leaving the hospital. An hour or two of sleep was possible if luck was on her side.

Lexi said her goodbyes, and Jessica climbed the stairs to the sound of Amber's grandparents oohing and aahing over her. She didn't even mind that she wouldn't be the one to christen the new rocker.

At Amanda's insistence, Jessica worked from home the first couple of months after Amber's birth. Her daughter was a treasure from the start. She wasn't colicky, she burped easily, and slept in four hour stretches after the first couple of weeks. Jessica imagined Danny looking down from above with a smug smile on his face saying, "See, she *was* listening when I asked her to be kind to her mommy." God, she missed him.

A few weeks before returning to work, Jessica began the search for a nanny. She interviewed seven candidates over the phone and immediately eliminated the one that smoked. She met the other six in a nearby coffee shop, eliminating another when she showed up in ratty jeans, a t-shirt, and dirty sneakers. The third disqualification was about transportation; the candidate did not own a car. References and background checks narrowed her candidates down to two. They were then invited to her home for a final interview to see how they interacted with Amber. Ellen came up with the idea of a Skype call to include her.

They both interviewed well, and each met the qualifications she was looking for, but Jessica was still hesitant. She wondered if the bar she set was so high that no one could meet her expectations. Ellen felt the same hesitancy, so Jessica went back to her search.

It was Lexi who saved the day. Didn't she always?

A nurse who worked on the same ward as Lexi had heard they were looking for a nanny. She suggested they meet her aunt, a retired nursing home director named Meg Williams. Meg had been a widow for the past five years and had one son who recently moved to Minnesota for a job promotion. Though she missed him and her grandchildren, she'd been born and raised in Sacramento and had lived in the same house for more than forty years. She couldn't bring herself to follow them.

Her grandkids would be off to college in the next couple of years. She was looking to fill the void by taking up childcare.

Meg was a cross between Mary Poppins and Nanny McPhee. It was as if she stepped out of the movie screen. Who could argue with that?

* * *

With Nanny Meg's help, Amber made it through her first year without a scratch, skipped the terrible twos, and passed through the incorrigible threes without incident.

Not long after her third birthday, Jessica began reading a series of articles to help families understand development achievements required before enrolling a child in preschool. Or, as Lexi quipped, *of course she read up on it.*

It seemed Amber was more than ready. She was certainly smart enough, and Meg agreed.

Maybe too smart as in "smart-ass." Jessica thought.

She answered a call from Meg shortly after Amber began preschool. Her daughter had been sent home early with a note from her teacher.

Jessica wanted to know what the note said but first asked, "Where's Amber?"

"In her room. She's on a time-out for now."

"Good. Can you read it to me?"

The sound of an envelope tearing, and the crinkle of paper came through the line. Meg cleared her throat and then read:

"My Dear Mrs. Langston: I'm afraid I had to send Amber home with an admonishment about her behavior in the school-yard at recess. Amber was observed punching her schoolmate, Roger Hawkins, in the nose."

Amber's nanny harrumphed and said, "She goes on to request that you keep Amber out of school for the rest of the week so she might learn a lesson and, further, that you have a talk with her about proper behavior. It's signed, *Thankfully yours, Miss Wilder.*"

"I'll talk with her and get to the bottom of this. At least she apparently didn't hurt him much."

Amber was in her room when Jessica got home. Meg ordered her to go to her room after dinner. She was reading a book, or at least pretending to, when Jessica entered after knocking.

Amber put the book down and met her mother's gaze defiantly.

Jessica thought, "Repentant? Hardly."

This was confirmed when Amber jutted out her chin and said, "I'm not going to say I'm sorry! He yanked my ponytail. He does it all the time when nobody's looking. And he calls me Red!"

Jessica sighed. How did she tell her three-year-old that the day would come when she would be thrilled to attract boys? She hoped bringing up her father would help. "Your daddy would have said *sticks and stones . . .*"

"No, he wouldn't! When he got bullied, he acted just like me! Aunt Lexi said so."

She was going to kill her sister. "Honey, you love preschool. You've made so many friends there. And you've told me you love your teacher. Would you give all that up because of one rotten apple?"

Amber looked stricken. "Miss Wilder says I can't come back?"

"Not yet. But she wants you to stay home for the rest of this week. Fortunately it's Wednesday, so you're missing only a couple of days of school. But there will be no television or playdates. As for changing your teacher's mind, how about apologizing to Roger and meaning it? Then you can apologize to Miss Wilder, too."

Jessica left her daughter to mull it over. She was pretty sure she made the options clear, but with Amber she could never quite tell.

"Amber was sent home from school today. Guess why?" Jessica said to Lexi when she called. "She gave a little boy a punch in the nose because he pulls her ponytail!"

"Hey! Way to go, Amber!"

"No. Not, the *way to go*. What if she had broken his nose? Apparently he didn't need treatment from the nurse. Amber loves preschool. She'll be crushed if she's not allowed back in."

"Well you must admit she's a chip off the old block. I can just picture Danny's reaction."

The next Tuesday when Jessica got home from work Meg said Amber had been in her room, without a peep except for saying she wanted to wait for her mother before she had dinner.

Jessica found her daughter with her arm around her teddy, Mr. Fluffle. He was still her favorite gift from Grandpa, even after all these years.

Amber tucked her chin under Mr. Fluffle's neck, apparently to avoid eye contact.

"Hi, sweety. Did everything go okay at school today?"

A shrug.

"Did you do what I suggested? Did you tell Roger and your teacher you were sorry?"

A nod.

"So, he's stopped pulling your hair?"

Another nod.

"And he's stopped calling you Red?"

Another nod.

"Well, that's great. He got the message, then. All's good, right?"

Amber shook her head and answered, "No!"

"What's wrong now?"

"He's calling me *poop-butt*."

7

Amber wandered the aisles of Just for Giggles looking at favors for her birthday party only a week away. This might have been her mission, but she returned again and again to the costume section.

Jessica was ready to throw up her hands and call it quits. But not really. Her daughter was like any kid in her favorite store and awestruck by the amazing array of costumes.

"Amber, your party is going to be in the King Arthur's Castle at Fairytale Town. That's why you picked the silk gown with the fur trim."

"But Mom, fairies have wings!"

Jessica sighed. She knew there was no dissuading her when her mind was set. "Let me see what you've got there."

Amber held the hanger up to her neck and spread out one of the wings. Her dimples flashed.

Aw, those dimples. Jessica had to admit it was pretty. Really pretty. The flowing dress in multiple shades of blue complimented Amber's hair beautifully. The wings were made of silky white gossamer fabric intertwined with gold thread. "All right, but you're wearing the medieval costume for Halloween. No arguing!"

What a relief when Amber did her happy dance.

Then they finally found the perfect party favors: mini magnetic drawing boards that would work for both girls and boys. Mission accomplished until Jessica spotted tiaras in the display case below the register. She wondered if fairies wore tiaras. No matter. This fairy would.

"We'll take one of those as well," Jessica said.

Amber clapped her hands.

The cashier asked, "Which one, ladies?"

"The blue one!" Amber shouted as she did another happy dance.

* * *

The weather in late March was iffy at best, but Amber's birthday dawned bright and clear, although a little chilly. It hadn't rained in a couple of weeks, so the grounds of Fairy-tale Town would be dry.

Part of Amber's birthday package included a t-shirt and button from the park, but her daughter had her heart set on wearing her fairy costume. Jessica held firm. Amber would change into her costume before heading into the castle.

They met at nine o'clock that morning in the lot near the entrance to the park where they made introductions and passed out name tags and maps. The party of twelve children and twelve moms descended on the park en masse.

As they entered, the kids immediately scattered before being reined in by their chaperones. They hit the Jack in the Beanstalk slide first. Beside the slide sat a giant gnarly foot in an open-toed sandal. Undoubtedly, the ogre's appendage. Jessica couldn't help thinking that only kids would enjoy crawling in and out of a hole in a giant ugly foot.

Roger's mother appeared beside her. "Kinda like trying to herd kittens. Am I right?"

Jessica nodded and laughed. "Yes, kittens high on catnip." She glanced at Pam Hawkins. "I'm glad Roger was able to make the party. I wanted to apologize for my daughter's behavior."

"No need. I know how four-year-old boys can be. He got a good talking to from me and his Dad. Roger swears he's not pulling Amber's ponytail anymore. So, was he fibbing? What does Amber say?"

"Well, he wasn't lying. He's not messing with her hair anymore. He's calling her poop-butt instead."

Pam burst out laughing before controlling herself. "I'm sorry. It's just so funny and exactly the sort of thing he'd do."

"Don't apologize. I had the same reaction."

"I'll have another talk with him."

"I wouldn't bother. These things have a way of working themselves out. Who knows, there might be a budding romance in progress."

"That's a thought we might want to keep just between us."

From the beanstalk slide they followed the kids as they walked the crooked mile to Farmer Brown's Barn.

They wandered around the farm display and the storybook animals.

Amber was in her element. She loved animals. There were little piglets, three of course, and a cow who looked spry for having jumped over the moon. Last, but hardly least, there was a docile donkey that seemed to love the attention of the children.

Just then, the donkey greeted them with a loud bray. Amber jumped up and down with delight. She was thrilled when one of the park staff led him out of his pen. Amber's smile was huge when her arms stole around the animal's neck, and she stood with her cheek nestled against his. She offered up an ear-to-ear grin for the photo.

They saw lambs and a spider that made Jessica step back, ignoring her daughter's teasing. Yes, she was terrified of arachnids and wasn't ashamed to admit it. She called on Amber to rid the house of them. Naturally, Amber was too kindhearted to squash a defenseless bug. She used a paper cup and flat piece of cardboard in the capture and release method. Jessica was convinced she recognized several repeat offenders.

A couple of turns down the spiral slide on the outside of the barn brought them to party time. They headed for the castle.

Amber changed into her fairy costume and entered the party chamber to a round of hoots and clapping. Jessica had fashioned a crown braid for her daughter's long hair to better hold the tiara.

Amber sat in the giant throne chair for her picture, then held court over her party. Peanut butter and jelly finger sandwiches, her favorite, were served with fruit juice boxes. Jessica took a picture of her when she tried on her costume, and then had the bakery put the edible image onto the cake. She didn't want to mar the image with candles, so she opted for a big number four instead.

Amber clapped her hands over her mouth, but her big smile peaked around her fingers. She blew out the candle, then joined in when everyone sang the happy birthday song.

Presents came next. Giftwrap flew everywhere, proving little girls did not care about preserving pretty paper and ribbons. There was a potpourri of gifts—books, arts and crafts supplies, stuffed animals. The one she clutched to her chest in delight was a fairy potions craft kit.

Amber's brow furrowed as she reached for the last gift—a plain paper bag. Some effort had been made to make it festive with multi-colored curly bows tied to the handle, but there was no card, and Amber's name was scrawled on the side of the bag in bright red crayon.

It was from a little girl named Annie. She was easy for Jessica to spot in the group because she was red with embarrassment.

A hush fell over the room as Amber opened the bag and pulled out a coloring book and a small box of stubby crayons. When she set it on the table, it opened to reveal several pages already filled with colors.

Without missing a beat, Amber glanced over at Annie and said, "Wow, you're really good at coloring in the lines. I'm terrible at it. Can you teach me sometime?"

Annie nodded and smiled, showing the large gap in her front teeth. The tension was broken, and the noise level rose again.

Jessica's heart nearly burst with pride. This was her special girl.

The party host brought out craft supplies. Amber had chosen the wand and sword craft to round out her birthday package.

The young host, an employee of the park, handed the sword-making kits to the boys and the wand making packages to the girls. Amber politely informed him she wanted to make a sword. No girly craft for her.

Roger took notice as well. When the swords came together, he challenged Amber to a duel. If he thought Amber fought like a girl, he had another think coming. At the end of three matches, the host declared a tie.

Pam winked at her across the table. Jessica winked back.

Jessica had a surprise for Amber after the castle party ended. The Fairytale Town theater group was putting on a production of *The Princess of Camelot* on the Mother Goose Stage. The story was about a lost princess and featured music, wizardry, and swords.

At the start of the party in the castle, several of the mothers found their way to the sloping lawn in front of the stage and spread their blankets, guaranteeing good seats.

Amber positively glowed with excitement as she watched the performance. Her delight knew no bounds when the princess of the story pointed at her and beckoned her to the stage. She turned and threw Jessica an ear-to-ear grin before standing up and making her way forward.

Jessica captured the day with her camcorder. She would return again and again to this one piece of footage because it caught her daughter in a perfect moment of happiness.

* * *

A few weeks after Amber's birthday, fences were mended between Roger and Amber. He was now the former bane of her existence. Jessica suspected the truce had a lot to do with the girly-girl fighting him to a draw, all while trying not to trip over her gown. Who said a combatant couldn't rumble and be stylish at the same time?

Jessica was surprised a few days later when Amber climbed into bed with her before dawn and asked, "Can I stay home today, Momma? I don't feel good."

Her daughter loved preschool. Jessica could count on the fingers of one hand the number of times Amber felt too sick to attend.

Jessica held her hand up, and Amber nuzzled her cheek against her mother's palm. "You don't feel warm. What's the matter, honey?"

"My tummy hurts." Jessica touched her stomach, and Amber cried out. Not a ruse then.

"It's still early, baby. Let me get you some of that Pepto Bismol Nanny Meg keeps special for you. We'll see how you feel in a couple of hours. How about that?"

"Okay."

Amber's stomach pain eased enough for her to fall asleep, and Jessica let Amber share her bed the rest of the night.

Morning brought more complaints of stomach trouble and a slight fever. Jessica was not too concerned. She hoped it was just a bug going around. Still, she was grateful when Meg said she'd keep a close eye on her.

When Jessica got home from work that night Amber was lying on the couch holding a hot water bottle on her stomach. Meg had taken her temperature and was reading the results. She urged her to drink some water, but Amber turned her face away and groaned.

Meg stared at Jessica, a look of concern marring her usually placid features. "A couple of degrees over. She's been complaining of a stomachache all day, and her appetite is down." Meg removed the water bottle and beckoned Jessica over. "I think her belly is swollen, too."

Jessica put her hand against Amber's belly. Meg was right. It felt swollen. "I'll see if I can get her in to see Dr. Wyatt tomorrow."

It was after hours, but fortunately the pediatrician's answering service was able to fit Amber in at four in the afternoon.

"I don't have court tomorrow, so I'll come home around three. That will give me plenty of time to get her to her appointment."

She spoke to Lexi later that night, and her sister put her mind at ease.

"Probably just a bug, like you said. But it doesn't hurt to get it checked out. Want me to come with?"

"No, it's your day off. Tell that hunky boyfriend of yours I said hi."

"Which one?"

"Very funny. Love you, bye."

Lexi tended to change boyfriends as often as she did shoes. Her sister wasn't flighty by nature; it was a serious commitment that was the monkey wrench.

A friend had talked her into a weekend Harley convention, where she met Matt Baumgartner, a dude on a Harley in full-out leather. It was a match made in heaven, and it didn't hurt that the man was gorgeous. He had a head of curly black hair. Lexi commented that she longed to run her fingers through it. While most of the bikers sported beards, he was clean-shaven, a feature she much appreciated.

He was a financial adviser, an entrepreneur invested in his own business who worked behind a desk. He wore button down shirts and Armani suits during the week and leathered up on weekends—an irresistible combination, Lexi explained.

Oh, Lexi loved him. Jessica had no doubt of that. She just had a hard time admitting it. Even to herself.

*   *   *

Dr. Raymond Wyatt was one of Jessica's favorite people. He had been from the start. His love of his profession was evident in the exam room where they waited. A mural against one wall depicted an underwater scene with cartoonish fish. A large red octopus appeared to be waving from the sea bottom. A number of those same fish adorned the ceiling above the exam table.

The doctor's roll-around computer stand was decorated with a hodge-podge collection of stickers. There was no rhyme or reason to it, footballs, basketballs, and soccer balls appeared alongside Disney characters. This had always been a happy place for her daughter.

Amber sat at the end of the exam table and studied the stickers. Jessica was heartened when her daughter perked up a little as she stared at the stand. "Mom, I like Doctor Wyatt, but there's no fairy stickers on it. Doesn't he like fairies?"

Sasha, Dr. Wyatt's nurse, came in on that last part. "Dr. Wyatt loves fairies. But his daughter won't give up any of her stickers."

"I have lots of them. Mom, can we bring some next time?"

Jessica nodded, "Absolutely."

Sasha was young and had a fresh scrubbed face. Her long hair was pulled up in a ponytail much like Amber's. She smiled and twirled her hair with her fingers. "Look at that, we're matchy, matchy."

Amber touched her own hair and started to smile before doubling over in pain.

Sasha tsked and smoothed Amber's hair back. "I'm just going to take your temperature and check your blood pressure, then the doctor will be right in." She pulled a pink and white polka dot hospital gown out of the cabinet and handed it to Jessica. "Amber can keep her underwear on."

Sasha turned just before opening the door. "Almost forgot, just wait till you see his bowtie and suspenders. They're his best yet!"

A few minutes later, Dr. Wyatt knocked and entered the room. Tall, with a stocky build, he had clear brown eyes and the coolest bowtie and suspenders. They lit up and blinked on and off.

Amber's dimples winked big at the sight. "Dr. Wyatt, you're all lighted up!"

"You like? Yeah, they're my daughter's favorites, too."

He sat at his computer, looking over the information on the screen, then took a couple of latex gloves out of a box near the sink.

"So, Little Miss Amber, I understand you're feeling a bit under the weather."

Amber's hand curled around her stomach. Her smile disappeared as she nodded.

Taking the stethoscope from around his neck, Dr. Wyatt scooted the stool over. "Well, let's have a listen and see if we can figure out what's going on."

He listened to her heart, checked her ears, and ran gentle fingers along the sides of her neck and behind her ears. He had her lie back and urged her hands away from her stomach. He applied pressure, first to the area away from the pain and then directly to the spot she was favoring.

Amber winced and cried out. Jessica stifled her own cry. She looked down at her daughter, then up at Dr. Wyatt, but he gave nothing away.

He lowered the gown to cover Amber's legs and helped her sit up. "Okay then, Miss Amber. That's it for now." He peeled off his rubber gloves and crossed to the hazardous waste bin, tossing them inside before turning to the sink to wash his hands.

"Jessica, you can help Amber get dressed. Nurse Sasha will take her to the children's lounge where she can relax while we talk in my office. It's right across the hall."

Jessica was suddenly trembling inside. If it was just a bug, he would have written a prescription and sent them on their way. He wanted to talk to her, but not in front of her daughter. Now, she was really worried.

She helped Amber put on her clothes. When Sasha led her out, Jessica crossed to Dr. Wyatt's office and sat in front of his desk.

"Jessica, I felt a lump when I examined Amber's belly. I'm going to order blood and urine tests. I'll also order an ultrasound that will allow us to better determine what we're dealing with. Now, I don't want you to worry. I know that the word *tumor* conjures up images of malignancy, but as often as not they are benign growths."

"But the pain . . ."

"It can simply be from tissue being displaced by the growth of the tumor. Let's not speculate until we know more. In the meantime, let's put Amber on a regimen of soft food and plenty of fluids."

Amber had been unable to keep anything down the last day and a half, so a urine sample was out of the question. Jessica promised to keep her hydrated and bring a sample back the next day. She fought to keep her emotions under control when Amber whimpered at each jab of the needle.

Amber was more animated on the drive home. Dr. Wyatt had given her a dose of children's Tylenol to ease her discomfort. Jessica turned onto her street and noticed Meg's Honda still in the driveway. Of course she had waited for their return. She was family, and Jessica felt so blessed to have her as part of their lives.

Amber had little appetite but they urged her to drink the chicken broth and juice before Jessica tucked her into bed.

Back in the kitchen, Jessica told Meg everything. The comfort of her arms was a welcome balm. "Thank you, Meg. I don't know what we'd do without you. Truly."

"I've made up your favorite cobb salad. Let me plate that up for you. There's a baguette from the bakery as well. Made fresh today."

"I can't."

"You need to keep up your strength. We don't want two patients on our hands. You call Lexi while I put it together for you."

She pulled her phone from her purse and called her sister. Lexi answered on the first ring. "Lexi. Please come."

"On my way."

* * *

The tests confirmed a mass. A biopsy confirmed malignancy. When the CT and MRI scans didn't give definitive answers, an MIBG scan finally confirmed the diagnosis—Neuroblastoma.

Dr. Wyatt referred Amber to an oncologist, Dr. Elizabeth Sullivan. "She's the top in her field," he said.

Days later, Jessica and Lexi sat in front of her desk and listened in stunned silence as she explained what it all meant.

"Neuroblastoma is a type of cancer that starts in immature nerve cells. They're called neuroblasts. In normal circumstances, these cells grow into working nerve cells. But this cancer causes those cells to grow uncontrollably, and they then form a solid tumor. The first step in Amber's treatment is radiation to try to shrink the tumor."

Jessica leaned forward. "That last scan, the MIBG? I understand it's a nuclear scan test and actual radioactive material is injected. How safe was that?"

"MIBG, *meta-iodobenzylguanidine*. It sounds scary, I know. Let me first say that the MIBG scan is the best test available to locate and confirm the presence of tumors of the nervous tissues. There is a relatively rare side effect of a rise in blood pressure, which usually resolves itself within a couple of days. Amber was closely monitored, and she came through the scan without any side effects."

Jessica was afraid to ask, but she had to know. "Did the scan tell you what stage Amber's cancer is in?"

"Neuroblastoma is divided into three stages. Low, intermediate, and high risk. Amber is in the high-risk stage."

Jessica felt the first tear in her heart. She reached for Lexi's hand and asked the only question that really mattered, "Is there a cure for this cancer?"

Dr. Sullivan hesitated.

That was all the answer Jessica needed. She covered her face with her hands and grabbed a tissue from the box on the desk to wipe at her tears.

The doctor looked from Lexi to Jessica. "Do you need a moment? I can . . ."

Jessica said, "No! No, please."

"All right. But just understand that the numbers I'm about to give you are based on statistical analysis. Please know that kids beat the odds all the time. For high-risk neuroblastoma, the five-year survival rate is around fifty percent."

With that, the tear in Jessica's heart became a chasm. A mewling cry sounded loud in the silent room. Jessica recognized it as her own but was helpless to stop it. Lexi stood and took her into her arms.

Dr. Sullivan stepped out.

Jessica pulled herself back together through sheer force of will. She kept reminding herself that her daughter's life was on the line. Falling apart was not an option.

Her tortured gaze met Dr. Sullivan's as she walked back into the room a short time later and sat behind her desk.

"What happens now?" Jessica asked. "What can we expect?"

"This stage of the disease means, in essence, that Amber is going to need longer, more aggressive treatments. As I said, we'll attempt to shrink the tumor with radiation. Then we'll follow up with chemo if that isn't successful."

Lexi spoke up and asked, "How *successful* has radiation and chemo proven to be for this cancer? Are there any clinical trials going on right now?"

"No treatment is a one-size-fits-all solution. Different patients respond to different treatments. Chemo and radiation have proven successful in some patients. We'll start there. We'll monitor Amber closely, and if those treatments don't do the trick, we'll move on to others. Clinical trials included."

Jessica's fear factor had been a six out of ten when she walked into that room. It shot up to ten as she listened to Dr. Sullivan explain the relentless disease weakening her daughter's tiny body and described the frightening treatments ahead.

She knew Amber was in good hands. Dr. Sullivan was patient with their endless questions. She even answered some they hadn't thought to ask. She gave them her undivided attention, never once glancing at the clock. Dr. Wyatt had said she was top in her field, and Jessica experienced that firsthand.

"I know this is overwhelming and there's no doubt it's going to take a toll on you. You're going to feel helpless. My suggestion would be to read as much as you can about this disease."

Lexi nodded. "Trust me, we will."

"Good. It will help you make informed decisions about Amber's care." Reaching across her desk, she picked up a folder and handed it to Jessica. "I had my assistant put together some resource data for you. I've also added contact information for the hospital's CLS, our child life specialist June Edwards. She's absolutely wonderful with children and heads our medical play program."

Jessica had never heard those words strung together. "Medical play program?"

"Yes. Tests and treatments are often a traumatic experience for children. June uses a combination of real and pretend equipment to help children become comfortable with medical procedures. Does Amber have a teddy bear?"

Lexi nodded, "Oh boy, does she ever. Mr. Fluffle was a gift from grandpa."

Dr. Sullivan smiled. "Perfect. She'll be able to take his blood pressure."

"Amber is going to love that." Jessica glanced through the folder. "I'll get in touch with June right away."

"Jessica, we're going to do everything we can to nourish Amber's body and mind so she can find the strength to fight this disease. But she's going to need your strength, too. Please take care of yourself. For you. For her."

They were mostly silent on the drive home. Lexi drove and held her hand, squeezing gently whenever she felt herself faltering.

Before pulling into the driveway Lexi cleared her throat and spoke softly, "Remember what Dr. Sullivan said . . . kids beat the odds all the time."

Jessica stepped from the garage into the kitchen, and there stood Danny's mother. Ellen opened her arms and Jessica walked into them. She was determined to stay strong, but all that fell apart when Ellen whispered, "I'm here, Jess. Whatever it is we'll get through this. I promise you that."

Jessica's tears soaked Ellen's blouse, but she seemed to pay it no mind as she stroked her hair. It soothed her as no words could. Finally stepping back, she asked, "Amber?"

"She's resting. I just looked in on her. She's all right, I promise."

Jessica nodded. She resisted the urge to check for herself. Not like this. The last thing she wanted to do was frighten her baby.

They sat at the table, and Meg poured them each a glass of iced tea. She set out a cookie tin, but it sat untouched.

Jessica told them the diagnosis and the next steps. She left out the prognosis for now. She couldn't bring herself to say the words. She just couldn't.

* * *

Jessica arranged a visit with June Edwards a couple of days later. Amber entered the medical playroom with Mr. Fluffle clutched to her chest. Her eyes widened to the size of saucers when she stepped through the door.

June came forward. "Jessica? Amber? I'm June Edwards. It's nice to meet you." She bent at the waist to peer at the teddy in Amber's arms. "And this must be Mr. Fluffle."

She nodded, "Yes. But he's afraid of needles."

"Okay. No needles for Mr. Fluffle today."

Amber looked around the room. "Momma says you have a machine here to check Mr. Fluffle, like the one Nurse Sasha put on my arm."

Jessica explained, "She had her blood pressure checked."

June nodded. "Why don't we bring him to the examination table?" Amber surprised them when she took the cuff and slipped it right around the teddy's arm and started squeezing the little airbag. The pointer rose above the red marker into the blue and she smiled. "Mr. Fluffle, you are A-OK!"

June produced a blank rag doll and encouraged Amber to draw herself. She picked up a red marker and added hair. She used black to draw in her eyes, brows and nose. She stopped and thought for a second and then drew a sad mouth.

Jessica felt a tug at her heart, but let June lead the conversation.

"Can you tell me why you drew the sad face?"

Amber grimaced and nudged at the plastic needle on the table with her finger. "I don't like sticks."

June pointed to a spot on the right side of the doll's chest. "Can you draw me a small circle right here." When Amber did as she asked June explained, "That's what we call an implantable venous port. That means it's going under the skin. You can just call it the port. That means you won't have to get needle sticks every time they have to give you medicine or take blood for testing."

"Is it going to hurt?"

Jessica caught herself unconsciously rubbing the spot on her own chest as June answered.

"Not at all. You'll be asleep. And it's pretty quick, so you won't have to stay in the hospital when it's done."

Amber was more relaxed after that. She got to listen to her teddy's heartbeat, made butterflies out of gauze and tape, and used several needles to do splatter painting on brightly colored craft paper.

Since at some point Amber's healthcare might include surgery for removal of the tumor, June brought out an anesthesia mask decorated with googly eyes. She explained that children were often fearful of the mask being placed over their face before surgery. She dipped the mask in a bowl of bubble solution and encouraged Amber to blow through the opening.

Amber's giggles were music to Jessica's ears.

8

Barely a week later, Jessica was helping Amber get ready for her first trip to the hospital to start radiation treatments. She took one of Amber's shift-type dresses off the hanger in the closet. The care team had recommended comfortable loose-fitting clothes.

Amber reached into her dresser drawer and pulled out her fairy warrior t-shirt and leggings.

A stand-off!

Jessica shook the hanger at her daughter. "Amber, we talked about this."

Her daughter's chin jutted out.

Ever the peacemaker, Ellen offered a solution. "How about if Amber wears her dress to the hospital. Then she can change to her t-shirt and leggings after her treatment, and we can stop at a nice place for ice cream if she feels okay?"

Thank God for Danny's mother. The last thing she wanted to do was fight with her daughter on this day, of all days. Jessica tucked the clothes into Amber's backpack. They headed out the door and were on their way.

Tristin, the radiation technician, led them back to the treatment room. A redhead like Amber and Jessica, she was bubbly and had a warm smile.

Jessica heard her daughter ask, "Will it hurt?" Tristin replied instantly, "Not a bit. It might be a little noisy, though."

The technician's words did little to ease Jessica's anxiety. She paced the narrow hall before settling into a chair against the wall. One of the arms had a loose screw, and she unconsciously tried again and again to tighten it. Her fingers were red and raw when the door opened nearly twenty minutes later.

Tristin held Amber's hand as she led her out. Amber's dimples were winking. A good sign.

Jessica looked back and forth between them. "That was quick. How did it go?"

Tristin smiled down at Amber. "Your daughter was a real trooper. Didn't move a muscle. Made my job super easy." She opened the door to the small dressing area and added, "I'll have some instructions ready for you when Amber is dressed."

"Okay."

"Good. I know her care team discussed the side effects Amber might experience, but these instructions will be a reminder and will guide you in dealing with them if they appear."

When they walked back out, Tristin handed Jessica a folder and bent to hug Amber. "I'll see you tomorrow."

It was Monday. Radiation treatments would continue once a day through Friday and start again the following week.

They joined Ellen in the outer waiting room, and Amber told her all about Tristin and the big scary machine. "But I was brave, Gammy. Tristin said so."

"I'm sure you were, my little ragamuffin."

Late in the afternoon Amber was fast asleep on the living room couch with Mr. Fluffle on her chest. She experienced a little nausea after her treatment but was faring well otherwise. Ellen sat knitting while Jessica was at the kitchen table catching up on her emails. The doorbell rang, waking Amber. She rubbed the sleep from her eyes.

Jessica waved Ellen back so she could answer the door herself.

Roger Hawkins stood on the porch. In one hand he held an envelope that nearly dwarfed him and a gaily colored gift bag in the other. His mother stood behind him.

Pam phoned earlier in the day asking if they could stop by. Her daughter loved surprises, so Jessica didn't mention the call to Amber.

Jessica held a finger to her lips and opened the door wide.

Mr. Fluffle went flying when Amber spotted Roger walking into the room.

Roger sat beside her on the couch and handed her the gifts.

She tried to open the flap of the envelope but couldn't manage it. Ellen stepped in to help. Amber opened the card, revealing a giant 3D pop-up garden of flowers and butterflies. The inscription and signatures were on a separate parchment. The calligraphy was beautiful, undoubtedly penned by Miss Wilder. Ellen read it aloud: *Amber, we miss you at school. We hope you get better real soon.*

Roger pointed at the parchment, "The whole class signed it. Miss Wilder, too."

Amber pulled the gift bag onto her lap. She pushed aside the tissue paper and pulled out a large mason jar. The frosted glass and soft glowing orange light inside highlighted the silhouette of a fairy swinging from the moon. Raffia yarn ribbon and a rose delicately wrapped the lid.

Amber hugged the jar to her chest and rewarded Roger with her biggest smile. "I love it! Thank you."

"Not me, my mom made it."

Amber set everything aside and crossed to give Pam a big hug. Then she grabbed the gifts and headed for the stairs. "Come on, Roger!"

Jessica stopped her before she could disappear. "Wait, let's get a picture. We can get it printed and send it on to your class with a thank-you note."

Amber positioned the card and the mason jar on the floor in front of her and rested her head on her hands. She smiled big. Jessica took a couple of shots.

Amber then jumped to her feet and headed for the stairs again. "Roger, come on!"

Jessica was delighted to see her daughter's enthusiasm. It was in these moments she felt certain Amber would beat the odds.

Pam glanced over at Jessica, a smile tugging at her lips. "Should we be worried?"

"Nah." Jessica smiled in return, "Who would have guessed, right?"

Ellen looked puzzled. Jessica reminded her of the feud between the two friends, and how it had become a thing of the past.

Ellen offered to make a fresh pot of coffee, and Jessica picked up the discarded gift bag from in front of the couch. She held it up for Pam's view, "You?"

"Nope, that was all Roger."

Who would have guessed?

*   *   *

Early on a Saturday morning a couple of weeks after radiation treatments began, Jessica woke to the feel of Amber's hand on her shoulder. Tears were streaming down her face.

Sleep gave way to panic. "Honey, are you okay? Does something hurt?"

Amber shook her head and held up her hand. Her fingers clutched long strands of hair.

Jessica urged Amber to climb on the bed, then put her arms around her and kissed the top of her head. "Oh, honey. Dr. Sullivan said this might happen. Tristin, too."

Amber only cried harder.

Jessica took the hair from Amber's fingers and carefully wrapped them in a tissue she pulled out of a box on the nightstand. She grabbed another tissue and dried her daughter's tears.

"Do you remember what Tristin said last week? She said her hair stylist works in a salon that can make a wig out of your hair. And no one will be able to tell the difference."

"I like Tristin."

"I do, too, baby. And she knows how important a girl's looks are. I tell you what. Why don't we go have a look-see? That way you can decide for yourself if you want a wig. Okay?"

"Can Gammy and Auntie Lexi come, too?"

"I'm sure they wouldn't miss it for the world."

Jessica got an appointment at Shear Delight for the following Monday after Amber's treatment. The salon was divided in two. The left was devoted to regular customers, and the right housed the wig side of the business.

Fran Kramer, their stylist, a woman in her early sixties greeted them warmly. She wore a colorful caftan and had a gorgeous mane of silver hair caught up in a loose chignon. She was a tall woman, and Amber had to tilt her head way back to look at her.

She led them to a lounge area with armchairs pulled up to a round glass coffee table. She offered refreshments and took a seat when they declined.

Fran spoke directly to Amber. Jessica liked her for that. "Amber, Tristin has told me so much about you. She says you're her favorite patient. She also told me all about your beautiful red hair." Fran looked over at Jessica. "Just like your mommy's. She's right, too. Your mom says you're thinking about maybe getting a wig made from your own hair."

Amber nodded, and Fran picked up a small album from the table.

"I know what you're going through is scary, and losing your hair can make you sad. What I have in this album are pictures of two little girls, just like you, who were going through the same thing. They decided they wanted a wig made. Would you like to look at the pictures?"

Jessica was happy to see Amber perk up.

Fran opened the album to the first sleeve of pictures, three in all. "This is Molly. There's a picture when she first came to the salon, a second picture when she was wearing the wig we made for her, and the third picture is the one her mommy sent me when Molly's hair grew back. Those pictures are not in order. Can you tell which one is the wig?"

Amber nodded and pointed at the one in the middle.

"Nope, it's this first one."

Amber's eyes grew big. "Can I guess again?"

"Sure. This is Angela. Which one do you think is the wig?"

Amber and Lexi picked the right picture but then had to admit it was a lucky guess. Jessica looked at her daughter. "So, what do you think, honey?"

Amber didn't hesitate. "Wig," she declared.

Fran settled Amber in the salon chair and took measurements of her head. She did some figuring on a pad of paper and gave Amber a coloring book and crayons to keep her entertained while she went back to the lounge area.

She sat across from Jessica and looked at her notes. "At least eight ounces of hair are needed to make a wig. Amber does have that and more. But to really give her the fullness she has now, you'll need to purchase supplemental hair. The wig manufacturer I use can help with that. They keep an inventory of donated hair on hand. And they'll make sure you're happy with the choice before it's added."

Jessica didn't hesitate, she reached behind her head and lifted her ponytail. "I think I've got all the supplemental hair they'll need." She would give anything to help her daughter.

Lexi whooped and slapped her legs. "I've been trying to talk her into a stylish do for years!"

Jessica refused the handful of hairstyle magazines Fran brought over. She put herself completely in Lexi's hands, insisting on only one caveat—absolutely no tinting. She closed her eyes and didn't open them, even when she felt the pull of the scissors.

She sat through a blow dry and the spritz of some kind of product. Fran's fingers pulled her hair this way and that.

Amber's words got her attention. "Oh, Momma, it looks bouncy!"

Now she *was* afraid to look. A short bob greeted her in the mirror. A short, jagged bob. *Oh boy.*

Fran gave it a final spritz and smiled. "It's known in the business as the low-fuss style."

Lexi gave it a two-thumbs up and high-fived Fran.

Ellen nodded. "It suits you."

Amber was next. After some debate, she agreed to let Fran shave her head. When the transformation was complete, though, she looked at her reflection in the mirror and grew teary-eyed.

Ellen retrieved a plastic bag she'd brought along. She pulled three knit caps out. Each had a flower accent. She spread them out on the shelf below the mirror. "Yellow, green, and blue, your favorite colors, punkin."

The caps explained the knitting needles Ellen was perpetually wielding. Jessica was so grateful for her presence. She'd become deeply, firmly, lovingly rooted in their lives. They were a family of the heart.

* * *

The initial side effects of Amber's radiation treatments were mild, but more distressing symptoms soon appeared in the days and weeks that followed—severe belly cramps, vomiting, and diarrhea wracked her little body. They pumped her full of antidiarrheal medication and pain relief medication and antibiotics to kill the bacteria in her intestines. When she had any appetite at all, she was restricted to a lactose-free, low-fat diet.

Adding to that, Amber had developed skin problems. The radiation treatment area had become red and blistered like a bad sunburn, a cruel joke because the area was sensitive to sunlight, robbing her daughter of the outdoor fun she loved. Dr. Sullivan said the skin irritation would gradually go away after the treatments stopped. This far into the treatments, Jessica couldn't see an end in sight.

When the end of radiation treatments finally came six weeks later, they hit a brick wall. Dr. Sullivan dealt the blow.

"Jessica, the results of the scan I ordered are back. They're not what we'd hoped for."

Jessica's heart sank. She reached for Ellen's hand. "What do they show?"

"The radiation has not shrunk the tumor. I'm afraid the cancer has spread to her chest."

The rock that lodged in her throat threatened to cut off her breath. She squeezed her mother-in-law's fingers so hard she knew they must hurt, but Ellen didn't pull away. It took every ounce of strength Jessica possessed to hold herself in check. She had to be strong for Amber.

"Is chemo next?" Radiation was hard. Chemo would likely be brutal. But if it was her daughter's only hope, then so be it.

"The next step will be the removal of the tumor. Then there's a treatment I'd like to discuss with you."

"Chemo?"

"Actually no. Do you remember the MIBG scan first administered to Amber to diagnose her illness?"

Jessica nodded, "Yes," she answered.

"A low-dose radioactive iodine was used to make the cancer cells show up on the scan. MIBG given with a higher-dose radioactive iodine has shown promise for killing the neuroblastoma cells."

A flicker of hope glimmered but soon went out. Hadn't she used those same words when advocating the radiation treatments?

Ellen spoke up beside her. "What will the MIBG treatments consist of?"

"The MIBG molecule will be combined with a higher-dose radioactive iodine and administered through a venous port. That will take under two hours. Amber won't experience any pain during those infusions. She'll stay in the hospital for a few days so she can be closely monitored."

Jessica remembered the medical play day. "June mentioned a port when Amber said she was afraid of needles, but she didn't go into detail."

"The port is a small, implantable reservoir with a thin silicone tube that's attached to a vein. It will be placed under the skin on the right side of Amber's chest. She will be put under general anesthesia, but the procedure takes only about ninety minutes."

"But higher dose radioactivity? Isn't that dangerous?" Jessica was having trouble wrapping her head around the idea.

"The benefit of MIBG is that only tumor cells absorb it, thus causing few problems in nearby healthy cells. However, because it's radioactive, Amber will get her treatments in a special room. It's the size of two hospital rooms, one of which acts as a suite for the parents. The therapy room itself is built with lead-lined walls and doors. Several lead shields will also be placed around Amber's bed to protect against any radiation coming from the treatment."

Jessica let go of Ellen's hand and leaned forward. "Will the lead shields allow me to be in the room with her while she'd getting the treatment?"

"The radioactive level in the room will be very high during the two-hour treatment and can continue to be so for the first twenty-four hours. During that time only her care team will have access. You'll be able to communicate with Amber through closed circuit TV or an iPad. There's also an observation window between the two rooms."

"After that first twenty-four-hour period, family members are encouraged to take on the task of caregiving."

"Given Amber's age, and how scary this can all be, having

you there to see to her basic needs will go a long way toward easing her anxiety. You'll wear a dosimeter—a badge that will measure the radiation you get from caring for Amber. Our staff will keep a close watch on that. She'll stay in the MIBG room for three to five days while the radiation level drops enough for her to go home."

Jessica remembered Amber's lack of appetite and the relentless nausea she'd suffered from the radiation treatments. "What about side effects?"

"Most children experience very few side effects. That's because this therapy stays in the area of the neuroblastoma. It can sometimes cause mild nausea and vomiting. Amber will feel tired or sluggish. It can affect the salivary glands, so there might be some swelling of her cheeks. In rare cases, it might cause high blood pressure, but that's temporary and passes quickly."

"While only tumor cells absorb the MIBG treatment, it does affect the bone marrow that makes blood cells. That can result in low blood counts for weeks afterwards. To counteract that, Amber is going to need an IV infusion of her own marrow. We'll collect those stem cells before treatments start."

Jessica sat back in the chair. She dug her nails into the palms of her hands hard enough to pierce the skin. "You're going to take bone marrow . . ." Jessica pictured it and was filled with horror.

"There's another, less invasive way to harvest stem cells. The procedure isn't painful, and Amber will be awake. It involves temporarily removing blood from her body, separating out the stem cells, and then returning it to her body. The whole process takes about three hours."

Jessica closed her eyes. Hope and fear played a tug of war inside her head.

Dr. Sullivan cleared her throat. "This is a lot to take in, I know, but I can't stress enough the need to move forward as quickly as possible. The first step will be to set up an appointment for you to meet with Amber's care team. They'll go over what we've covered and offer more detailed information. You'll also need to go through special training before Amber's admitted."

"There's an opening on Wednesday at 10:00 a.m. I'll pencil you in. Think about it tonight and let me know in the morning if you want to go ahead with the treatment."

Jessica shook her head. "No need. I'll be there." The decision came easily; the alternative was unthinkable.

9

When Jessica and Ellen returned home after the consultation, neither was surprised to see Lexi's Honda parked at the curb. The dashboard clock showed half-past ten, so her sister must have headed over right after her shift.

Meg and Lexi were seated at the kitchen table with coffee cups in hand when they walked through the door.

Jessica looked at Meg, "Amber?"

"She's napping."

Jessica set her purse on the kitchen counter and headed for the stairs. "I'll just be a minute."

She quietly turned the knob and stepped into Amber's room, meaning to take a quick peek to reassure herself she was all right. Amber sat up and held out her arms. Jessica was dismayed when she saw the dark circles under her daughter's eyes.

Jessica crossed the room, moved Mr. Fluffle aside and lay down beside her. She held up her hand, and Amber nuzzled her cheek against it.

"Hi, sweetie. Nanny Meg said you were napping. I'm sorry I woke you."

"It's okay, Momma. I wasn't sleeping. I was having tea with Mr. Fluffle." She reached under her pillow and produced two little teacups. "Please don't tell Nanny Meg."

Jessica took the cups out of Amber's hand and set them on the nightstand. "I won't, but how about taking that nap now? I'll stay here until you fall asleep. Okay?"

"Okay."

When Amber finally dozed off, Jessica rejoined the women in the kitchen. She looked over at Meg, "Sorry. I got sidetracked. Amber was only pretending to sleep. She was enjoying a spot of tea with Mr. Fluffle. Let's keep that to ourselves, though. I promised I wouldn't tattle."

They chuckled, glad for a light moment in an otherwise wretched day.

Lexi cracked her knuckle, a nervous habit from childhood. "Ellen filled us in. You know I'm here. Whatever you need, I'm here."

Jessica took a sip from the cup of tea Meg poured for her. The hot liquid sloshed over when Jessica set her cup down with suddenly nerveless fingers. A brown stain spread across the placemat. She ignored it.

"How am I going to tell her?"

Lexi reached over and blotted the spill. "You're going to be meeting with her care team, and Ellen said you'll be going through training. I'd hold off saying anything until then. They deal with these situations all the time. They'll have some suggestions."

Jessica looked across the table at her sister. "You're right."

Lexi offered a half-hearted smile. "Aren't I always?"

* * *

Everything moved quickly after that. Just a few weeks after the surgery to remove Amber's tumor, Jessica was helping her choose her *besty* for the long hospital stay.

Jessica picked up her teddy. "How 'bout Mr. Fluffle?"

Amber shook her head. "No, Momma. I can't lose Mr. Fluffle!" Then she burst into tears.

Jessica couldn't believe she'd forgotten the caution about bringing toys from home. She quickly backpedaled. "Honey, you don't have to take one of your friends from home. The hospital is going to have lots of toys for you."

Lexi walked in the door jangling her keys. "Come on guys, we've got to get moving!" She noticed Amber's tears and slipped the keys into her pocket. "What's the matter, honey? I thought you were excited about glowing in the dark."

Jessica answered for her, "She wants to take a friend from home, but she's scared the radiation will hurt them."

Lexi marched over to the bookshelf and picked up the mason jar. "Well, how about Twinkle?" Amber's name for the fairy in the jar. "She's already radioactive. Where do you think that orange glow comes from?"

Problem solved.

Ellen waited for them at the front door. When Amber stepped off the last step, Ellen took her hand and led her to the car.

While Amber was distracted, Lexi whispered to Jessica, "Roger's mom can put together another mason jar, right?"

Jessica whispered back, "I'm counting on it."

After securing Amber into her booster seat, Ellen went around to the front passenger door while Lexi got behind the wheel.

Jessica was grateful for that. The need to be near her daughter was overwhelming, especially now, en route to the hospital.

Ellen and Lexi walked with them as far as the entrance doors. They exchanged hugs, holding their emotions in check. No sad faces. The experience was frightening enough without adding more anxiety to it.

As Amber was checked in, a familiar figure appeared— June Edwards, officially known as the hospital's child life specialist, unofficially known as her daughter's guardian angel.

She led them back to the oncology ward and the MIBG unit. They entered the parent suite first where Jessica placed their bags and pulled Twinkle from one of them. She handed the jar to her daughter.

June bent down to look at the jar in Amber's hands. "What's this?"

Amber held it out. "It's Twinkle. She's a fairy. My Auntie Lexi says she'll be all right cuz she's already radioactive. See, she's glowing."

"She sure is. You know, fairies are magical creatures. It's said they bring good luck."

Jessica dearly hoped that was true.

Amber looked apprehensive and clutched Twinkle to her chest when they walked toward the door to the treatment room. Then, her face lit up at the sight of the bedspread. It was pink, her favorite color, and had a fairy motif.

The kindhearted gesture filled Jessica with a swell of gratitude. She realized superheroes come in many forms.

✳ ✳ ✳

The treatment began the next morning. As promised, a window into the MIBG room allowed Jessica to observe the procedure.

Amber seemed to be doing well. She didn't appear in distress. She watched the activity around her, turning often to look at her as if to reassure herself she was still there.

The window was high up on the wall, so the lone chair in the room was useless. Jessica didn't know how long she stood there before June's reflection appeared behind her. She was holding a tall stool. Jessica sat and nodded her thanks without taking her eyes off Amber. She would never let her guard down.

When the procedure was over, Jessica took advantage of the video conferencing feature installed in the suite.

"Honey, you did so well. I'm so proud of you. How are you feeling?"

"K."

Amber soon nodded off. Jessica was expecting that. Fatigue was high on the list of side effects.

Jessica picked up a book she brought along. After a few pages, she gave up and returned to watching the rise and fall of her daughter's chest. She must have been having a happy dream because her face broke into a smile and her dimples flashed.

A flashback struck without warning. Danny. Their last communication. That dazzling smile . . .

She took several deep breaths, but the tears came anyway. She closed her eyes, fighting for control. Amber's voice pulled her back.

"Don't cry Momma. It's okay. It doesn't hurt, I swear."

How could it be that her daughter was concerned for *her*? That sweet, precious little girl was worried about her. Jessica's heart was near to bursting with love.

"I wasn't crying about you, baby. It was just a bad dream."
And a little white lie, she thought.

Just a little white lie . . .

* * *

The five days Amber spent in the MIBG room were
uneventful except for a handful of bouts with nausea and a
rise in blood pressure that quickly passed. After the initial
twenty-four hours, Jessica was able to see to her daily routine.
The biggest hurdle Amber had to overcome was boredom. She
watched all the videos provided by the hospital staff twice.
The games the hospital provided helped, but limited mobility for an otherwise very active four-year-old was torture.

The day the radiation levels were low enough for
discharge was the happiest for both of them. The fight wasn't
over by any means, but allowing a little normalcy back into
their lives was a relief. Amber would be back in a few weeks
for an infusion of the harvested stem cells and more scans
would be taken to determine if the treatment worked.

For the time being, that all faded into the background as
they made their way out of the ward.

Jessica wished she could thank the entire care team, but
that wasn't possible in the busy ward. The radiation was low,
but not completely gone. Amber couldn't have close contact
with anyone for the next seven days. She gave everyone she
passed a huge smile and enthusiastic wave. She blew kisses to
June. But the best part was the wheelchair ride through the
corridors. "Zoom. Zoom, Momma, faster!"

Jessica loved hearing this. Her daughter was back, and Jessica felt she could finally breathe again. Still, she kept up the slow and steady pace.

Ellen stood beside the car in the pick-up lane at the front of the hospital. They loaded up, hoping the experience would retreat into a distant memory.

Amber startled them with a shriek from the backseat, "Momma! Twinkle. I forgot her. We have to go back!"

Jessica glanced over at Ellen, who nodded. "I didn't forget her. She's in my bag in the trunk." She was thankful she asked Ellen to pick up Twinkle's identical twin from Pam.

As a nurse, Lexi had to be careful about coming into contact with radiation, so she called Amber before her shift. Jessica was in the shower. Ellen took the cell phone to Amber's room. The rules were strict: avoid close contact as much as possible. She put it on speaker and stood at the foot of her bed. Not ideal, but it worked.

Amber's whole room had been plasticized, including Mr. Fluffle. She understood the need for the precautions. Her teddy was still her constant companion, plastic and all.

While Amber slept, Ellen took her turn in the shower and put the clothes she had worn to the hospital in the washer with Jessica's.

She joined Jessica in the living room where music played softly. She smiled and shook her head. "Your secret is out. Amber knows Twinkle's an imposter. Apparently, there was a magic marker spot on the bottom of the original mason jar. She asked Lexi and me to keep it a secret. She didn't want you to feel bad."

"That's my girl. A real softy, like her daddy."

"Yep, that same big heart." Ellen reached over for her knitting bag. She pulled out a brown and blue variegated yarn skein that matched Twinkle's dress. "By the way, have you heard from Fran about Amber's wig?"

"Yes, it's done. I've made an appointment for next week. It's a surprise for Amber when she's no longer radioactive."

Amber was more herself with each day that passed. The week in quarantine came to an end, and she was practically bouncing up and down on the way to the salon.

The wig transformed her daughter. Amber was truly back. Once again, the little girl with the strawberry curls. Jessica was certain that Danny's dimples were flashing right then.

Amber did a fashion week catwalk around the salon. She did *Project Runway* proud. The applause was thunderous as she made her exit.

Jessica convinced Ellen to take a week off to go home and recoup. The infusion appointment was a full week off, and Amber was doing well. Meg was nearby as well.

"I don't know, Jess. What if—"

"You need a break, Ellen. If anything happens, I'll call. I promise."

"You're right. Daniel has been urging the same thing."

* * *

Amber begged to have Roger over. It was ironic how the two combatants had connected.. A dose of Roger was just what her daughter needed to take her mind off everything she'd been through. She called Pam and arranged for him to come for a visit the following day.

Roger had barely stepped through the doorway when Amber yanked him toward the staircase. Pam watched them disappear and laughed. "Wow, that was quite a welcome. She's either glad to see him, or she's desperate for company."

"A little of both, I think. Would you like to come in? I've got blueberry muffins and fresh coffee."

"Muffins, yum."

They sat at the kitchen table, and Jessica filled Pam in on Amber's treatment process. "It's been a harrowing time, for sure. But she's making great progress."

"I googled neuroblastoma after we last talked. I read about that MIBG treatment. The idea that it searches out and kills the cancer cells . . . wow. That's like sci-fi. Hard to imagine."

"Yep. I was there the whole time, and it's still hard to believe."

Excited voices sounded from above and Pam rose to her feet. "I'd best be heading out. I'll be back this afternoon. You're sure that's not too much for Amber? Call me if we need to cut his visit short."

"I think she'll be fine. Thanks for bringing Roger over for a playdate."

After Jessica walked Pam to the door, she took out her laptop. Since Amber's diagnosis she kept a hand—more like a finger—in the firm's operations. She was doing little more than paralegal work. Amanda was fine with whatever time off was needed; Jessica was certain of that, but she felt duty bound to offer what she could.

A few hours later, she shut down her computer and phoned Gino's, their favorite pizzeria. She called up the stairs that pizza was on the way. That announcement was met with cheers.

She was putting the morning dishes in the dishwasher when the doorbell rang.

Jessica was shocked to find Chloe on her doorstep. Had something happened to Ellen? Or Daniel? That thought was ridiculous. She had spoken with Ellen just that morning.

"Chloe, hello. What a surprise!"

"Bill's attending a realtors' conference in San Francisco. I couldn't be this close and not visit. I'm just sorry I haven't made it here sooner."

Amber's head appeared over the railing. "Momma, is the pizz—Auntie Chloe!"

She disappeared again before Chloe could reply. The reason was apparent when she came back down the stairs holding the storybook her aunt sent her.

Jessica explained, "It's her prized possession."

Amber settled on the couch with Chloe on one side of her and Roger on the other. She handed the book to her aunt. "Can you read it, Auntie Chloe?"

Jessica said, "Amber could probably recite the entire book from memory, but she loves having it read to her aloud."

Chloe cleared her throat and began at the cover. "*Tales of the Brave Fairies, A Story for Amber . . .*"

Roger's eyes grew big. Jessica could see he was impressed. The book told the story of three fairies. Twinkle, Dee Dee, and Amber, of course. In the story each fairy had to perform a special act of bravery. At the end, the queen of the fairies awarded each of them a special wand to spread magical dust.

While Chloe read, Jessica was thinking about the personalized inscription—*For Amber, the bravest little fairy.*

"Thank you, Auntie Chloe. You are the best story reader ever."

The lunch with Roger and Amber was a test of Jessica's endurance as the kids volleyed coded silliness across the kitchen table. She glanced at Chloe and shook her head. Her sister-in-law responded with a roll of her eyes. Luckily, Pam arrived to pick up her son. Soon after that Amber lay down for a nap.

Chloe helped Jessica straighten up the kitchen before they retreated to the living room where her sister-in-law regaled her with stories about the early years in the Langston household.

"Danny once took my favorite doll hostage and held her for ransom. Claimed she was in a cold dark room. He even played a recording of her cries for help."

Jessica burst out laughing. "A recording? How in the world did he manage that?"

"I'm pretty sure his friend Brian lent a helping hand. It sounded suspiciously like a scene from *Silence of the Lambs*. Of course, Mom forbade us from ever watching scary movies, but that never stopped us."

"So, what was the ransom demand?"

"A family size bag of Pop Rocks candy. It took my whole allowance for the week to buy them."

"Did you get her back?"

"Sure did. Safe and sound. I have no idea where they got them, but a tiny set of handcuffs hung from one wrist. I'm not kidding, I still have the doll. I'll show it to you some time."

Jessica was trying to imagine Danny playing wicked tricks on his sisters when she heard Amber's scream. She rushed up the stairs with Chloe right behind.

They found her in the bathroom. Blood was streaming from her nose, and she was choking on the blood that backed into her throat.

Chloe rushed through Jessica's bedroom door, snatched the phone off the nightstand and dialed 911.

* * *

They wouldn't let Jessica accompany Amber through the double doors of the ER, so she paced just outside until Chloe came in from the parking lot and gently took her hand, leading the way to a nearby waiting room.

The ER was busy, and the waiting room was crowded. Jessica paid no attention. Seated in one of the armchairs, she stared at her feet, seeing nothing. She was racked by guilt. She let Amber do too much, too soon. She should have kept a closer watch on her. Had her carelessness cost her everything?

Chloe left for a time and then returned and handed her a cup of coffee. She nodded her thanks and tried to lift it to her mouth, but her hands shook so hard she gave up and held it between her knees. After a few minutes, Chloe pried it from her hands and set it aside.

Jessica refused to move from her seat. She rarely raised her eyes above her clenched hands. After what seemed like hours, a pair of white women's clogs finally appeared in her line of vision.

Dr. Sullivan said her name, but she couldn't bring herself to look up.

"Jessica, it's all right. Amber is in a stable condition."

Amber was asleep when Jessica was finally allowed to see her. The paperwork had gone through to admit her, and they were waiting on a room before transferring her to the pediatric ward.

Dr. Sullivan explained that Amber's uncontrolled bleeding was caused by a low platelet count. Blood transfusions helped stabilize her, but they scheduled her for the stem cell infusion early the next morning.

The low blood counts were worrisome. She said Amber would remain in the hospital as a precaution. Scans would also be run to determine whether the neuroblastoma had spread.

With Meg's help, Cloe put together an overnight bag and brought it to Jessica.

"Thank you so much, Chloe. I don't know what I would have done without you here."

"I'm so glad I was, but I have to get back to San Francisco. Mom is on her way. Love you, Sis."

Jessica gave her an extra squeeze before stepping back. "Love you, too."

When Chloe left, Jessica sat beside Amber's hospital bed and watched her breathe. Another hospital stay, more transfusions, more scans. At least this time she wouldn't have to leave her daughter's side.

10

Three days after Amber was admitted, Jessica sat beside her hospital bed and tried to hold things together. Ellen had gone to the cafeteria for coffee.

Amber, so tiny and pale, was a ghost of the vibrant, spirited little girl she'd once been. The transformation was unbearable to watch. Jessica wanted to take her daughter into her arms and infuse her with the strength she needed to fight off the cancer cells. How much more could Amber take? The thought of more treatments terrified Jessica. Worse still was the thought of no more treatments.

Amber awoke when the door to the room opened. She recoiled in fear.

Jessica felt a stab to her heart. She reached for her daughter's hand and turned to face what was to come.

The wide smile on Dr. Sullivan's face said it all. Lexi and Ellen entered behind the doctor, smiling just as broadly. Lexi carried a ceramic teddy bear holding a balloon. Written across the rubber surface in black marker was *Amber 10, Cancer 0!* She removed the water pitcher and tumbler from the over-the-bed table and set the teddy on it, turning it so it faced Amber.

Lexi held up her hand. "How about a high-five?"

Amber looked to her mother. Jessica nodded, "I think what your Auntie Lexi's trying to tell you is that you are one lucky little girl. You beat the cancer, baby."

Amber grinned, and gave Lexi a high-five, adding a fist bump.

Dr. Sullivan made some notes on Amber's chart and slapped it back into the holder. "What say we get rid of that port?"

Amber put her palm over the chemo port peeking out of her hospital gown. Fear filled her eyes again. "Will it hurt?"

"Not a bit."

Amber stared wide-eyed at Dr. Sullivan.

Beth held up the chest piece of her stethoscope and raised her right hand. Her version of a pinky-swear.

* * *

Jessica hadn't planned for Amber's discharge. Luckily, her sister had it covered.

Lexi produced a shopping bag she had hidden behind her back. Amber gasped when she pulled out a t-shirt that pictured a beautiful fairy in flight holding a sword aloft. Then she squealed in delight when she held it out for a closer look. The face of the fairy was her own. It read: *Amber, the bravest fairy warrior of them all*!

Shedding her hospital gown proved frustrating. Amber's enthusiasm was boundless, but her body would take some time to catch up. Jessica helped her change and led her to the mirror tacked to the bathroom door. Amber preened for a moment before giving Lexi a big hug.

"It's me! It's really me! Thank you, Auntie Lexi. It's the best t-shirt ever!"

Jessica held back tears with some effort. God, she loved her sister.

Two hours later, the chemo port had been removed and the discharge paperwork was completed. Another surprise awaited Amber in the corridor. All the ward staff lined the hallway. They were clapping. Amber beamed as her fist pumped the air.

Remission. If the English language had a more beautiful word, Jessica could not name one.

They passed the nurses station, now hidden behind giant fruit baskets hastily ordered by Jessica as a thank-you gift. There weren't enough thanks in the world to express her gratitude for all everyone there had done for her little girl, but she hoped to God she would never see them again.

* * *

A month later, life seemed calmer. Amber's hair was slowly growing back, though she still wore her wig with pride. Her appetite was back, and Jessica savored the moments when her daughter begged for pizza or had tea and crumpets with Mr. Fluffle.

Still, any little sound of distress sent Jessica's heart racing. The panic attacks finally subsided when Amber's stomach growled, and she reached for the phone to dial 911. She found she could laugh after all.

Their lives were also about to take another turn for the better.

On a cold, drizzly Saturday in early December, Amber was spending the afternoon at Roger's house. Lexi and Jessica were vegging out in front of the television watching old reruns of *Grey's Anatomy*. Jessica still questioned why her sister liked medical drama when she lived it five days a week.

Lexi's answer—*Dr. McDreamy.*

Lexi kicked off her shoes and stacked some throw pillows under her feet. Jessica noticed her sister's ankles were swollen. She thought back on lunch and how Lexi had opted for a salad rather than the spicy burritos she usually favored. And she'd been moody lately, blaming her boyfriend for that.

Yeah, he was to blame all right.

Jessica mentally slapped her forehead. She grabbed the remote and hit pause.

"So, when are you going to fess up?"

"I don't have to. You've obviously already guessed."

"Does Matt know . . . wait. You haven't told him. I know you haven't, otherwise there'd be a ring on your finger!"

"That's where you're wrong. He knows. And he did try to put a ring on it, but I'm not sure he's ready for fatherhood. A shotgun wedding does not make for a great start to a marriage."

Jessica wanted to hit replay on that ridiculous statement and force her sister to listen to herself. "Matthew Baumgartner might be an only child, but he coaches little league baseball in his very limited spare time. The oldest kid on that team is six, for heaven's sake! I'd say that's the definition of a man who loves kids. And you'd hardly be forcing him into anything. Matt's crazy about you."

"Don't push, Jess."

"Am I at least allowed to ask when you're due? I'll skip the part about how it happened."

"Somewhere around the fourth of July. I've got an appointment for an ultrasound on Tuesday. Want to come?"

"Perfect. No court that day. I'll drive."

* * *

Jessica felt her enthusiasm slowly fade as they headed toward the hospital entrance. Memories of the past year threatened to overwhelm her, and she stopped outside the sliding glass doors of the lobby. She realized Lexi was oblivious to her distress as she walked on, still chattering.

"I don't want to know the sex, so don't . . ."

Lexi stopped midway across the lobby, turned and walked back out. "God, Sis. I'm sorry. You don't have to come in. There's that Starbucks across the street. Wait for me there. I'll call you when I'm done."

"No, it's okay. Just give me a minute. I'll meet you in the waiting room."

Lexi had checked in and taken a seat by the time Jessica joined her. They were both silent. Lexi reached over and squeezed her hand before picking up a magazine from the side table.

The ultrasound technician was a perky twenty-something girl named Caitlyn. She sported stylish horn-rimmed glasses, and her scrubs were the color of bubble gum. Her enthusiasm for her work was evident as she squirted gel on Lexi's stomach and held up the wand, "Do we want to know if it's a boy or a girl?"

Lexi answered, "No!"

Jessica answered, "Yes!"

Caitlyn merely raised an eyebrow, waiting patiently. She undoubtedly had witnessed this clash many times. "Momma, make a command decision?"

Lexi sighed. "I guess it's a yes. Otherwise, my sister will hound me to death."

Jessica's excitement bubbled back. A new beginning.

Jessica sat in the passenger seat on the ride home, holding up the ultrasound image of her nephew and studying it closely. "Have you thought of a name?"

Lexi glanced over. Her features softened. "Kevin."

"Kevin Baumgartner. Has a nice ring to it"

"Don't push, Jess."

"Sorry," she lied. *She was not sorry at all.*

Amber broke into her happy dance when she found out about her cousin Kevin. She insisted her aunt make a copy of the ultrasound picture, so she could put it on the refrigerator. They used the copier in Jessica's office and Meg got a magnet from a kitchen drawer. Amber gave Kevin the place of honor in the center of the refrigerator. She leaned over and kissed her cousin before stepping back and clapping her hands.

While Jessica made some phone calls, Amber retrieved Mr. Fluffle from her room along with her tea set. She poured him a cup, offering one to Lexi before filling her teddy in on the news of the day.

Her aunt played along for a few minutes before setting her cup down and excusing herself.

Amber turned on the TV and was about to settle down on her bean bag when she remembered her favorite socks were in the clothes basket in the laundry room. She hit the pause button on the remote and headed down the hall to retrieve them.

The door to the bathroom wasn't closed all the way, and Amber paused when she heard her aunt crying. She peeked in and saw Lexi sitting on the lid of the toilet with Kevin's picture clutched in her hand.

Amber pushed the door open. Lexi looked up and put the photo on top of the sink vanity. She opened her arms, and Amber crawled onto her lap.

"Why are you sad, Auntie Lexi? Cousin Kevin wouldn't want you to cry."

"I'm not crying about your cousin Kevin, honey. Women who are going to have babies cry all the time. For no reason at all."

"I love Matt. Kevin's going to love him, too. He's going to be so happy to have a daddy. I wish my daddy were here."

Lexi set her back on her feet. "You'd best get back to Mr. Fluffle, you don't want to leave him alone with the remote control for too long."

When Amber scampered off, Lexi splashed water on her face. She got the hand towel off the rack and gave it a fierce scrub. She picked up Kevin's picture, folding it carefully before tucking it into her pocket. Then she retrieved her phone from her purse on the kitchen counter. She walked to the laundry room at the end of the hall to get away from the noise of the television.

Matt answered on the second ring. "Lexi?"

"What do you think of the name Kevin?"

She heard his release of breath. "I'm okay with that."

"Well, then my answer is yes. That's if the offer is still open?"

* * *

One week following Matt's second proposal, Jessica stood with Lexi outside Iridessa's Bridal in the downtown plaza, a stone's throw from the state capitol.

Jessica was certain that given her druthers, her sister would have opted for a drive-through ceremony with an Elvis impersonator officiating, so she was surprised when Lexi showed her the shop's website. Surprise turned to understanding when she read the advertisement: *Iridessa's Bridal. Whether you're seeking a traditional dress, or searching for that uniquely you look, come check out our selection.*

It was fifteen minutes before opening, and Lexi paced impatiently in front of the shop, pausing often to peer inside.

A woman walked out from behind a curtain and saw Lexi at the door. She pulled a key ring from her pocket and opened it. A bell sounded loudly above their heads.

"Good morning, ladies. I'm sorry to keep you waiting. My shop is a popular spot, but I don't usually have customers waiting at the door when I open."

She held out her hand. "Luna."

Lexi and Jessica introduced themselves. The shop owner was near their age and sported a short pixie and had flashing blue eyes.

"So, which of you is the bride-to-be?"

Lexi raised her hand.

Luna eyed her up and down and smiled. "I'm guessing you're interested in the uniquely you line?"

Lexi nodded and glanced around the shop. She eyed the hanging gowns and frowned.

Luna explained, "There's an area beyond that curtain for my specialty attire. Give me a minute while I cash up the register, and we'll head on through."

Jessica picked up one of the business cards from the counter. "Irridessa, I love the name of your shop."

"It's named for my mother. She passed the shop on to me when she moved on to her *grand reward*." Luna laughed. "It's not what you think. My mother's grand reward is a condo in Florida. My family has always been into the mystical universe. I think you'd agree that Irridessa and Luna would top any list of the ultimate magical baby names."

Luna closed the register and led the way to the back of the shop. She pulled some chairs closer for them. "Can I ask what the wedding venue is?"

Lexi looked sheepish, "Vegas."

"How do you feel about pantsuits?"

Lexi grinned. "Tell me more."

"They're a growing trend for Vegas weddings. Most brides love to parade around in their wedding finery but it's hard maneuvering through the casinos in a full gown. Even when the skirt can be hiked up in back."

Luna went to the rack against the wall. She pushed aside hangers until she found the one she was looking for. "What about a train?"

"They're not my thing."

"Reserve your judgment. I'm guessing a size six?"

"At least for now."

Luna undoubtedly got her meaning but didn't comment. "Why don't you step behind that screen and try it on. It shows much better that way."

Jessica gasped when Lexi came out from behind the screen. The jumpsuit was made of stretch crepe. The bodice was beautifully embroidered with a delicate floral pattern, and the slim leg pants fell to just above the ankle. They were embellished with pearl buttons. Pure Lexi.

Luna removed a final item from the bag and held it up. It was a train made of tulle, the ends were embroidered in the same pattern as the bodice "I know you said you aren't into trains, but I think this combines the best of both worlds. It's both traditional *and* unique. It's also completely detachable."

Luna was right. It was the perfect complement to the pantsuit.

Lexi badgered Jessica into a maid-of-honor pantsuit in a gorgeous emerald green, before they headed for home.

* * *

Lexi's wedding could best be described as an elopement, just not in the traditional sense. But when had her sister ever followed convention?

A couple of weeks following the visit to Irridessa, they were flying to Vegas. The timing happened to coincide with a Harley convention in Henderson, Nevada, about sixteen miles southeast of Las Vegas. It was a long-planned trip, so Lexi figured why not combine their two passions—motorcycles *and* each other. Jessica suspected that Amber had played a big part in the chapel decision versus a courthouse. She would have been heartbroken not to be the flower girl.

Kyle Gallagher, Matt's best friend and best man, drove his Range Rover from Sacramento pulling a trailer carrying their Harleys. Jessica knew Lexi was holding out hope that something might develop between her and Kyle. Wasn't going to happen. Oh, she had nothing against bad boy good looks. Motorcycles, on the other hand, were not *her* thing. Still, he was good company on those occasions they found themselves thrown together.

The *Forever and a Day Wedding Chapel* was on a quiet street off the strip. Despite its kitschy name, it had a simple design, with a vaulted ceiling and two tall arched windows behind the pulpit. The sun bounced off the crystals of the massive chandelier hanging from a beam above their heads, casting spots of rainbows all over the chapel.

Amber walked down the aisle carrying a flower girl basket of yellow calla lilies. They matched the color of her yellow gown perfectly.

Jessica came next. Her hands trembled around the stem of the single pink calla lily. The chapel was practically empty, but that took nothing away from the solemnity of the ceremony. She was so happy for her sister.

Jessica smiled as she stood abreast of Matt, then took her place beside Amber. The big, brawny biker dude appeared ready to keel over when the music began, and they turned to face the front of the chapel.

Lexi slowly made her way up the aisle to an acoustic rendition of Elvis Presley's "Can't Help Falling in Love." She had managed to get the king into the ceremony after all. She held a single white calla lily, and her face was partially obscured by a peek-a-boo blusher veil, the *something borrowed* from her sister. The train belled out like a cloud behind her.

Their vows were traditional with one exception. A videographer had come with the wedding package, and they'd decided to break the news of their impending family in a unique way. Matt added to the last line, "I will love and cherish you and our son, Kevin, all the days of my life."

A trip to Matt's hometown of Bakersfield was planned for after their Harley convention honeymoon. Jessica wondered how his parents would feel about the elopement. Disappointed, certainly. But she figured the *fait accompli* would be tempered by the news there was a new Baumgartner on the way.

* * *

Matt secured rooms at the Circus Circus Hotel and Casino. He insisted it was their favorite. Jessica suspected, and rightly so, that it was a ruse concocted for Amber's benefit.

After the ceremony, they all headed for the Adventuredome, a combination circus and amusement park. Kyle, too. They made a quick stop at the hotel rooms where Amber changed her clothes and Lexi detached her train. Then they were off.

Amber was nearly back to being fully healthy. Her hair had grown in though she still wore the wig, and her appetite had returned with a vengeance. Despite that, she was still not a hundred percent.

Her stubborn streak had returned as well. They stood in front of the stroller-for-rent booth, and Amber's chin jutted out. "Those are for babies. I'm not a baby!"

Matt saved the day. "How about a piggyback ride?" Jessica could have kissed him. He was going to make such a *great* dad.

Kyle further endeared himself when he offered to take turns.

They watched acrobats perform hair-raising feats. They all rode the giant merry-go-round. They ate cotton candy and caramel corn, some of which ended up in Matt's hair. He took it in stride.

Amber spotted a clown making balloon animals and clapped her hands when she saw him making poodle dogs for a group of girls gathered around him. Lots of kids were afraid of clowns, but not her brave girl. Amber's eyes widened in wonderment when he made a sword for a little boy in a wheelchair. *Uh, oh,* Jessica thought.

The clown turned to Amber and asked what color dog she'd like him to make.

"I'd like a sword, please."

Lexi piped up, "Yes, you're looking at a genuine warrior princess."

"A sword it is! What color hilt would you like?"

"Yellow, please."

Her good girl pointed the sword up toward the sky, not once trying to stab anyone with it.

Matt spotted an arcade booth and headed in that direction. The booth was a giant water-gun game. He bought each of them a try, but Lexi and Jessica gave Amber their tickets. Kyle watched from the sidelines.

Matt went head-to-head against his niece. The first two tries were a bust. On the third try the bell behind Amber's number seven rang out loudly.

Amber jumped up and down with joy when the barker handed her a big pink teddy bear with a pink and white polka dot bow. Matt's consolation prize was a hand-sized version. The game was totally rigged of course, Amber's water stream landed nowhere near the target. Jessica pulled Matt in for a cheek peck. "Thank you."

He winked. "No idea what you're talking about."

Jessica had to purchase another suitcase for Amber's winnings and the sundry memorabilia she scored in Vegas. She packed the balloon sword in a separate compartment. The clown said the foil balloon could last weeks if they were careful. She just hoped it made it home safe. The trip was about her aunt and uncles wedding, but they made it about Amber, too. Jessica was so grateful to Lexi and Matt, the new six foot-five member of the family.

On the plane back, Jessica dozed off. She woke to the feel of Amber pulling on her sleeve.

"Mom, do you think Mr. Fluffle will like his new family? He's been single for a long time."

She was referring, of course, to Miss Daisy, the new pink teddy and her little boy Junior. Matt's consolation prize. "Miss Daisy is gorgeous, and Mr. Fluffle is going to make a great dad. I think he's going to be a very happy man."

Lexi's early July due date whizzed by. Jessica checked in with her and Matt every day, but it appeared her nephew was not ready to make an appearance. Court had just recessed for the day on July 10th, when Jessica turned on her phone. The text from Matt jumped out at her: "Lexi's in labor. Come quick!"

When she arrived, Jessica heard Lexi's screams from the moment she stepped out of the elevator. She entered the labor room and would have laughed if her brother-in-law hadn't appeared ready to throw-up, pass out, or both.

She urged Matt into a chair and advised him to lower his head between his legs and breathe. "Take a deep breath, Matt. Everything's going to be fine. She'll forget she hates you the minute they put Kevin in her arms."

"The hell I will!"

Jessica tried not to laugh as she stood next to the bed and took Lexi's hand. She remembered her own labor pains and the car ride to the hospital. She kept the smirk off her face with some effort. "Remember your breathing exercises: hee-hee-hoo, pant-pant-blow."

Kevin Jackson Baumgartner made his debut at 7:15 p.m. on July 10, 2010, weighing a whopping nine pounds, six ounces and measuring in at 21.9 inches. Ouch. The *little* guy had a head full of wet dark curls.

Once the umbilical cord was cut, Dr. Sherman placed him on Lexi's chest for some skin-to-skin contact. A nurse draped a blanket over the two of them.

Now recovered, Matt stepped up to the bed. He moved the blanket aside and studied his son's long legs. "Yep, point guard for the Sacramento Kings. Three pointers all the way!"

* * *

Slowly, their lives returned to normal. Because of the time off due to her illness, there was some question as to whether

Amber possessed the basic academic and social skills to start kindergarten. Jessica met with the school administrator, Mrs. Sutton.

Jessica handled the situation with aplomb. Instead of pointing out this was kindergarten, not Harvard, she suggested Amber be tested. She could sense that the buttoned-down, bun-haired administrator thought it would be a waste of time, but this woman knew nothing about her warrior princess. She had better than rudimentary proficiency when it came to reading and math. Jessica had to wear earplugs whenever Roger visited as they marched up and down the stairs singing the alphabet song at the top of their lungs. And for fun, they counted to fifty coming down the stairs, then continued the count from fifty-one to one hundred heading back up.

As for social skills, no problem there. She was her daddy's little girl.

Amber could read every book on the shelf in her room, and not just from memory. Jessica knew this because she was her daughter's captive audience.

After the screening, bun lady declared her daughter gifted.

Jessica drove Amber to her first day of class with mixed feelings. Letting go was so hard. She still suffered flashbacks of her daughter on a gurney covered by a blood-soaked sheet while the ambulance screamed toward the hospital. But she knew that chaining Amber to the memory of her battle with cancer wasn't the answer.

PART III

Endings and Beginnings

11

Sacramento, California 2018

W as her daughter's cancer back? Those words ran through Jessica's mind again and again as she sat in Dr. Sullivan's office in the heart of Old Sacramento. Amber was thirteen. She'd been in remission for nine years, and the yearly checkups had become almost routine.

Jessica crossed her arms, digging her nails into the soft skin to stop trembling. She desperately tried to distract herself with the view outside the window. Tourists crowded the sidewalks of the storefronts which resembled Gold Rush era shops, as tears welled in her eyes and blurred her vision.

Beth entered the room a few minutes later. She took the stethoscope from around her neck and placed it on the corner of her desk. It was telling when she bypassed her chair and took a seat beside Jessica.

Jessica stared down at her lap. She was trembling again. She finally met Beth's gaze. The awful sorrow reflected in the doctor's eyes was her undoing. She shook her head, once, then again. "No. Please . . . no."

Beth grasped her hands. "I'm sorry Jess. I'm so sorry."

Jessica felt the bile rise in her throat and jumped up. She looked frantically around the room.

Beth rose and quickly crossed to a door behind her desk. She threw it open, and Jessica lurched through, slamming the door closed behind her.

Beth knocked and entered ten minutes later. Jessica was sitting on the tile floor with her back against the wall. Her knees were drawn up to her chest, and she had a wad of damp paper towels pressed to her face.

Jessica made no sound as Beth gently removed the paper towels from her grasp and steered her to a nearby bench. She made no protest as Beth took a jogging suit from the locker beside the bench and helped her change.

Seated once more in Beth's office, Jessica sat in silence for a moment. When she finally spoke, her voice was a low, sorrowful whisper. "How long?"

"A few months, maybe a little longer . . ."

Jessica wandered the streets of Old Sacramento after leaving Beth's office. She knew her sister would be waiting for an update, so she sent a quick text to Lexi and turned off her phone.

She thought about returning to her car and heading to the office. But first she had to pull herself together. She strolled along the wooden boardwalk, looking into store windows. They were all a blur of shapes and colors. She passed sight-seers, but their chatter fell on deaf ears.

Three months, maybe more were Beth's words. Some would say she should be grateful for the gift of nine years. Of course, she was grateful. As the years went by, they were so hopeful. New drugs, new treatments, the promise of a cure right around the corner. Now, what she feared most had come to pass; the neuroblastoma had spread. There were no options. It came down to Amber's quality of life in the time she had remaining. Jessica thought about the next few months and closed her eyes against the images. "Oh God . . . why?" she whispered.

She passed Sidle Up, one of Lexi's favorite pubs. She was tempted to lose herself in a martini glass, but she doubted they stocked enough gin to block her tortured thoughts. She walked on.

She somehow ended up at the entrance to Just for Giggles, a favorite of tourists and locals alike and Amber's favorite shop in past years. She hesitated on the doorstep before a group of teenagers jostled her, taking the decision out of her hands.

The shop hadn't changed much. It was stacked floor to ceiling with every outrageous novelty item imaginable. Pink flamingos, skulls, and crazy colored wigs. Jessica wandered through the store, avoiding one aisle. Despite her misgivings, she found herself drawn to the costume section. She recalled that as early as ages two and three, Amber knew her own mind. She always chose her own characters, and age four was the year of the magical fairies. Jessica suspected that the wings played a big part in that choice.

This brought to mind her daughter's fourth birthday when Amber dressed as a fairy. The same year she was diagnosed with cancer.

Jessica pushed aside hanger after hanger in search of something she couldn't articulate. She left the store empty-handed, knowing that for the sake of her sanity she had to leave those memories behind.

At the parking garage she turned her phone back on and called Lexi from the car. Her sister answered on the first ring.

"Jess, I got your message."

"Can you talk? Where's Amber?"

"She and Kev and are up in his room totally engrossed in a new PlayStation game. Roger, too. What did Dr. Sullivan say?"

"It's back. Her cancer's back. Three months . . . Oh, God, Lexi, that's all the time she's got left."

"Are you all right? Do you need me to come get you?"

Jessica pulled herself together with some effort. "No, it's okay. I need to talk to Amanda and arrange for a leave of absence."

"Okay. Listen, the kids have been talking about taking in the latest Avengers movie. There's a showing at ten past four. I'll drop them off and come over so we can talk. Does that give you enough time?"

"Yeah, that's perfect. Thanks, Sis."

The traffic back to the office was mercifully light. Jessica was lost in her thoughts, wondering how she was going to tell her daughter there would be no more birthdays.

The law offices of Marsden, Walker, and Hall occupied a good chunk of the seventeenth floor of the Esquire Plaza Center on K Street. The beautiful tower building offered breathtaking views of the heart of downtown Sacramento, but today the scenery seemed a dull background.

Jessica set her purse on top of her desk and headed to her boss's office. Amanda Marsden was on the phone. She waved her in and quickly ended the call. She came from around her desk and took Jessica into her arms.

Amanda, her boss and mentor, had become a close friend. She reached behind Jessica and closed her office door. She led her to a couch near the windows and grasped her hands. She said nothing.

Jessica was grateful she didn't have to repeat Amber's prognosis. She didn't think she could bear it. "I'm going to need to take some time off from work. A few months, maybe longer."

Amanda silenced her with a shake of her head. "Jess, whatever you need."

"My caseload is crazy right now."

"You've put in almost as many billable hours in the past year as me. Your last extended *vacation* was spent in the hospital when they removed your appendix. Take as much time as you need."

There had been one other leave of absence . . . nine years earlier when Amber was four. Shying away from those memories, Jessica pulled her thoughts back to the present. She offered a weak smile. "Thank you. It's Friday, so if it's all right, on Monday I'll gather my case files and make notes on the progress of each."

"Perfectly fine. Turn them over to me, and I'll distribute the load accordingly."

Amanda squeezed her hands. "If you want to get away from the city, you can use our cabin in Placerville. It's just a few blocks over from the house your rented . . ."

Jessica knew what she was referring to—when Amber beat the odds at age five, and they finally took a real vacation.

Amanda cleared her throat. "We haven't made good use of the cabin in years. We've often thought of putting it up for sale."

"I don't know how to thank you. We have a lot of good memories of staying in Placerville. It's still one of our favorite day trip spots."

"It's settled then. I'll have the keys for you on Monday."

The drive home from the office was short. Jessica leaned forward and crossed her arms over the steering wheel as the garage door closed behind her. She finally allowed the tears to spill, stirring only when her leg muscles cramped. She swayed as she got out of the car, unsteady on her feet.

In the kitchen, she automatically dropped her keys and purse on the counter, grabbed a cup from the cupboard, filled it with water and heated it in the microwave. She didn't realize she'd forgotten the tea bag until she took a sip.

Her phone rang.

"I'm a block away, Lexi said. See you in two."

Jessica opened the door as Lexi stepped onto the porch. She fell into her arms and held on tight, desperately in need of her sister's strength.

When she finally pulled herself together, they moved into the living room.

They sat on the couch and Lexi took her hand. "Tell me everything."

Jessica could barely get the words out. "It's back. And it's spread. Oh God Lexi, how am I going to tell her?"

"You'll find the words. And I'm here for you. I'm here for both of you. We'll get through this together."

* * *

Jessica heard the car pull into the driveway. She opened the front door as Amber came running up, excitement and happiness written all over her face.

"Hi, Mom. *Avengers Endgame* was the best! Of course, that blabbermouth Kev gave away the ending like he always does."

She hung her backpack on the hall tree and turned around. She went still.

"Mom?"

She knows, Jessica thought. *Of course, she knows.*

"Baby . . ."

Before she could say more, Amber cut her off, "It's back, isn't it?"

They sat in the living room and Jessica explained the diagnosis as gently as she could. She didn't know where Amber found the strength to accept it. She supposed her daughter had been preparing for that eventuality most of her young life.

"How long?"

She couldn't lie, much as she wanted to. "Three months, maybe a little longer."

"But I feel fine."

"Beth explained that your health won't decline all at once. It will be gradual. What do you think about getting away from the city? Amanda offered us the use of her cabin in Placerville."

"I've always loved it there."

"Good! We can leave early Tuesday morning."

Later that night after dinner, Amber stretched out on the sofa with her head in Jessica's lap.

"Mom . . ."

What honey?"

"I know Grandma and Grandpa will need to be told, but I can't bear the idea of a death watch. Can it be just the two of us for now?"

"All right. I'm sure they'll understand."

"And can you promise me one thing? Can you promise me my last days won't be spent in a hospital?"

Jessica cupped her daughter's face. We'll handle this any way you say. Do you hear me? *Whatever* you want."

* * *

Jessica made the familiar drive along Highway 50 to Placerville with a heavy heart. Amber lay fast asleep in the reclined seat beside her. She knew her daughter's lack of energy was one of the first signs of her declining health.

Was she wrong to take her away from the city? She thought back to when she brought up the idea of going to the cabin. Amber liked the idea. The times they visited the old mining town over the years brought back so many happy memories. She was certain it *was* the right move..

Amber woke up as they exited the highway into downtown Placerville. "We're here! I love Placerville, it's so . . . old."

"I think the word you're looking for is historic."

"Yeah, historic. Do you think they still have those free stagecoach rides?"

"We can find out easily enough." While Amber craned her neck to take in the sights, Jessica's mood lightened.

"Mom, look! There's that saloon with the hanging man. It's all boarded up. Do you think it closed down?"

"No. I read that Hangman's Tree is being renovated. Did you know that statue went missing once?"

"What happened? Did they have to make another statue?"

"Nope. Someone found it. The owner had it repaired and re-hung it."

"That's so cool."

Jessica handed her phone to Amber. "Honey, can you open my email and find the message from Amanda. It's got directions to the cabin."

Amber scrolled through the emails. "Mom! Did you see the street address?"

"No, I didn't. Why?"

"5539 *Dead Possum Lane*?!"

"What? Oh, honey. I had no idea." She watched helplessly as Amber turned her face to the window, her shoulders shaking.

"Could be worse," Amber said without turning.

"What?"

"Could be *Dead End Lane.*"

Jessica realized her daughter's shoulders were shaking with laughter, not tears. She quickly got into the spirit of it. "Or *Demise Lane.*"

"*Departure Lane.*"

"*Moribund Lane.*"

They laughed so hard Jessica was afraid she might run someone down. She pulled into a grocery store parking lot. "Good place to stop. We're going to need supplies."

* * *

It turned out Dead Possum Lane *was* a dead-end street. More laughter as they spotted the road sign.

They left their bags and supplies in the car while they explored the surroundings. There was a wooden deck at the rear of the cabin. An old porch swing and an umbrella table with a couple of Adirondack chairs sat in the middle. Amber headed directly for the swing. The contraption creaked and strained with every movement.

"I call dibs on this swing," she announced. "It's been sitting here waiting and rusting just for me."

Jessica eyed the chairs and winced. They were traditional in the rustic setting but didn't look comfortable or inviting. "Okay, come on, let's check out the inside."

They let themselves in and Jessica was immediately drawn to the pentagon-shaped window. The view was spectacular. The other striking feature of the great room was the logs in the ceiling. The builder had somehow managed to maintain the shape of the tree in its original form.

The décor, however, screamed 1960s retro, although Jessica suspected the chrome metal dining table and red vinyl chairs were not original pieces. Regardless of this, she found the furnishings charming.

Amber piped up beside her, "Mom, this furniture is—"

As if on cue, they both quoted Lexi's favorite saying, "It was ugly then, and it's ugly now." Their laughter echoed through the rafters.

Amber fingered a doily, "I kinda like it." She picked up a remote control from the coffee table. "This looks state-of-the-art, though."

"If that makes you happy, have a look at what's in the console. Amanda said to enjoy ourselves."

Amber opened the console and squealed with delight at the large cache of games. While she rummaged through the cabinet, Jessica checked out the kitchen. She picked up a business card propped against a bowl of teakwood fruit in the center of the table. The card was from a cleaning service thanking them for their business.

The rest of the cabin sported two fair-sized bedrooms with a Jack and Jill bathroom. The small loft, however, left barely enough room for two small people to turn around. Tight as it might be, she suspected Amber and her cousin Kevin would probably still insist on sharing the space until . . . She pushed her dark thoughts away.

She came back down the stairs and called out, "Amber, how about we unload the car?"

After putting everything away, Amber retreated to her bedroom, cell phone in hand, and Jessica headed for the back deck with throw pillows and her laptop. The trees afforded her plenty of shade at that time of day, so she left her hat and suntan lotion behind. She dashed off an email to Amanda thanking her for the use of the cabin and clued her in on a particularly gnarly custody case she had handed off.

She closed her laptop and picked up her phone, placing a call to Amber's grandmother. Ellen answered after a couple of rings.

"Jessica, hello. How is everything going there? You moved into the cabin today, right? How is Amber doing?"

"Yes, we're in, and it's ideal for our needs. Amber is— Ellen, she's the picture of health. I find myself forgetting sometimes why we're here. She has a little less energy, maybe. But that's all."

"That's good to hear. What are your thoughts about a visit?"

"About that. Amber is adamant about not wanting everyone to rush here for what she calls a 'death watch.' Her words, not mine. Let's give her a little time. I know it's not her intent to shut anyone out."

"Of course. We'll wait to hear from you. Give her our love."

They ate a simple dinner of pasta dressed with butter and garlic and a tossed salad. Amber helped clear the dishes and then headed for the couch and the PlayStation.

Jessica watched as her daughter set a tangled mess of wiring on her lap. She explained what she was going to do as she started untangling everything. Jessica only half listened as Amber tossed out words like *HDMI, in port and out port.*

Jessica mumbled a reply, pretending to have a clue. As if. She poured a glass of Chablis and settled into an oversized recliner. She found an old 2017 *People* magazine in the side pocket of the chair. Blake Shelton's pearly whites flashed out at her. Sexiest man alive, indeed.

The long day had taken its toll, and Jessica soon nodded off. The room was dark when she opened her eyes and saw Amber was asleep on the couch. It was nearly eleven, way past their bedtime. She roused herself and gently shook Amber's shoulder, "Honey, wake up. Let's go to bed."

Amber turned her head away and hugged the throw pillow tighter.

"Come on sleepyhead. You'll find your bed is comfier than that lumpy couch."

"You're waking me up so I can go to sleep?"

"You'll thank me in the morning."

* * *

Amber's distressed cries awakened Jessica before dawn. She hurried into the bedroom and relaxed when she saw her daughter was sound asleep. She stretched out beside her, and they both slept until the morning sunlight peeked through the curtains.

Jessica loved watching Amber's morning ritual. Her eyes popped open and then immediately closed again. She knuckled away the sleep. A huge yawn followed.

"Mom, you know you have a perfectly good bed right on the other side of that door."

"I was lonesome."

"Mmm. Do you know what you need?"

"Oh, I can't wait to hear this one. What do I need?"

"A man."

Jessica raised herself on her elbow and bent over her daughter. "A man? You are officially banned from watching that sappy movie again. I *do not* need a man to *complete me*!"

"But *Jerry McGuire* is a great love story. We've watched it dozens of times."

"Yeah, well, not anymore."

It wasn't as if she never dated. One relationship lasted nearly six months. A record. And it wasn't that she measured them against Danny. Jessica was fully aware that her marriage had never moved beyond the honeymoon stage. She had no yardstick for comparison.

Jessica patted the bed, urging her daughter to come closer.

Amber nuzzled her cheek against Jessica's palm, a gesture of comfort carried over from early childhood.

"Mom?" Serious now.

"What, honey?"

Amber took so long to answer that Jessica thought she might have fallen back to sleep. When she spoke, it was barely above a whisper, "Can we pretend my story has a happy ending?"

12

A week after their move to Placerville, Amber sat atop a split-rail fence at the back of the property, a daily routine since they settled in. The afternoon sun was high in the sky. It broke through the latticework of leaves and brightened the gloomy forest floor. She closed her eyes to let it warm her face and dry her tears.

Yes, they agreed to treat this like any other vacation. They mostly succeeded, if one discounted the times at night when she heard her mother crying behind the closed door of her bedroom, and her own escape out here where only tall pines and an occasional owl bore witness to her own moments of weakness.

Amber lowered her chin to her chest but didn't open her eyes. Her time out for mourning what lay ahead was over for the day. She breathed in the rich earthy smell of the forest; this was one of her favorite things about the outdoors.

Her eyes popped open at the sound of leaves rustling nearby. There she was again, the same fawn she'd seen yesterday and the day before that. It was her; the chewed off tip of her left ear left no doubt.

Amber didn't move or make a sound, lest she scare her away. She scanned the forest, searching for the mother. After spotting the deer for the second day in a row, she looked up baby deer. This wasn't uncommon. The article said they were often left alone when their mothers foraged for food or when danger threatened.

Jane Doe . . . yeah, she named her, not that she was planning anything. Aside from the question of legality, the idea of confining a wild animal was abhorrent to her. But the fawn seemed to be venturing closer each day and there was no law against admiring the deer with the big almond shaped eyes from afar.

The muscles in Amber's legs cramped. Jane Doe startled and slipped away when she jumped down from the fence. Probably just as well.

Amber entered the kitchen through the slider and got herself a glass of orange juice. Her mom looked up and smiled. She sat with her feet up in the recliner, an open book in her lap.

"Hey, you. Did Jane Doe pay another visit?"

"Mm-hmm. Inched a little closer, too."

"Speaking of Jane Doe, we missed the season finale of *My Spirited Daughter.* You up to watching it now? It's a two-parter, but we missed a week, so we should have both episodes."

In addition to all the bells and whistles of the game console, it appeared Amanda had signed up for every streaming service available.

"Yes! Let me wash my hands. Go ahead and start it up."

The crime drama was about a teen girl named Isabella who dies and comes back to haunt her dad, a homicide detective.

Amber slumped onto the sofa and put her stocking feet on the coffee table. "This is the episode about the serial killer, right?

Jessica pointed the remote at the television. "Yep."

The final episode ended with Detective Stanton in the ICU near death from a knife wound. Amber threw a pillow across the room. "I hate cliffhangers! I hate it when they leave a major character clinging to life."

Watching a good show helped them forget for a little while. Then just like that, reality would punch Jessica in the gut. Amber wouldn't be around for another season. Suddenly, Jessica felt the swell of impotent rage boiling up. She wanted to pick up the remote and hurl it after the pillow. Instead, she turned it off and watched helplessly as Amber rose and headed for the hallway, slamming the bathroom door behind her.

Jessica picked up the book she had set aside earlier. She set it back on the end table when she couldn't focus.

Amber came back, sprawled out on the sofa and reached for her earbuds.

Jessica tried to lighten the mood. "Your Aunt Lexi called earlier. Said she's heading up this way tomorrow. Kevin's coming along, too. She said she's got a surprise for you."

"What kind of surprise?" There was little enthusiasm in her voice.

"Beats me. She didn't let me in on it. You know your Auntie." Of course, Jessica knew the surprise; she just didn't want to give it away. It was big. It was *great* big. She was tempted, *sorely* tempted after what just happened. But, if something didn't work out, she couldn't bear the thought of Amber's disappointment.

The following afternoon, Lexi entered the cabin after a brief knock. An excited Kevin came in behind her.

Jessica closed the email she was reading and set her laptop aside.

Amber paused the game she was playing on her phone and removed her earbuds. In the past she would have jumped up to enthusiastically greet her cousin. Instead, she remained where she was.

Lexi and Jessica exchanged looks. Lexi's was full of confidence, and Jessica hoped she was right. Her sister headed for the kitchen, waving a large envelope around in the air. "Come here you two. I've got news."

Amber's look darted between her cousin and her aunt. "What kind of news?"

Jessica got up and headed over, "Better humor her, or we won't find out."

When they were finally seated, Lexi slapped the envelope in the center of the table. Amber leaned over to get a better look, but there were no markings on it. She turned it over and looked at her aunt.

"Can I open it?"

Lexi smiled, "Hard to figure out what's inside if you don't."

Amber frowned when she pulled out a smaller envelope marked Southwest Airlines. "Am I going somewhere?"

"Will you please just open the envelope! Anyone ever tell you you're a trial and a tribulation?"

"Mom says it all the time." She opened the flap, spilling its contents onto her lap. She picked up two Olympia Gate Studios VIP passes with one hand and two Southwest airline tickets with the other. She looked closer. They were for the following weekend. "How did you manage this? I know these things get booked up fast. This is only six days from now!"

"You have your Uncle Matt to thank. He knows somebody who knows somebody."

Amber came out of her chair and hugged Lexi. "This is great. Thank you!"

Kevin was practically bouncing on the balls of his feet. "We're coming, too!"

Amber looked over at Kevin. "Come on, let's get online and check it out."

Jessica smiled at Lexi as the kids headed up to the loft. "Why don't we grab some iced tea and go out on the patio."

They sat in the Adirondack chairs, a large bag of chips on the table between them.

Jessica took a sip of her tea and eyed her sister over the rim of the glass. "You didn't tell her the best part. How in the world did Matt swing a visit to the set of *My Spirited Daughter*?"

"I wasn't kidding. He does know someone who knows a studio exec. Matt's in Anaheim right now setting up a deal with a big client who apparently has major connections on the Hollywood scene."

"Wow, that's incredible. She's going to be over the moon when she walks onto that set. You didn't tell Kevin about the surprise, right?"

Lexi got a chip out of the bag and pointed it at her sister. "I love my kid. Wouldn't trade him for the world. But he's a blabbermouth. Always has been."

* * *

Matt had arranged for first class seats on the Southwest flight. Amber and Kevin sat side by side, talking non-stop about everything the Olympia Studios tour had to offer. Kevin couldn't stop talking about the Need for Speed roller coaster. The park website claimed the G force was off the charts reaching speeds over sixty miles-an-hour. It also boasted one of the longest dives in the world.

Jessica sat across the aisle from Kevin and couldn't help hearing the conversation. "So, you like roller coasters, huh? Which are your favorites?"

"The biggest, scariest, and fastest!"

Jessica smiled and nodded. Then she turned to her sister. Her voice didn't carry across the aisle. "I hope you're not putting him behind the wheel of a car anytime soon."

"I'm not putting him behind the wheel of a go-cart anytime soon."

Matt met them at the Hollywood Burbank Airport. Amber almost knocked him over when she threw herself into his arms.

He set her back on her feet and chuckled, "I guess I did good, huh?"

Amber nodded, "You're the best uncle ever!"

A limo picked them up from the hotel early the next morning, courtesy of the best uncle ever.

They arrived at the Olympia lot to discover they were booked for a *personal* VIP tour. Tegan, their guide, was a tall, gangly ball of energy. She was so energetic that Jessica feared the girl's ponytail would smack her in the face if she got too close.

The tour started, and they moved toward the line forming to board the trolley. Tegan called them back.

"You won't be touring on the trolley. Our transportation is back here." She led them to a golf cart with a colorful canopy overhead.

Jessica looked at Lexi in wide-eyed amazement. Exactly who was the *someone* Matt had been talking to?

While the trolley headed off to the east, Tegan zipped along at a good clip toward the back lots. She kept up a steady chatter.

"You're all in for a real treat. I got my orders from the top studio exec. Full VIP treatment. The works! Don't see *that* too often."

Amber glanced over at her. "What exactly is the works?"

Tegan only smiled. "You'll see."

She stopped near the front doors of a massive concrete structure with Stage 20 printed on the side. As they approached the entrance, Tegan held up her hand to quiet them as they listened for sounds coming from inside.

A sign was posted just outside the doors. Amber noticed it first and gasped. It read, *MY SPIRITED DAUGHTER*. It was a safety precaution warning about keeping the fire lanes clear, but she didn't read beyond the first three words.

"Oh my God! We're visiting the set of . . ." Her voice trailed off. "I'm going to get to see the squad room?" She stopped just short of turning a cartwheel.

Tegan laughed. "Let me guess. Your favorite TV show, right? Mine, too."

The first thing they noticed was the thirty-foot ceiling and the different shaped lights that hung from the rafters. On their right, something that looked like a giant shower curtain hung from floor to ceiling. Tegan called it a painted sheet and explained the track ran the entire length of the set. One sheet depicted daytime, and another depicted nighttime.

Jessica could barely contain her excitement about what she knew was waiting for Amber. They climbed some steps and walked onto the set.

Because everyone was a fan of the show, they had more than a passing acquaintance with the room where they stood. The first thing Amber spotted was the chest-high counter where Officer Huxley Brooks, a.k.a. Hux, often stood. She glanced down at the worn linoleum that cushioned many a perp's head in takedowns. Above it hung the large bulletin board where missing persons and wanted posters fought for space.

Jessica pulled out her camcorder and looked at Tegan, who nodded. "Can you excuse me for just a minute? Have a seat over there. I'll be right back."

Soon after she left, they heard heavy footfalls on the staircase. Amber's eyes widened when Russ Ward, who played Hux, walked through the door in full uniform.

Lexi leaned toward Jessica and whispered, "Oh my, he's even better looking in the flesh!"

Jessica just rolled her eyes.

Russ came over for a handshake. He was as imposing in the flesh as he appeared on television. He had the build of a linebacker and the gruff, case-hardened persona of his TV character. A real cops cop. He was all smiles as he approached.

"Rumor has it we have a big fan in our midst." He looked from Kevin to Amber.

Amber snapped out, "Let's remember, eyes and ears out there!" a line Hux was well-known for.

"Clearly, you've got the lingo down pat. How about we check out the rest of the set? Follow me. I'm playing tour guide for this part of your visit."

Amber glanced around and asked hopefully, "Is filming going on today?"

"Nope, the season's a wrap, but there's a few of us still in the city."

Jessica was surprised Amber didn't pick up on the subtle hint.

He took them through to a set that housed the morning briefing room where Hux marshalled the troops, then into an adjoining area containing the holding cells which appeared ancient and rusted. Each one had a bed, a porcelain toilet and a sink. They were all attached to the wall and had seen better days. Talk about realism.

He explained, "Those sinks and toilets are real, but there are no water pipes on the set, so each has a water storage unit behind it. The show would never have an inmate sitting on the toilet, but there are occasions when a scene calls for someone to toss their cookies." He laughed at his own joke, showing perfect white teeth.

Hux's office was next. Glass windows faced a narrow hallway. It looked so real, down to the well-worn leather seat behind his paper littered desk. He pointed out the push button phone and the computer monitor, explaining they were real but not hooked up to any power source.

The phone rang, startling them. Russ smiled and lifted the receiver. He listened for a moment then answered, "On our way."

They stopped outside a door labeled Interrogation Room One and there was that smile again. He opened the door and Amber stepped through first and then abruptly stopped, covering her mouth with her hands.

Here, finally, was the *great big* surprise.

Samantha Evans, who played Bella Stanton, the spirited daughter, sat in a straight chair behind a table. Even without makeup, the young actress was pretty, just like her on-film persona with her blonde ombre hair color and short sassy curls.

She waved her hand in the air and said, "Hi. Sorry it's just me. My *pretend* dad is out of the country right now."

Introductions were made all around. Amber got over being star struck long enough to find her tongue. "Is this really happening? I can't believe you're here right now . . . I can't believe *I'm* here right now!"

"So, you're obviously a fan. How did you like season two? Were you bummed out by the finale? My Twitter account lit up like the Times Square Christmas tree."

Amber only nodded. Jessica suspected she was worried the tears would come again and she would feel silly about crying over a make-believe plot.

"We just wrapped up season three. If you promise not to spill the beans, and, Mom, if you could shut that recorder off for just a sec, I'll let you in on the best kept secret in Hollywood."

Amber nodded again, dimples flashing this time. Kevin crossed his heart and held up his right hand.

"Dad is going to spend a week in the hospital and a month recuperating, but he's going to be just fine. Aside from driving me crazy with his complaints about being cooped up. I spend a lot of time disappearing in a huff. The producers briefly toyed with the idea of killing off Dad and having the two of us haunt Hux, but it was decided to keep the storyline intact."

Amber high-fived her. Jessica had been wondering if the actors were told about Amber's diagnosis. The secret reveal pretty much confirmed they had been given the heads-up. Yet they treated her like any other young visitor to the set. Jessica loved them for that.

Samantha stood up and motioned Amber over. "You know, if we were still filming, we'd have you on as an extra." She scratched her chin as she thought it over. "I've got an idea you might like. Your mom's got that camcorder. What say we do a short scene? Russ is somewhere still around. I'm sure we can think up some kind of action."

They put their heads together and came up with a scene where Amber would barge through the doors of the squad room yelling about a stabbing nearby. Kevin would run in behind her.

Bella hopped up onto the counter where her character's ghost often planted herself for some excitement in the busy station house, and the action began. Amber ran head long into Hux, who tried to calm her.

Jessica captured it all. She was no cinematographer, but she managed to record them without too much fumbling around. Amber did a pretty good job of playing a young girl reporting a crime in progress, and Kevin did a pretty good job of looking like a kid scared out of his wits. Having Bella and Hux in the scene was the cherry on the cake.

When their impromptu scene was completed, they spent a little more time with the actors. Amber's biggest ask was for Samantha. She wanted to know if it was hard playing a ghost no one else could see but her dad.

Russ scoffed and answered for her. "She's got it easy. It's the rest of us who have to ignore her when she pulls her shenanigans."

"He hates it when I try to give him a headache by sticking my fingers into his head. I don't touch him. It only appears that way—all part of the special effects. But he's still such a baby about it."

They laughed and said their reluctant goodbyes when Tegan showed up to continue the tour.

After hugs all around and a tight squeeze for Amber, they were heading out the door when Samantha called them back. She walked behind the counter and pulled out a fancy box and handed it to Amber. The lid had the Olympia Gate Studio logo embossed on it.

Amber opened the box with trembling fingers. A photo album nestled inside tissue paper. It was filled with photos of the cast and crew and the *My Spirited Daughter* set. It also had pictures of *Bella* and *Hux* autographed with a personal message for Amber.

Amber had tears in her eyes when she threw her arms around Samantha and Russ in turn.

Finally, they got back in the golf cart with Tegan, and she drove them out of the back lots and into the heart of the Olympia Studios theme park.

Kevin could barely contain his excitement. "Where are we going next? You know, my favorite coaster is The Need for Speed!"

Tegan nodded, "My kid brother's all about those big coasters too. I promise it's on the to-do list. But first, we're heading for the special effects live show. You'll like it, I promise."

At the theater entrance, they were directed to Gate A on the left side of the building. Tegan led them in ahead of everyone in line. She sat them in a reserved seating area where they had a great view of the stage. Amber whispered something to Tegan when Kevin wasn't looking.

The show proved to be a little cheesy, but fun. The special effects were pretty cool, especially when they set the stuntman on fire. Growing up, she had watched her share of the classic horror movies. Nanny Meg was vigilant, but Roger had been her co-conspirator and they streamed many a show with her laptop. The bloodier, the better.

For a while after that, Amber traded the shower for tub baths. She figured her mom got wise to her when they started watching scary movies together. Nanny Meg joined them, but only occasionally.

A number of Olympia Studios blockbuster hits over the years were horror movies. Kevin's big moment came. Tegan winked at Amber when he was picked from the audience. He practically skipped onto the stage for the next special effect demonstration. In the background stood some of the most famous horror movie wax figures.

The crew rolled a large box onto the stage. Kevin stood behind it between the two hosts. The young woman picked up a sword and waved it menacingly in the air. Putting it back down, she grabbed a machete. She then cut through Kevin's forearm. He let out a blood curdling scream while blood spurted out.

Aunt Lexi recorded the whole thing so Kevin would have the proof along with bragging rights. They posed for a photo with the monsters in the background. Kevin handed over his phone and moved closer to a very scary vampire. He hammed it up, of course. Then he screamed for real when the monster grabbed him by the shoulders and bared his teeth.

The recording would undoubtedly feature a lot of wobbly motion as Lexi hooted with laughter. "Oh, I'm going to get some big mileage out of that! My son, the tough guy, scream-ing like a girl!"

Amber nodded, "Oh, yeah. He's not going to be able to live that one down!"

The final special effect was an outer space scene. They brought up a young couple from the audience. They dressed him in a space suit. He was directed toward the back of the stage where one stagehand fitted him with a helmet, and another gave instructions to his girlfriend on how to use a joystick to control his flight. Once he was hooked up, he went from being flipped upside down to being dragged along the floor, then he flew high over the audience, all the while yell-ing, only to have his voice was drowned out by laughter.

Kevin was bummed. "I should have waited. I could have been picked to be the astronaut!"

Tegan leaned over his shoulder from behind. "Remem-ber, the whole idea of special effects is to make you believe what you're seeing."

Amber overheard the conversation and glanced at her cousin. He didn't look convinced. He smiled at Tegan and gave her a thumbs up when it was revealed at the end that the audience member hadn't soared over the stage. It was a stunt double.

Outside the theater, Amber begged off continuing the tour. She was feeling tired and achy and knew she'd reached her limit.

She hugged her cousin. "Hey Kev, I'm not gonna make it. You go on that coaster twice, once for you and once for me. Okay?"

* * *

Amber rested while Jessica caught up on emails back at the hotel room. More herself after a couple of hours, she was all smiles when Kevin burst into the hotel room when her mother opened the door. He was giddy with excitement when he told her about all the cool rides.

"Course, no movie stars showed up for *me*."

"Kevin!" Lexi scolded.

He toed the rug and clasped his hands behind his back. "Sorry." He looked at Amber. "I'm really sorry."

"That's okay. I'd totally feel the same."

Lexi and Kevin headed back to their room to get ready for dinner. Matt had promised a special dining experience, but Amber had something else in mind.

"Mom, I'd like to surprise Uncle Matt and Aunt Lexi with some time to themselves. Is it okay if I invite Kev back here for a sleepover?"

"Sure, honey. That's a nice thing to do. I'm sure your uncle will appreciate it."

Matt answered the knock. Tears filled Amber's eyes when she wrapped her arms around him.

Matt seemed flustered by the gesture. "Oh, hey now . . ."

Amber kissed his cheek before pulling back. "Uncle Matt, thank you for the best day ever."

"You're welcome." He looked over her shoulder. "Where's your mom?"

"You made this trip all about me, so I'm taking Kev for a sleepover, so you and Aunt Lexi can enjoy yourselves." She looked across the room at her cousin. "How about it, Kev?"

Kevin grabbed his backpack and joined her before she finished her sentence. As they headed down the hall, he waved at his dad over his shoulder.

Matt closed the door behind them and walked over to the dresser to retrieve his phone. He looked at Lexi as he cancelled their dinner reservations.

Slinging her purse over her shoulder, Lexi frowned. "We're not going out to dinner?"

"Nope. I thought we could order room service. After."

"After what?"

He didn't take his eyes off her as he loosened his tie and stepped closer. When he started unbuttoning his shirt, she let her purse slide to the floor.

* * *

Amber and Kevin ate room service pizza. It wasn't half bad. Her mother retreated to the garden tub and Amber settled on one of the two king beds to watch *The Fate of the Furious* with Kevin. She knew her cousin loved the Fast and Furious movies. They came in a close second to giant roller coasters. She figured she owed him.

After the opening credits, Kevin paused the movie and looked over at Amber. "I meant it. I'm really sorry about that stupid remark about movie stars."

"Don't be a putz. We had a great day, didn't we?"

Kevin gave her a thumbs up and started the movie again. He hit the pause button a short time later.

Amber sighed heavily. "Now what?"

He chewed his lower lip before answering. "Do you think much about what happens when . . . I mean after—"

Amber knew he was thinking about Paul Walker, one of the original *Fast and Furious* actors who'd died in a car crash during a charity event. "After I die, you mean?"

Kevin nodded. "Yeah. The whole idea of you looking down on me from up there kinda freaks me out. Ya know? I mean, will you be watching me when I take a dump?"

Amber burst out laughing. "How 'bout I promise to close my eyes?"

13

A couple of days into July saw Amber's spirits wane along with her stamina. She rarely ventured beyond the immediate vicinity of the cabin and missed her daily chats with Jane Doe.

To her surprise, after only a couple of missed meets, Amber woke from a nap on the swing to find her little friend standing at the edge of the patio. Amber slipped down and cautiously approached the deer. She slowly held out her hand, ready to pull back if Jane Doe spooked.

When she stood perfectly still, Amber gently stroked her head. She spoke softly to her. "I guess you missed me too, huh? Will your mommy find you here?" She asked, although she suspected the deer was an orphan.

Amber sat on the raised wood patio and dangled her legs over the edge, ignoring the prickles of the rough lumber against her skin.

"It's got to be hard for you, out there all alone. Just so you know, I would adopt you in a hot New York minute. But first, I'm pretty sure it's against the law. And second, I'm not gonna be around for much longer, and I'm not talking about going home from my vacation. I mean I'm literally not going to be around much longer."

Out of the corner of her eye she glimpsed her mom standing at the open slider. When she retreated, Amber continued,

"Sorry to bother you with all this, but what are friends for, right? If you want to bail, I'll understand. Or you can just tune me out and go to sleep. I won't know the difference since you can nap with your eyes open. I read that on the internet."

When Jane Doe didn't move, Amber nodded. "Okay then. I've been spending a lot of time looking up dying. I won't bore you with the details. I like the idea that I'll get to see my dad. He died before I was born, so I never knew him. Heard a lot of stories though. I'm told I'm a lot like him." She poked her cheek. "The dimples for sure. I'm an Aries, too. Aries are known to be excessively positive if you believe in that sort of thing."

Amber plucked at a thread in the seam of her jeans. "My favorite story about my dad is how he talked Mom into holding a conversation with him on the phone when he called the wrong number. Want to hear what his favorite saying was?"

Jane Doe restlessly pawed at the ground.

"I'll take that as a yes. Anyway, he called it the wrong number and the right connection. Yeah, cheesy. But sweet, too, right? I've heard Mom's side of the story. I kinda like the idea of getting my Dad's side of it."

Amber reached up again, running her fingers through the fur on Jane Doe's foreleg. "Want to know something else? I'm scared." She leaned her head against Jane Doe's neck and closed her eyes. "I'm really scared."

When the sun had dipped below the tree line later that evening, a loud thump sounded from the patio slider. It was hard enough to rattle the blinds.

Jessica's hand reached out to stop Amber from investigating. She went into the kitchen and flipped off the light while simultaneously illuminating the patio. She peered out the window above the sink. Spying the cause of the disturbance, she moved to the slider and reached for the wand to move the blinds back. "What on earth . . .? It's Jane Doe!"

"Really?" They both stared out at the deer, too stunned to move. Amber recovered first and reached for the lock handle, flipping it up and pushing the slider open.

Unperturbed by the two humans staring open-mouthed, Jane Doe proceeded to step inside.

Jessica looked at the deer, then at her daughter. "Has she done this before?"

"No! I swear. She's never come closer than the edge of the patio. What are we going to do?"

"Well, I don't want to scare her away, and I don't think we can force her out if she's gets stubborn. Let's leave the slider open. Maybe she'll go back out on her own. Put that bowl of fruit in the fridge. We don't want her trying to eat it. Let's go into the living room."

"And what, act natural? Pretend like this isn't the most bizarre thing ever?"

Jessica nodded. "Yeah, something like that."

Jessica moved to the recliner. Amber perched on the edge of the couch. They tried to ignore the *elephant* in the room. It was a stalemate long enough that Jessica picked up a magazine and Amber reached for her phone. She pretended nonchalance as she scrolled the internet for articles about deer behavior.

They were both startled when they heard the clicking sound of hoofs coming closer. Suddenly Jane Doe came around the end of the couch to the center of the room to lie down, tucking her legs under her.

Amber looked at her mom, "Now what?"

"We should call the ranger station." One look at her daughter's face told her what she thought of that. Jessica was torn. Calling them was the right thing to do, but she knew it would break Amber's heart. The baby deer was her biggest source of comfort right now. "Okay, let's look at this from a practical standpoint."

"Like what?"

"I'm pretty sure there are no handbooks about this kind of thing. If she sleeps in here, is she going to wake us up to let her go outside?"

Amber couldn't help it. She tried to hold the laughter in, but it bubbled out. "No, but what about installing a doggy door?"

"Very funny."

"Mom, I'll sit up for a while. I'm not sleepy. Besides, I like hanging out with Jane Doe. She never contradicts me or tells me what to do."

"Back to Hollywood for you. Apparently, stand-up is your shtick."

"It would work if my sidekick, Jane Doe, is willing to make an appearance. I don't think she'd like flying though."

Jane Doe, who'd been immobile throughout the conversation, luckily ended the debate. She got up and made her way to the slider without so much as a by-your-leave.

* * *

Amber sat in one of the deck chairs a few days later, trying to catch some rays from the sun. When her phone pinged, she fished it out of her pocket. It was July 10th, and her calendar was reminding her it was her cousin's birthday.

She quickly texted Kevin a happy birthday GIF. He was celebrating his eighth birthday at the Marvel Superhero Island in Orlando, Florida. He texted back a picture Lexi had taken of him and his father on one of the rollercoaster rides. She somehow managed to capture them in the middle of open-mouthed screams.

She held out her phone to Jane Doe who sat beside her. "Real wusses, right? I was supposed to be on that trip, too. But I'm glad for Kev; he's having the time of his life." Amber liked to think that Jane Doe listened with a sympathetic ear.

"Wait here. I have to show my mom this picture."

Jessica was unloading the dishwasher. "Did you hear from Kevin? Lexi says he's wearing them out."

"Yep. Here's a picture of him and Matt on a rollercoaster. It's probably the biggest, fastest, and scariest." She held up her phone.

Jessica knew Amber had been excited about going to Orlando for her cousin's birthday. She also knew her daughter wouldn't welcome her pity, so she kept silent.

"Hey, Mom. I'm a little tired. I think I'm going to lie down for a while."

"Okay, honey. The sun's high in the sky, so I'm going to take advantage of it. I'll wake you in a couple of hours for dinner."

Amber smiled. Her mother's idea of sunbathing involved a full cover up routine: a floppy hat, sunglasses, and the highest SPF sunblock on the market. She called it the curse of the redhead. There was a time when she worried about that, too.

Amber headed for the bedroom. Jane Doe came through the slider and followed. A common occurrence these days.

Jessica woke Amber a couple of hours later, then returned to the kitchen to toss the salad she'd thrown together earlier.

Jane Doe was absent, undoubtedly out in search of her own meal.

Amber buttered a piece of French bread and munched while her mother set everything on the table.

Jessica speared a tomato slice and savored its sweetness. She waved the fork in the air, "I got a call from Pam Baumgartner earlier. She and Larry are heading up to Tahoe in the morning. Wanted to know if I'd be willing to let Roger come for a visit and spend the night."

"You said yes, right?"

"Of course. They'll be here around ten in the morning."

Roger was absolutely the best medicine anyone could have given Amber. His parents didn't linger since they were on their way to a round of golf with friends. Amber barely allowed Roger to carry his overnight bag up to the loft before she whisked him out onto the back patio.

Jessica smiled, remembering the little hellion who'd pulled on her daughter's ponytail and called her names. Who would have guessed?

Jane Doe lay just beyond the patio chewing on grasses, her eyes closed. She stood, suddenly alert and sniffing the air. Amber and Roger had just moved out onto the deck. She eyed Roger for a few moments before deciding he wasn't a threat and made her way up the steps. She settled beside Amber as she dropped onto the swing. The deer was her usual taciturn self.

Roger tried unsuccessfully to get comfortable in the Adirondack chair. "Throw me one of those pillows, will ya?"

"You can come sit on the swing if you'd like."

"Nah, I don't want to chance spooking her." He caught the pillow one handed and stuffed it behind his back. "So, she just showed up here one day?"

"Not here. I used to venture out to the edge of the property. That's where I first spotted her."

"Do you think her momma's dead?"

Amber nodded. "Something happened. I don't like to think what."

"I like her name. Jane Doe. It's so you. Is she like, your pet?"

"She's nobody's anything." Amber explained with some aggravation.

"Sorry, just trying to wrap my head around this. It's like the coolest thing ever. And she sleeps with her eyes open?"

"Yeah, sometimes. Deer have to be constantly on alert out in the wild. Here, near the cabin, maybe not so much."

"Cool."

Jessica called them in for lunch.

They got up, and Roger looked over at Jane Doe. "Will she follow us in?"

"Not while we're eating. Can't chance tempting her with people food. We close the screen door. Since that first time, she seems to have accepted it."

After lunch, Amber got the camcorder out, intending to play the video of her on-screen debut at Olympia Studios. But first, she insisted that Roger had to watch at least one episode of the show so he'd get the gist of the plot.

Jessica cleaned up the dishes and retreated to the patio to catch up on her reading. One episode soon turned into four as the show hooked him in. Jessica heard the conversation through the screen. Roger declared Bella to be a total fox. She noticed his voice oftentimes cracked. He had also hit a growth spurt. Ah, puberty.

✳ ✳ ✳

Reese Connors leaned back in his chair at the ranger station and stared morosely at the mound of paper cluttering every spare inch of the desk. This was his least favorite part of being a forest ranger.

He picked up the discarded note from earlier in the day. It didn't amount to much, just an FYI about a possible orphaned baby deer hanging around a cabin on Dead Possum Lane. It was Amanda Marsden's cabin, to be exact. The Marsden's were long-time friends, and the cabin stood mostly empty these days. Was it empty now?

He never went into any situation blind. He supposed it was a throwback to his time in Iraq. He sent Amanda an email at the beginning of his shift. He reached for his phone but then remembered it was out of juice and the charging cable was in his truck.

A glance at his watch showed it was nearly five o'clock, time to head out—but where to? Home or the cabin? He debated about heading home. Instead, he booted up his computer and opened his email.

There was a response from Amanda. The cabin was apparently occupied. An associate of the firm, Jessica Langston and her daughter Amber, were in residence for the next few months. Hmm . . . Curiosity trumped fatigue.

The image that popped up from the law firm's website was of an attractive woman who had earned her B.A. from Berkeley with honors. Her Doctor of Jurisprudence was from Stanford Law, where she had graduated Summa Cum Laude. She had been published in the school's Law Review and was an active member in the Family Law Society and Youth

Advocacy Association. She sounded like a devoted mother, but he couldn't help wondering why there was no mention of a Mr. Langston.

Throwing his hat on the front seat of the Land Rover, Reese drove to the cabin, running his hand over his five o'clock shadow before heading for the door.

The lady in question answered his knock. He doffed his hat and noticed the lack of a wedding ring.

She looked at him, then eyed the truck in the driveway carefully. "Can I help you?"

Reese nodded. "Yes, ma'am. Reese Connors, with the U.S. Forest Service. Is this a good time? May I come in?"

Jessica motioned him in. "We're just sitting down to eat."

"I can come back at a better time."

"No need for that. It's only pizza. You're welcome to join us. There's plenty."

"Thanks for the offer, but I'm meeting some friends for dinner."

A cup of coffee, then?"

"I'd welcome that, thanks."

"Black?"

Reese nodded, watching as she turned toward the kitchen. He followed the shapely jeans across the cabin and took a seat at the small table. Marshalling back his wayward thoughts, he smiled at the young girl across the table. Since she was the spitting image of the woman standing at the kitchen counter, he had a pretty good idea this was Amber. The boy at her side looked curious but offered no comment.

Jessica set a large mug in front of him and sat. She dropped a tea bag into her own cup before looking up expectantly. "So, what brings you here, Ranger Connors?"

"Please call me Reese."

Remembering her manners, Jessica made introductions. "Jessica Langston. This is my daughter, Amber, and her friend, Roger."

"I try to get out and greet new residents as time allows, but I'm afraid this is more of an official call."

Roger looked intrigued. Amber eyed him suspiciously. Unperturbed, Jessica calmly bounced her tea bag up and down several times then scooped it up with her spoon and placed it on the saucer. She took a sip before asking, "An official call?"

Reese nearly squirmed under her scrutiny. He could well imagine her arguing her case in front of a judge. He cleared his throat and soldiered on. "There's been a report of an attempt to domesticate a wild animal."

At that moment a loud thump sounded against the glass behind him. Reese turned in his chair. The proof of the report stood just outside.

Amber got up and opened the slider, after which the deer walked through and proceeded to the living room where she made herself comfortable on the rug in front of the fireplace hearth. Ignoring the drama in the room, she began grooming herself.

Reese suddenly found himself at war with what he considered his duty and his awe at the surprising development. He took a second sip of his coffee before clearing his throat again. "Well, can't say I've ever encountered a situation quite like this."

Amber raised her hand and spoke before her mother could respond. "She just showed up one day. I promise I didn't lure her here. At first, she only watched me from a distance. Then she started venturing closer and following me around when I was outside. One night, she did what you just saw.

We were scared she'd hurt herself, so we let her come in. I read up on deer and I know it's illegal to domesticate them. We didn't know what to do. And, like I said, we were scared she'd hurt herself."

Reese found himself admiring the young girl. He wondered if she planned on being a lawyer like her mom. She certainly put up a good case for the defense. He glanced again at the deer. Obviously, she was there by choice. Still, he knew the inherent danger. "You don't feed her, right?"

Amber was indignant. "No, of course not!"

Jessica grasped Amber's hand. "As my daughter said, she's read up on it. So, have I. We know that supplemental feeding can do more harm than good. There is the real risk to the deer's health."

"Aside from that, as she matures, she will most likely return to the wild. If she becomes accustomed to being fed, she'll find it difficult to forage for food. We are very careful about not leaving any kind of food out, especially fruit, where she can get into it."

"We would never do anything to hurt Jane Doe!" Amber said.

Reese's lips twitched at that. "Jane Doe?"

Amber ducked her head and blushed. "It's just something I call her. It's not like she answers to it."

Reese took a last drink of coffee and stood. "I'll be filing my report and . . ."

Amber looked apprehensive for the first time. "Are we in trouble?"

He pretended to mull it over. He knew he wouldn't be filing a report. It wasn't a deliberate attempt to domesticate.

More an extraordinary event. Still, it wouldn't hurt to let them stew. And it would give him an excuse for a return visit.

"Not my call. But, given the circumstances, I don't foresee much more than a warning. Well, I'd best be heading out."

Jessica stood and saw him out. She stepped onto the porch and closed the door softly behind her.

"Ranger Connors, one more thing. I hope you see that no mischief took place here. Jane Doe means the world to my daughter. To both of us. I give you my word no harm will come to her at our hands."

This woman undoubtedly commanded a courtroom, but the soft appeal in her eyes was disarming. "To be honest, no one has made a formal complaint, so resolution is at my sole discretion. I see nothing right now that bears further action. I'll be checking back from time to time. Maybe I'll take you up on that offer of a meal?"

She was a little miffed that he hadn't reassured her until now. But a win was a win. "Sure, any time. Enjoy the rest of your evening."

Jessica joined Amber and Roger back at the kitchen table and gave her daughter a reassuring smile. "Everything's fine. Ranger Connors won't be filing an official report."

Amber's relief was palpable. "So, we're not in any kind of trouble?"

"No trouble. He'll be back occasionally to keep an eye on Jane Doe, but other than that, all's good."

Amber gave her mother a cheeky grin. "Is he coming back to check out Jane Doe or you?"

Jessica flashed her daughter a look, choosing not to answer.

They were up early the next morning, and Jessica decided on a grocery store run. Normally, Amber would accompany her, but with Roger there, she doubted the idea of buying groceries would appeal to her daughter or their guest.

Jane Doe again appeared at the slider, so Amber and Roger opted to sit out on the patio. This time, he sat in the swing alongside her.

He set it in motion. Cringing at the loud creaking noise it made, he stopped it with the toe of his shoe.

"Did your parents say when they'd be back down the mountain?"

"Yeah. Around eleven. I've had fun, and it was cool meeting Jane Doe."

Roger turned halfway toward her, studying her face. "I wanted to tell you how sorry I am about . . . you know."

"Thanks. And thanks for not treating me with kid gloves. I want to feel normal. For as long as I can, anyway."

"Do you think about it much?"

"You mean dying? Yeah it's kinda hard not to. I've read up on it a lot. Wondering how it's going to feel. Will I just close my eyes and not wake up? Will it hurt?" For a moment, Amber's thoughts turned to what lay in store for her before she shut them down. "My Aunt Lexi's a nurse. I know she'd never let me suffer."

"If you ever need to talk, you know you can call me, right?"

"I know. Thanks."

Roger put his hand on her cheek. She took comfort in his touch till he leaned closer, and she realized what was coming. She jerked back. "What are you doing?"

"I'm sorry. That was dumb."

"So, what were you gonna do? Give the dying girl her first kiss?"

Amber became silent for a long time. He looked surprised when she took his hand and said, "I wasn't expecting it, that's all. I'll be ready next time."

Roger was flummoxed but still game to try. He touched her lips with his. But as he pulled his head back, he frowned.

"Did you feel anything? Do you want to try again?"

Amber gave it some thought. "Will you be offended if I say no?"

"No. Because it kind of felt like kissing my sister, if I had one."

"Or like me kissing Kevin."

"Gross!" Roger declared.

"Gross!" Amber repeated.

14

A week later, Amber answered a knock to find Ranger Connors at the door. She held a finger up to her lips and whispered, "Mom's on a Zoom call. Meet me around back."

Amber watched the ranger climb the steps of the deck. She wondered about the reason for his visit. Was he just checking in, like her mother said he would? Or was it another *official* call?

He settled in the deck chair. Amber breathed easier when he smiled.

He glanced over at Jane Doe, "A catchy name, you gave her. She's a mystery, that's for sure."

They watched as she made her way to Amber's side and settled on an old rug next to the swing.

Amber reached out and stroked her head. "Speaking of mysteries, crime shows are kinda my thing." She shrugged.

"What's your favorite? Wait, let me guess—*My Spirited Daughter*. Am I right?"

Amber rolled her eyes. "Well, duh. Are you a fan?"

"Not my usual thing. But Katie, my niece, is a big fan. She streams it whenever she comes up for a visit. It's not half bad."

"My Uncle Matt is a financial advisor and one of his client's is a big wig at Olympia Gate Studies. I got to visit the set. I met Bella, and Hux too. The season was over, but we did a scene where I run into the station to report a crime. My cousin Kevin had a part too. It was awesome!"

"Get out! Katie's going to freak when I tell her. Maybe I can bring her by on her next visit?"

"Yeah, maybe." Not wanting to dwell on the chances of that, she changed the subject. "I've been wondering something. Are you a forest ranger or a park ranger?"

"Forest ranger."

"What's the difference?"

"A lot of people think national parks and national forests are the same thing. It's a common misconception. National parks are designated strictly for preservation of natural and historic resources. National forests are designated for resource preservation as well, but there's more variety to it."

"Like what?"

"Lumber, minerals, even cattle grazing."

"Cattle grazing? *Really*?"

"Scout's honor."

"Do you get a chance to milk many cows?"

He chuckled. "Cattle grazing is confined to national grasslands. Not much call for that around here."

Amber nodded at the firearm strapped to his waist. "You carry a gun. Are you a cop?"

"My official title is LEO."

"Leo?"

"Not as fanciful as it sounds. It stands for law enforcement officer, not the Zodiac sign for the lion."

She wasn't deterred in the least. "Have you ever had to fire it?"

"Thankfully, no." Her disappointment must have shown on her face because he threw her a crumb. "I once assisted in a drug raid, though."

"Cool."

"I guess you could say I represent the long arm of the law since I'm sworn to protect natural resources, forest service staff and forest visitors. But mostly I enforce traffic laws, investigate timber theft, and do public outreach."

Amber mulled that over. "Okay, I get it."

"A little known fact is that the forest Service *does* employ special agents."

"Really?"

"Yep. They're plainclothes investigators. They carry concealed weapons and make arrests."

"Special agents? Wow."

"I know special agent sounds way cooler than ranger, but a lot of their time is spent in surveillance. Me, I'd rather surveil nature."

Her mom stepped out onto the deck. "Ranger Connors, I didn't realize you were here."

"Call me Reese. And I just stopped by to check up on things." He glanced over at Jane Doe. "Your little visitor appears to be doing just fine."

"I'm about to throw together some lunch. Nothing fancy, just toasted cheese. Would you like to join us?"

"Sure, thanks."

Jessica brewed a fresh pot of coffee and handed Reese a mug before she moved back and forth between the counter and the stove as she spread butter on the bread, added cheese, and put it in a frying pan.

Amber watched the ranger's eyes follow her mother. She was right, Jane Doe was no longer the reason for his visits. Her mom was oblivious to it, of course. Hmm . . .

Jessica got plates out of the cupboard while Amber retrieved a large bag of chips and emptied it into a bowl.

From the table Reese asked, "Do you have any jam by chance?"

Amber opened the fridge and took out a large jar. "Is grape jelly okay?"

"Yep, grape's my favorite."

When they were finally seated, Reese cut his sandwich in half. Because it was made from two large slices of sourdough, they were good-sized halves. Amber watched as he pulled the bread back and slathered the jam on one side and then did the same to the other half of the sandwich. He then added potato chips

He smiled at them. "This is my idea of *sweet and salty*."

Amber was never one to be outdone. She proceeded to corrupt her own grilled cheese in the same way. She took a big bite and declared, "Delish!"

Her mom just shook her head and ate her boring sandwich.

Reese swallowed the last bite and wiped his mouth. "Do an internet search on grilled cheese sandwiches sometime. You'd be surprised at the concoctions people come up with."

Amber pulled her phone from her back pocket. She looked at her mom. Phones were usually a no-no at the table. Jessica nodded her okay. "Here it is, fifty insanely good grilled cheese recipes. Listen to this! S'mores grilled cheese. Mac and cheese—and pizza grilled cheese!"

While Amber retreated to her bedroom to text Roger about grilled cheese sandwiches, Jessica saw Reese to the door.

He stepped outside and donned his hat. "Thanks again for lunch. I hope I didn't create a grilled cheese monster."

Jessica laughed. "I have a feeling my next grocery bill is going to make me wince."

"Well, goodbye then."

"Goodbye Ranger, uh, Reese."

Jessica was loading the dishwasher when Amber sat on the barstool. She would have recognized the twinkle in her daughter's eyes had she glanced back right then.

"Ranger Reese is nice. Aunt Lexi would call him a hottie."

"I'm sure she would."

"Carries a gun, too."

"And undoubtedly knows how to use it. Yes, he's nice, well spoken, wears a uniform, and carries a gun. That about covers it, right? Quit trying to play matchmaker."

She grinned at her mother's back. So, she *had* noticed.

* * *

Amber agreed to a family get-together, and the Langston clan gathered en masse at the cabin the following weekend. They were joined by the family Baumgartner and two-thirds of the Hawkins family. Her Uncle Warren emerged from the first rental car early Friday morning, followed by her grandfather and her Uncle Bill.

A second rental driven by her Aunt Chloe pulled up next. It carried her grandmother, her aunt Ginny, and her cousin Hailey. Only Michael and Bill Junior were missing.

"Mike and Bill are on a gad-about in Australia," her Aunt Ginny explained. "They send their love."

They piled inside the cabin with everyone talking at once. It was all Amber had wished for. No long faces. A celebration, not a death watch.

No more than a half hour later, Lexi and Matt arrived with Kevin. Roger and his mom were right behind them.

Her mom set out snacks and drinks on the kitchen counter and everyone helped themselves.

Amber motioned for Hailey, Kevin, and Roger to join her on the back patio, leaving the adults to catch up on life's events.

Hailey was especially keen to see the remarkable Jane Doe. Of all her cousins, Hailey was closest to her age. They were distant cousins, literally, but had grown close through frequent gab sessions by phone and the annual family meets. They shared the Langston dimples, they were both total fans of *My Spirited Daughter*, and they were both particularly fond of critters.

Jane Doe stood at the tree line, just beyond the property fence. Amber cautioned them about how they should behave. "Let's sit at the edge of the deck. She'll come close if we keep still. She's gotten used to having people around."

After a while, Jane Doe ventured toward them. Amber nodded at Hailey, "You can pet her if you like. She's very docile."

Hailey reached out her hand and ran her fingers gently over the deer's head. She spoke barely above a whisper, "Wow, I can't believe this. She's beautiful. Her fur is so soft."

Kevin ran his hand over her back. "Amber says she can sleep with her eyes open. It's so she can be alert to danger."

"You said she sleeps in your room as well?" Hailey shook her head in wonder.

Roger stretched his legs out, careful not to startle Jane Doe. "It's like she thinks of herself as a member of the family."

"She *is* a member of the family." Amber stated emphatically.

She noticed several of the adults had gathered at the slider to look out at Jane Doe. Amber was glad they hadn't piled onto the patio. She was thankful for that.

They rose to go inside, and Hailey looked back at Jane Doe. "You said she goes inside the cabin too? Will she come in now?"

"Probably not. That's a big crowd in there."

Amber was right. Jane Doe retreated back into the forest.

That afternoon Matt unveiled the off-road motorcycle he had strapped down in the back of his pickup. It had a sidecar with a bench big enough to fit two.

Her uncle spent the afternoon motoring through the woods around the cabin and giving them rides up and down the dead-end road. Jane Doe got into the spirit as well. It was as if she thought they were racing, trotting alongside them, then taking leaping jumps ahead.

After dinner, Roger's mom said she was heading out. She didn't want to navigate the mountain after dark.

Amber walked Roger and his mom to the car. Before he could open the door to the backseat, she hugged him. His sorrowful demeanor told her he knew, as she did, that this was likely the last time they would see each other.

Amber pinched his cheek. "Don't go all soppy on me. It's okay, you hear?"

He swallowed hard and nodded.

"And you know what . . . I'm really glad you pulled my ponytail and called me red."

Roger managed a smile. "And I'm really glad you punched me in the nose."

To finish off the evening on a high note, they sat down to watch the pilot of *My Spirited Daughter*. Next, they watched Amber and Kevin's screen debut. A standing ovation finished the night's entertainment.

The adults left to return to the nearby B&B they rented for the weekend. Kevin made for the loft.

Hailey bedded down in Amber's room on a roll-away bed.

Her cousin teased her about Roger. She was convinced they were hiding a secret crush.

"Oh yeah. It all started when I was three."

She had her cousin in stitches as she recounted the events leading to her long friendship with Roger.

After a while Hailey grew serious. "I know you want this weekend to be about fun and family. But I just want to tell you I'm going to miss you, cuz. I'm sorry. I just had to tell you that."

"It's okay, Hailey. I get it." Amber turned on her side and looked at her in the dim light from the moon shining through the window. "If I tell you something, do you promise to keep it to yourself?"

"Yes."

"I was looking on the internet for information about how people dispose of ashes. You know, like out at sea. Some have paperweights made, or jewelry containers. But I found something kinda neat."

"Kinda neat?"

"It's called Better Place Forests. Your ashes are mixed with soil and placed at the base of a tree in a protected forest. You even get to choose the tree and the site, like if you want one near a stream."

"That does sound cool. Will there be a headstone marking the spot?"

"Not a headstone, but a bronze marker on the ground, and I can choose the inscription. A memorial service is held at the site, too. And there can be more than just my ashes under my tree. That means Mom and I can be together forever." Amber felt a lump rise in her throat. Hailey grasped her hand.

Amber took a deep breath to calm herself. "Anyway, what's more cool is that they plant new saplings. The website says they partner with a nonprofit called One Tree Planted to help reforest America."

"Wow."

"I'm still checking it out. I haven't decided yet."

"Don't worry. I won't say anything."

* * *

The family weekend coincided with a big Placerville tradition—the annual Hangtown Wagon Train Days. After lunch, Ellen joined Jessica, Lexi, and the kids for the trip into town while the other adults headed for the Red Hawk Casino, another ten minutes down the highway.

Festivities were due to start at two. They parked as Main Street filled with locals and tourists alike. They were lucky to find a free patch of sidewalk in the shade not far from the Bell Tower. They spread out their blankets and folding chairs and settled in. Jessica brought a hamper filled with munchies and several thermoses of Kool Aid and began filling paper cups.

Ever the impatient one, Kevin, took a bite of muffin and whined, "How much longer before they get here?"

Ellen looked at her watch. "Not much longer. Just another twenty minutes or so."

"Does anyone know where the wagon train starts?" Amber asked. "Is it somewhere here in town?"

A deep male voice answered from behind them. "Oh, the journey starts a lot further out than the town limits."

Reese came forward, standing next to a free spot on the blanket spread out near Jessica. Looking down at her, he tilted his head, asking "Mind if I join you?"

Lexi scooted over to give him room and answered, "Please, do." She held out her hand.

Jessica recognized that look and introduced them. "This is Amber's Aunt Lexi, my sister."

"Reese Connors." He shook her hand and stretched out between them.

"And this is Ellen, Amber's grandmother and her cousin Hailey."

Jessica could well imagine the grilling that was in store for her, especially from Lexi.

"Hi, Ranger Reese. Further out where?" Amber asked.

"It starts in Zephyr Cove, which is about a sixty-five-mile trek to Placerville."

"Wow. They actually come over the mountain on an old wagon trail?"

"No, they travel mostly by way of Highway 50. The trip takes seven days. You can either join the fun for a day or for the whole trip. They break camp every night and cook over an open fire."

Kevin piped up about that information. "Do they have to rub two sticks together to start the fire?"

"Not sure how successful that would be. The wagons are all authentic vintage replicas, though."

Kevin threw his mom a pleading look. "Can we do it next year, please, please . . . please?"

"You might be able to talk your dad into it. My idea of roughing it is a hotel room without a television. And I like my mattress too much to stretch out on the ground."

Reese grinned. "The kids love it. High schoolers, too."
This last said with a look at Amber.

Amber averted her gaze. She was saved from replying
when a couple of highway patrol cars started down main
street, sirens blaring, followed by the lumbering wagon train.
The crowd went wild. People stood, clapping, cheering, and
throwing out wolf whistles.

There was a pause for introductions and speeches. When
everyone disembarked from the wagons, the town celebration
turned to Wild West entertainment, complete with gun fights,
lassoing competitions and tomahawk throwing.

A live band began setting up on a raised stage. Soon country music blasted from giant speakers and dancing followed.

Amber wasn't surprised when Ranger Reese stood and
offered her mother his hand.

"Oh, I'm no dancer. Especially not country."

"Just follow my lead."

She finally stood. Aunt Lexi's hand at her back probably
had something to do with it.

After a few missteps her mom had no trouble keeping
up. When the song ended and everyone moved into position
for a line dance, Amber was proud to see her mom was game
for that as well.

Amber reached to grab her phone to record it. When she
turned back a pair of jean-clad legs had moved into her line
of vision. They seemed to go on forever.

"Hey."

His face came into view and Amber caught her breath.
Fourteen, maybe fifteen. And he was a dream. He had green
eyes and long lashes. His hair was dark and curly.

He cleared his throat and said, "I noticed the toe-tapping. Looked like you're really enjoying the music. Would you like to dance? I'm Nathan, by the way."

She found herself echoing her mother's words, "I'm Amber, and I'm not much of a dancer. Especially not country dancing."

"Go on Cuz, it'll be fun," Hailey urged.

He held out his hand to her and said, "We can practice on the sidelines. There's an alleyway alongside that hardware store. And I'm a good teacher."

She had no idea why he picked her, but she'd follow him anywhere.

Her Aunt Lexi, who'd witnessed the whole exchange, winked at her.

She felt better when she saw the alleyway was empty.

"So, we'll start with a simple two-step and then a promenade. We'll move slowly at first. The easiest way to show you the steps is to face each other and hold hands."

He smiled and added, "Let's put a little space between us so you don't step on my feet. You're going to be moving backward and I'm going to be moving forward. I'll start with my left foot first; you'll start with your right. That way we make sure our feet are lining up and we're moving at the same speed."

"Ready?"

No, she thought. But she nodded.

"Remember, you start off with your right foot."

Naturally she started with her left foot first, throwing them off balance. "Told ya I wasn't much of a dancer."

"That was just your first try. Give it a chance."

After another false start, she relaxed, and it went more smoothly.

"Okay, that's good. You've got it down pat. You're a natural."

"A natural disaster, maybe."

Nathan laughed. "We're going to do that again, but this time we're going to be walking two quicks and two slows. Ready?"

"Sure." How hard could it be?

"So, it's quick, quick, followed by slow, slow."

They went through the moves six more times. Each went a little better than the last.

"Now we're going to go into the dancing position. For this, I'm not going to be directly in front of you, but I'll be a little off to the side. That'll allow our feet to go outside and inside. By the way, if I step on your feet, it's technically your fault."

"Excuse me?"

"The reason it's your fault is because I'm going to be dancing to the music. You're the follower and you'll be dancing to stay in sync with me. So don't blame me if I scuff up your sneakers."

"And if you end up with a black eye, it will be technically your fault since it's a reflex reaction on my part."

He held up his left hand and Amber grasped it.

"Since I'm taller than you, we'll raise our hands to your nose height." He took her left hand and placed it on his shoulder. His palm was warm against her back through the thin material of her blouse. She tingled from the contact.

"Just one more thing, the two-step is a progressive dance. Nothing really complicated about that, it just means we'll be travelling around counterclockwise."

This move went a lot smoother. She was surprised by how much she was enjoying herself. Probably had a lot to do with being this close to cowboy hottie, as her aunt would say.

"This is kinda fun."

"It is. You want to try another move?"

"Okay."

"This one's the promenade."

The promenade was easy, it was the same basic steps—quick, quick, slow slow. In the first lesson their bodies were in what Nathan called the closed position. Now they'd be opening their bodies to the side and moving forward with their arms and hands stretched out, but not so far out as to mimic the Spanish dancers with the rose between their teeth.

After several practice runs, Nathan stopped and nodded toward the band and the dancing which was still going strong. "What do you think—want to give it a go?"

Amber was never more angry with her body than she was at that moment. "I really want to, but I'm kind of tired. I'm sorry."

"No worries. We can tackle it some other time. These shindigs go on all summer long. And when the weather gets bad, they move indoors."

She didn't want to break the wonderful spell of the moment so she nodded.

Nathan took her hand and led her back toward the festivities. "There's some picnic tables set up on the other side of the stage. The ice cream shop is open. Want to grab some cones?"

"Sure, that sounds good."

Amber saved their spot while Nathan went inside. Ten minutes later he walked out with a giant banana split with three scoops of ice cream, chocolate and butter scotch syrup, and tall mounds of whipped cream. Plus two cherries.

"Nathan, I asked for a single strawberry scoop in a cup!"

He offered her one of the cherries before popping the other in his mouth. "The strawberry scoop in the middle is yours."

"So, where did you pick up the dance moves? You're super good at it."

"It runs in the family. My mom teaches music at the high school and plays the piano. See that guy next to the drummer playing the fiddle? That's my dad. He's the barber in town. Sings in a barbershop quartet too."

"Do you play an instrument as well?"

"Several. My favorite is the violin."

"Really? What other instruments do you play?"

"Piano of course. Plus drums and a little harmonica. What about you?"

"I am definitely not musically inclined."

"I meant what do you like to do."

"My life isn't as exciting as yours. I mostly listen to music, play video games with my cousin Kev, and read everything I can get my hands on." She flashed him the dimples as she added, "And my BFF is a deer named Jane Doe. At least for the summer."

"Uh . . . what?"

"It's true. She just showed up one day like a lost puppy. I don't like to think what happened to her mother. She knocks on the slider to be let in and she—"

"Wait. She comes inside?"

"Yep. She likes to sit by the fire and even sleeps in my room sometimes. She's a good listener too. I share all my secrets and worries. She doesn't offer much advice, and I sometimes think I put her to sleep. Did you know deer can sleep with their eyes open?"

Amber realized she'd said too much when Nathan's brow furrowed.

"Worries? What sort of things worry you?"

She should be honest with him, but she couldn't bring herself to tell him. It had been a perfect day. She wanted just one perfect day when cancer didn't overshadow her happiness.

"Silly girl stuff. Jane Doe rolls her eyes at most of it."

They exchanged numbers and promised to connect soon. Nathan walked her back to the family. Amber made introductions before he said his goodbyes.

She looked at her aunt expectantly, certain a comment was coming.

"Such a handsome young man. Seemed real taken with you."

That night, after lights out, her cousin Hailey spoke up from her bed, "He's really into you."

Amber didn't need to ask who. "I know. The way he looked at me, the way he made me feel . . . just once I wanted to be that special in someone's eyes."

* * *

The following afternoon Amber woke from a nap on the couch and found herself alone in the cabin. The noise from out back signaled everyone had retreated to the patio where a barbeque was in progress.

When she got up from her makeshift bed on the couch, she looked through the front window and spotted her grandfather's head and shoulders. She hadn't had a chance to talk to him one-on-one since the start of the weekend, so she made her way out the front door.

Her Grandpa smiled and patted the bench seat. "Hey, honey, how about joining an old man for a quiet moment away from the hoopla?"

"You bet." Amber sat beside him. He put his arm around her shoulders and kissed her forehead before settling back.

"How'd that wagon train celebration go yesterday? Your grandma told me how it started out in Zephyr Cove and the trek takes seven days, ending here on Main Street."

"It was really cool. Kev, being Kev, thought it would be more fun with a runaway horse."

"And what about you? A runaway horse? Or one moseying along?"

Amber ducked her head. "Well, yeah, who wouldn't want the excitement of a careening wagon?"

"You remind me so much of your dad. He was fearless, too."

"Tell me about him Grandpa."

"I remember there was a park near the house. It had a small wading pool. Practically from the time he could walk, we'd find your dad in that pool till he turned into a prune. You might think he was training for the Olympics, but in truth he was doing little more than dragging himself along the bottom."

"One day, when he was about five, Chloe took him to the public swimming pool. They came out onto the pool deck and before she knew it, he jumped into the deep end. When she recovered from her shock and started to dive in after him, she saw his head bob up midway across. He then proceeded to use his arms and legs to propel himself the rest of the way. He grinned and beckoned his sister to join him. Your dad was fearless and daring . . . and so full of life."

"I wish I'd had the chance to know him."

They sat quietly for a moment, each lost in their thoughts. Amber laid her head on his chest and whispered, "I've read all these different stories about near-death experiences where people claim to have seen loved ones waiting to greet them. There's a bunch of stuff online about it. They're called NDEs. I hope it's true, Grandpa. I hope he's there waiting for me." Her grandfather didn't say anything for a long time, prompting her to ask, "Do you want me to carry a message for you?"

She felt a shudder run through him before he responded. "There's no need for that, little one. I talk to your dad all the time. And before you ask, no, he doesn't answer. At least not with words. I'm sure you've heard about the research into that as well. They're called ADCs, after-death communication."

"What's it like?"

"There was this one time I was reminiscing about a fishing trip we'd been on when he was just six. I laughed and reminded him how he couldn't bring himself to hook a worm and kill a poor defenseless living thing. Just then, a breeze picked up strong enough to ruffle the hair on my head. A wind that was there, then just as quickly gone."

"Maybe between us, Dad and I can conjure up a tornado."

He kissed the top of her head again. This time she felt the moisture from his tears.

* * *

The following week Amber was on the swing conversing with her little friend. "So, what do you think? Would you have picked Jane Doe if you'd had your druthers? I looked up deer names on the internet. Can you believe there was a post with 168 suggestions for what to name a deer?"

She picked up her phone and scrolled through the list. "I'll pick out some of *my* favorites. Let me know if any strike your fancy. Ooh, here's some that are kind of pretty. The meaning is listed, too. *Niabi*: Native American for small deer. I don't know about that one. You might not always be small. How about *Ceren*. Oh, wait, it's Turkish for young gazelle. How about this one: *Ayala*. It's Hebrew for fawn or deer."

She heard Reese coming up the stairs. "I like that name, *Ayala*. What's with the sudden interest in names? Planning on getting a pet?"

"I was asking Jane Doe if she'd like to pick her own name."

"How's it going?"

"No hits yet."

"Maybe she's happy with Jane Doe." Reese sat and removed his hat, running his fingers through his close-cropped hair. "Is your mom on another conference call?"

"No, she's lying down with a headache. I've never liked my name that much. Don't tell my mom, okay? Could be worse, I guess."

"Worse how?"

"I could have been named after her favorite drink."

"What's your mom's favorite drink?"

"Fuzzy navel."

Reese laughed.

Amber smiled, but quickly became solemn. "You know a lot about this area, right? I mean you knew all about the history of the wagon train celebration. And you're a ranger."

"Lived here all my life. Been a ranger the past ten years. What's on your mind?"

"I've been reading about something called Better Place Forests. There's one not too far from here. Near Pollock Pines."

"Yep. I know about it. In fact, I looked into it for my mom. She was really taken with the idea. It's legit if that's what you're wondering. Gives back to the environment, too. Is there someone you know whose thinking about it? They give tours, and the website has a lot of information as well. I'd highly recommend it."

Amber spoke before she thought better of it, "It's for me, Ranger Reese. I got sick with neuroblastoma when I was a kid. I was one of the lucky ones, went into remission. But it's back."

He looked down at his hands for a moment. She could sense him grappling with the news, but he simply said, "I'm really sorry to hear that." His phone rang, and he glanced at the readout. "Sorry, I have to take this."

"Connors here." He listened and then replied, "On my way."

Before he stood, he pulled a card from his wallet. Using the pencil from the small notebook in his shirt pocket, he wrote on the back. "If you need anything, anything at all. Day or night, here's my number. Office, cell, and home numbers. Anytime. You understand?"

Amber watched him walk away and felt better for the telling.

And it was time to tell the truth one more time. Nathan had called twice and left messages for her, but she hadn't returned his calls. She picked up her phone and dialed.

He answered on the first ring. "Hey Amber, wow . . . I was wondering what was going on, I mean did I—"

"You didn't do anything wrong. I'm the one being an idiot."

"You're not an idiot. Far from it."

"Yeah, well I'll repeat one of my mother's favorite sayings—the jury is still out on that one. But there's something I need to talk to you about. Any chance you can come over?"

"I'm just finishing helping my dad with the lawn clippings. How about an hour from now?"

She gave him the address and went inside to get a book to distract herself. She read a couple of chapters before she closed her eyes and was soon asleep.

The sound of a loud engine in the distance woke her. Jane Doe rose and was quickly gone.

Amber watched as Nathan pulled up on a bright red ATV, cut the engine and doffed his helmet. "Want to go for a ride?" he asked with a grin.

Glad for the reprieve, Amber nodded. "Just let me check with my mom."

She turned to see her mother standing at the slider with an ice pack in her hand. She looked over the ATV and asked, "Do you have a license to drive that?"

"No mam, but I've taken the required safety training course and have an ATV safety certificate. Both are required by DMV. I got that training a few months ago when I turned fifteen. I've got the certificate in my wallet if you'd like to see it."

"No need. Go have fun."

Nathan handed her a helmet, and they were off. He stopped in a field of flowers and pulled a blanket from his backpack.

Amber sat with her legs tucked under her. Nathan stretched out beside her.

She was reminded of the time eight years before when she was rescued by a search and rescue team. She looked at Nathan and knew she couldn't put it off any longer.

"Nathan, I have to tell you something, and I'm sorry I didn't tell you right off. I was diagnosed with a cancer called neuroblastoma when I four years old. I've been in remission for eight years, but it's back. This is my last summer . . ."

He sat up and opened his arms.

"What can I do? Name it."

It felt so good to be held. She could hear his heart beating strong. "This is what I need. Exactly this."

He lifted her chin and kissed her. It was achingly gentle.

He said nothing, just held her tighter.

Exactly this . . .

15

As July drew to a close, Jessica watched her daughter experience fewer bursts of energy, replaced by longer stretches of exhaustion. She brought in a hospital bed, so Amber could wake up to the panoramic view of the forest through the wall of windows in the living room.

Amber was peacefully sleeping with Jane Doe—her constant companion these days—lying on the rug nearby.

Savoring the quiet, Jessica sat in a deck chair on the patio, pulled her hat brim further down over her eyes to shield herself from the sun, and drifted off. She woke to Amber's voice beside her.

"Mom?"

Amber sat in the new comfy porch swing they purchased. It was bigger and quieter than its ancient predecessor. The second accessory tore at Jessica's heart, a rollator walker. An image from years past came to mind. Amber, riding her ten-speed, ponytail flying behind her.

Jessica stretched and asked, "What time is it?"

"Almost noon."

"Oh. I should get lunch started."

"Wait, Mom. I need to talk to you about something I found on the internet."

"What is it, honey?"

"It's called Better Place Forests. It's an alternative to being buried in a cemetery."

Jessica felt her throat constrict. She swallowed back the words that immediately came to mind . . . too soon, plenty of time. "Better Place Forests?"

"The company's dedicated to the conservation of its memorial forests. They're private forests, and my ashes would be spread under a tree I get to pick. The website says they plant saplings for each tree that's purchased. A bronze plaque would be placed at the base of the tree and I'd get to choose the inscription. There's an on-line guided tour, but I really want to visit the forest. It's only fifteen miles from here, near Pollock Pines."

"And it's a bona fide company? Not a fly-by-night?" Jessica paused, then added, "I'm sorry, of course you would have checked that out first off."

"Yeah, I did. It's accredited by the Better Business Bureau. And I've been talking to Ranger Reese. He said his mom asked him to look into it for her, so I asked him what kind of tree I should pick."

"You talked to Reese about it?"

"I figured if anyone knew something about these forests, it's him. I don't know that much about trees. He said his choice would be the ponderosa pine. Says the bark smells like butterscotch. They grow up to two hundred feet and can live for more than five hundred years."

Jessica wasn't surprised Amber had opened up to the ranger. He'd become somewhat of a fixture around the place, dropping by a couple of times a week. Her daughter didn't trust just anyone with her prognosis. That spoke volumes about the measure of the man she'd taken into her confidence.

Jessica picked up her phone. "I'll look up the number and call for an appointment."

"Ask if Thursday afternoon is available. I asked Ranger Reese if he could be there too. I hope that's okay?"

"Of course it's okay."

"He said the tours last about sixty to ninety minutes. They have a motorized vehicle, too, for those who have trouble walking."

"Wow, you've been busy. Why am I just hearing about this?"

"I'm my mother's daughter," Amber replied with a sheepish grin. "Once I sink my teeth into something, I don't let go."

What could she say to that? Jessica punched in the number and got through right away. The woman who answered the phone said her name was Allie. She checked the schedule and said they had an opening that Thursday at one o'clock. Jessica gave Amber a thumbs up. Allie asked for her email and said she'd send a link so they could do an online tour of the forest. That way they wouldn't spend time looking at trees in a setting in which they might not be interested.

Jessica rose to her feet when she finished the call. "Let's go inside. Our guide's name is Allie. She sounds very nice. She's sending me an email with a link to the forest. She said it sits on one hundred seventy-two acres and advised that it's best to have an idea of the trees and settings you're interested in."

They settled on the couch, and Jessica opened her laptop. She brought up Allie's email and clicked on the link, then handed it to Amber.

Amber's eyes widened. "This is great. There's a view of the tree up close, then it opens up so you can see what's around it, too. It says here the legacy tree comes with two spreading rights and two hundred reforestation saplings. The legacy tree is what we're interested in, right?"

Jessica nodded, "Yes, so let me grab a pen and paper and we'll write down the ones you want to look at."

There were sixteen legacy trees to choose from, and Amber studied each one closely. She settled on four she wanted to see.

Reese had some errands to run that Thursday, so he arranged to meet them at the Better Place Forests' *Welcome House*. The name immediately gave Jessica a good feeling.

When they stepped out of the car, Jessica retrieved Amber's walker, and they headed for the entrance.

"Wow, Mom. Look at that. The visitor center is beautiful."

Jessica had read about it on the company website. It was beautiful, and as advertised— completely in harmony with the surrounding forest.

Jessica spotted Reese chatting with a young woman with ash blond hair pulled up on top of her head and secured with a giant barrette. Her face was fresh scrubbed and make-up-free. She had a deep tan that showed she spent a lot of time outdoors. She greeted them with a wide smile.

"Amber? Jessica? I'm Allie. It's so nice to meet you." Her smile never wavered when she looked at Amber. "Ranger Connors tells me you're especially interested in the ponderosa pine trees. They're my favorite too. We were just discussing the aroma that comes off the bark. I say vanilla. He says butterscotch."

Reese cupped his hand around his mouth and whispered in an aside, "Butterscotch!"

Jessica spoke with Allie after her initial call. She felt compelled to explain the circumstances of their interest in the memorial forest. Now, meeting her, she realized the caution had been unnecessary.

Jessica looked around for an office where they could talk, but Allie surprised her. She got right to the business of the tree.

"Amber, did you look over the ponderosa pines available? Did you make a list of the ones you want to see?"

Jessica pulled the list from her purse and handed it to Allie.

"Perfect. We can head out if you'd like."

Amber didn't hesitate. "Yes, please."

Allie led the way to the back of the building where an ATV waited. Luckily there was room for four people. Amber rode shotgun while Jessica and Reese took up the rear, the folded-up walker anchored between them.

Amber gave the off-road vehicle the once over. "I bet this can do some awesome wheelies."

Allie looked at Amber over her sunglasses. "Are you a big ATV rally fan?"

"My friend Roger watches them on YouTube all the time."

"Yeah, they can be fun. But we won't be doing much off-road wheeling. The path that runs through that section of the forest is fairly sedate."

Amber looked a little disappointed. "So, where are we headed?"

"The ponderosas are located in the section of the forest called Pearly Everlasting."

"Is that named for, like, the pearly gates?"

"No, that's the name of the wildflowers this area is known for. They're native to Northern and Central California. They bloom from late summer to early fall."

Reese spoke up at that. "And they're a sight to behold."

Allie stopped just past a wooden sign with the words *Pearly Everlasting* carved into it. "Here we are."

Reese pulled out Amber's walker and unfolded it for her.

Jessica was relieved to see that this section was flat. With care, Amber would be able to navigate the forest floor.

Reese placed his hand against a nearby tree. "The ponderosa pine is known for being plucky and resilient."

Jessica watched her daughter's eyes light up. She could easily read Amber's thoughts, *Plucky and resilient, like me.*

"If you look closely, the bark of the *juvenile* ponderosa pine tree is blackish brown. As the tree matures, the bark will change color to an orange red. That's when it gets it . . ." Reese glanced over at Allie with a grin, "butterscotch aroma."

Amber turned to Allie. "How do I know which trees are available?"

"Each available tree has a coin-like tag, about the size of a quarter, with a number on it. They're recorded with their GPS location." She pulled her iPad from the ATV. "I can make a list of your favorites, or, if you find the one that speaks to you, we'll tag it. Your mom told me you're interested in the legacy trees. Let's check out the ones you picked."

As they headed back to the vehicle, Amber gasped. "Mom, look. That's Jane Doe!"

They all turned to look. Jessica thought the deer was too far away to say for certain. Jane Doe would have practically had to sprint alongside the car to be there at that exact moment. Still, she didn't want to burst her daughter's bubble. "I don't know. Maybe."

Allie looked at the deer, then back at Amber. "Jane Doe?"

Amber looked sheepish. "Sorry, inside joke." She glanced around the meadow. "So, the forest is open to wildlife?"

"A lot of the forest is open land. Some parts of it are fenced, but the fencing is wildlife friendly."

"So, deer can wander in and out?"

"Deer like that one are among our most frequent visitors, along with all manner of forest critters."

Jessica felt a tug at her heart when Amber's dimples flashed. The sight was so rare these days.

"Want to hear about one particular critter uniquely tied to the ponderosa?" Reese asked.

Amber rolled her eyes, "Well, duh."

"It's the Abert's squirrel." He got out his phone and tapped the screen, holding it up for Amber to see. "Take a look."

Jessica took a peek as well. She'd never seen anything like it. It had big ears, *very big* ears, and appeared larger than the squirrels she was used to seeing. It had a white belly and long fluffy white tail. The squirrel's back was dark gray with a reddish-brown patch.

Amber smiled, "Wow, those are some honking big ears! And super furry."

"Yeah, those tufts of fur earned it the nickname *tassel eared squirrel*."

Reese tapped the screen a couple of more times. "What you just saw was the squirrel in the winter. Here it is during the summer."

They took another look. The transformation was wild.

Amber grasped his hand and pulled it closer. "Wow, talk about casting off their winter coat! Even the fur in its ears is gone. Why do they call them Abert's squirrels?"

Allie fielded that one. "They're named in honor of John James Abert, an American naturalist from the 1800s.

Amber nodded and mumbled, "Cool."

"So, are you ready to pick your tree?"

Jessica moved to Amber's side, alert for any mishap with the walker. She was grateful when Reese took up a position on her other side.

The first couple of trees didn't *speak* to Amber, so they moved on to the third. The sun had broken through the canopy of trees surrounding it and warmed that area of the forest enough for the aroma to tickle their senses.

Amber took a deep breath. Ever the diplomat, she declared, "Definitely . . . a blend of butterscotch *and* vanilla!" Just then, a slight breeze kicked up and a pinecone fell near her feet.

Reese smiled. "Well, I'd say that's definitely a sign."

Amber wrapped her arms around the tree and rested her cheek against the bark. "This is it. This is the one." Silently, she added, *Thanks, Daddy.*

Allie smiled and nodded. "Okay, then. We can head back to the office and start the process."

Jessica glanced at Amber and hesitated. She could see her daughter's energy waning.

Reese came to the rescue once again. "How about I take Amber home and stick around until you're finished? I've got my laptop, so I'll catch up on some emails. Take your time. We'll be fine."

"I'd appreciate that. Thank you."

After they left, Allie led Jessica to the office where they'd completed the necessary paperwork after which she closed the folder and set it aside. "Jessica, I'm glad we have this chance to talk privately. I'd like to convey how very sorry I am about Amber. She's a very special young lady, and I want to give you my promise that I'll do my best to see that the memorial goes smoothly."

"Thank you for the reassurance, but I sensed that deep commitment from you at the start. Can I ask you something?"

"Of course."

"How do you do it? I mean, I understand the draw of being out here in this beautiful forest. Still, it must be difficult."

"You're right. I love the outdoors. My fondest memories are of camping trips with my family. These protected forests are a haven from the hustle and bustle of the city. Yes, there is the somber side of the business, but thinking back on today and Amber's delight when she found her tree, knowing I had a part in putting that smile on her face . . . It's the most rewarding part of what I do."

"It's wonderful to know your calling. You're very good at it. Today was perfect, thanks to you."

"One thing before you go. I'd like to email you a link to our Better Place Forests blog. It's a really good resource for families. You'll find articles about support groups, including where to find one, how to cope during the first holiday without your loved one, and the one I've received the most positive feedback on—how your diet can impact the way you cope with grief. There are many more articles relating to a variety of topics. And the blog is updated frequently."

"Yes, please send me the link." Jessica wasn't sure she was ready for that next step, but she loved that the company was not all about the big sell.

* * *

Amber was napping on the couch when Jessica walked into the cabin. She set her purse and sunglasses on the table inside the door and joined Reese at the kitchen table.

She spoke in a hushed tone. "Has she been asleep long?"

"About an hour." He took a drink of his iced tea and nodded at the glass in his hand. "Helped myself. Hope that's okay."

"*Mi casa, su casa*. Join me on the patio?" She took his glass and refilled it, pouring one for herself as well.

She sat in the deck chair beside his. "Thanks for bringing her back here. And thanks for being there today. I know Amber appreciated it."

"That's one special young lady you've got there. I don't know many adults who could handle themselves as well, me included."

"I think the planning of it helps her forget . . . no, not forget. It helps her deal with it. Does that make sense?"

Reece replied, "Yes, it does. She's never struck me as someone who would go down without a fight. I think those who are facing death fall into two categories. The ones who succumb and those who face every day with a purpose. The planning, the action itself, gives her a reason to get up every morning, a reason not to sink into a well of hopelessness. I admire the hell out of that."

"Amber's always been a fighter. She was diagnosed at age four. I don't know if she told you that. A year of brutal treatments. She was so brave through all of it."

Jessica buried her face in her hands. She felt the vibration of his chair scraping, his hands urging her up into his arms. She let his strength enfold her, hardly remembering to breathe.

They stood for a long time. Her tears dried, and still she didn't pull away. She had fought this battle alone for so long.

It felt good to lean on someone else for a change. She pulled back reluctantly. "I'm sorry."

"Don't be. I'm glad I was here for you, Jess."

She tugged at the fabric of his shirt that was wet from her tears.

He grasped her hand. "It'll dry. The snot might cake up a bit, though."

She laughed and pushed him away. "I'd offer to wash it, but you don't appear to have an undershirt on. And there's an impressionable young teen on the premises."

"Yeah, we wouldn't want to give her the wrong idea." He bent his head and briefly touched her lips with his.

Before she could react, he turned toward the slider, glass in hand. "I need to head out. I wrote my cell number on the pad stuck to the fridge. Call me if you need anything." His demeanor was measured and reassuring. "Anything at all, Jess. I mean that. Don't feel you have to go through this alone."

Jessica stood with her fingers to her lips long after the door closed behind him. She told herself it didn't mean anything. A kiss of comfort, to show support. Nothing more.

She walked back inside and caught her daughter grinning from ear to ear. So, she'd seen the kiss. She crossed to the kitchen, rinsing and placing the glasses in the dishwasher with a clatter.

Amber leaned over and said, "Don't worry, Jane Doe. Ranger Reese wasn't here to check up on you. He had more important things on his mind."

* * *

The following morning Amber called Nathan to see if he would be stopping by. She hoped she hadn't scared him away.

He answered, and commented, "Hey, I was just about to call you. Is today a good day to come over?"

"Yes, how about eleven o'clock? We can do lunch, and you'll finally get to meet Jane Doe. That's if you don't scare her off with the ATV again. And can you bring your violin?"

"It's only a couple of miles, I can hoof it . . . no pun intended."

Her mom was folding clothes in the laundry room, so Amber got out of bed and used her walker to maneuver to the back of the cabin.

"Hey Mom, I called Nathan, and he said he could make it. He'll be here for lunch."

"Good. How about Chinese?"

Amber thought about the bed in the living room. "Can we eat out on the patio?"

"You bet. I'll set out the TV trays."

"Thanks Mom, I'm going to take a shower."

Soon after the doorbell rang her mom led Nathan through the cabin and onto the deck.

He had a big smile on his face and carried his violin case tucked under one arm. Jane Doe looked up but didn't move from Amber's side.

Nathan set down the case and then squatted beside Jane Doe. He reached out then pulled his hand back, looking up at Amber.

"It's okay, you can pet her. She's used to it."

"Wow. She's really something."

After lunch, her mom came out to the patio with her purse and car keys in hand.

"I've got to make a run to the store. Are you guys okay out here? I won't be long."

"Yeah, we're fine. Take your time."

When she'd left, Amber talked about Better Place Forests and the plans for her memorial.

"I've been giving it a lot of thought, and everything is pretty much set. I picked my tree. It's in a section of the forest called Pearly Everlasting. Cool, huh? It's actually the name of a wildflower that grows there. And my Cousin Hailey is going to sing 'Wind Beneath My Wings.' That's for my mom."

Nathan nodded, "That's a good choice. Did you want me to accompany her? Is that why you had me bring the violin?"

"No, she's going to sing it a cappella. I've got something else in mind for you. My dad was killed in the Iraqi war before I was born. And I want to honor him. I also want to do something special for my grandfather. My father's name is Daniel. Danny for short. Do you know the song, 'Danny Boy?' Okay, lame! Of course you do."

"The tune to 'Danny Boy' is 'Londonderry Air.' Something interesting . . . that tune preceded the song and there were other songs and hymns set to that same melody. Uh, sorry. I got off track there. Are you asking me to play it at your memorial? My dad and I often play at memorial services." He sat in the deck chair and pulled up his violin case. "Would you like me to play it for you?"

It was melancholy and haunting and beautiful all at the same time. It brought tears to her eyes.

When he finished, he set the violin back in its case and came to sit beside her on the swing. He put his arm around her, and she kissed his cheek.

"Thank you. You've no idea how much that means to me."

"I think I do."

* * *

When Amber wasn't resting, her laptop was her constant companion, along with Jane Doe, of course. She planned everything down to the last detail.

Amber's declining health made further trips to the forest impossible, so Allie arranged Zoom meetings. Better Place Forests could host up to thirty celebrants. Amber explained that was how she wanted to think of the invitees. Not mourners, not grievers, but celebrants. She chose the picture for her memorial card, one with her biggest smile and dimples flashing deep.

When they ended the Zoom meeting, Amber set aside her laptop and turned to her mom. "Do you think Uncle Matt would be willing to officiate?"

Jessica swallowed the lump in her throat. Matt had always thought of Amber as his own daughter. "I think he'd be honored. Just ignore any protests he might make about not being qualified to do it."

"How can he refuse a dying wish, right?" This she asked with a smile.

"That's the spirit. Use the guilt card. Works every time."

Amber chewed on her lip for several moments before asking in a whisper, "Allie said I can use up to a hundred eighty characters for the inscription on my memorial plaque. What do you think of *Amber Langston . . . My spirit roams free, healthy and whole at last.*"

Jessica turned and cupped her daughter's face with her hands. She kissed her forehead and looked into her eyes. "That is absolutely beautiful. It'll lift my spirits every time I read it."

* * *

Later that evening, Aunt Lexi answered her call.

"Hi Aunt Lexi. Is Uncle Matt there? Can I talk to him?" Amber asked.

"Hi, honey. He sure is. He's tinkering out in the garage. Let me get him for you. "Everything okay there?"

"Yeah, everything's fine. I just want to ask him something."

The sound of her footsteps walking through the house came through the receiver.

"Hey, Babe, Amber's on the phone for you!"

The noise of an engine revving cut off abruptly. "Hey, Amber. What's up?"

"Hi, Uncle Matt. Aunt Lexi told you Mom and I are planning my memorial, right?"

"Yes, honey, she did. Do you need some advice about that?"

"No. I was wondering if you'd be willing to officiate."

"Oh. Oh, wow. He was silent for a moment. He cleared his throat before replying. "I'm honored that you'd ask. You have my promise I'll do you proud."

"I know you will. Thanks, Uncle Matt."

Matt switched off his phone and headed into the house.

Lexi was sprawled out in his recliner. He idly thought about getting her one for her birthday.

She hit the remote to silence the television and asked, "What was all that about? Is Amber all right?"

"What? Oh, yeah. She sounded fine. It's just that she asked me to officiate at her memorial. Can you believe it?"

Lexi let her head roll back. "I think that's an excellent idea. You know she loves you. I'm not surprised at all. You accepted, right?"

"I told her I'd do her proud."

"And you will. She's like her mother in a lot of ways. Trust me, she'll have it all mapped out for you."

A week later, Lexi woke from a sound sleep to the ring of her cell phone. She looked at the readout. Her sister's number. It was 3:00 a.m.

"Jess?"

"We're at Marshall's Medical Center Hospital. It just came on so fast, Lexi. There wasn't any warning. She was in so much pain, I called an ambulance. I didn't know what else to do."

"Jess, listen to me. You did the right thing, I promise. Have they admitted her? How is she?"

"Yes, she's been admitted. She's sleeping right now. I explained to the doctors that you'll be acting as her hospice nurse."

"Okay, good. I'll make arrangements for my leave of absence today. They're expecting it, so that won't be a problem. I'll be there tomorrow, and we'll get everything sorted out so we can get her released as soon as possible. You hang in there. Everything will work out, I promise."

When Lexi walked into Amber's hospital room the next day, she was sleeping. Jessica sat next to the bed with her arms crossed tightly over her chest, and she was shaking so hard her teeth chattered.

Lexi took Jessica into her arms. "I'm here now. I've got you. We'll have Amber out of here in no time."

Lexi stepped into the hallway to consult with Amber's doctor about her release and home care.

Back in the hospital room, Lexi urged Jessica away from the bed, out of Amber's earshot in case she woke up. She took hold of her sister's hands, "Jess, we knew this was coming. I know it's almost an impossible ask, but you need to readjust your thinking; hoping for more time is the wrong focus. For Amber's sake, our focus has to be on making her last days as comfortable as possible."

Amber was back in the cabin in no time with her Aunt Lexi taking care of every detail. As she tucked the covers around Amber's waist, there was a knock at the door. Jessica answered it.

The nurse from hospice care stood on the porch. She wore light blue scrubs and appeared to be in her mid- to late fifties. Her features were unremarkable. Then she smiled, and her whole face lit up. "Mrs. Langston? Hi, I'm Deb Morris from Daylily."

"Call me Jessica." Since Amber was resting, she led Deb to the kitchen where Lexi sat with a large mug of coffee in hand. "This is my sister Lexi. Can I get you something to drink?"

Deb took a seat and shook her head. "Thanks, I'm fine. As I said on the phone, I wanted to stop by and introduce myself. Lexi, I understand you'll be acting as Amber's care provider, and that's wonderful."

Jessica took Lexi's hand and nodded her agreement.

"The vendor indicated the medical supplies were dropped off. Was it all in order?"

Lexi answered for them, "Yes, I went through everything."

"Good. And I'll be stopping by frequently to check up on things. But please don't hesitate to call any time of day or night if something arises."

A loud thump sounded at the slider.

Amber spoke up from across the room. Her voice was weak, but accusatory, "Mom, you didn't forget about Jane Doe, did you?"

"Yeah, afraid I did." Jessica got up and opened the slider.

Jane Doe soon settled beside Amber's bed.

Deb won them over when she simply smiled at the deer. Jessica imagined she'd likely seen a lot over her career.

The next morning, Jessica answered a phone call from Ellen. She was on her way from the airport, and Matt was driving her up the hill. They would arrive within the hour.

Jess watched Lexi check Amber's vital signs. "That was Ellen calling from the airport. Matt's driving her up. Thanks, Sis. I should have called first thing."

"This is the first day you haven't been in a panic. And the first day you've taken a deep breath. Don't be so hard on yourself."

Jessica nodded. Lexi was right.

The knock on the door half an hour later, announced another surprise. Nanny Meg stood on the landing, suitcase beside her. Her arms were crossed over her ample chest.

Uh Oh. Jessica knew that stance. She recognized that look. She was in for an ear full. Now she knew how her daughter felt all those years ago when her nanny levelled that look at her.

"Your sister tells me you're not taking care of yourself. I'm here to put a stop to that nonsense!" Meg scanned the room. "But first, where's my little darlin?"

Amber's reply came from the bed. "Over here, Nanny Meg."

Meg headed across the room, leaving Jessica to bring in her suitcase.

"Well, isn't this a fancy set up! Glad to see you remember your old nanny."

Amber smiled. "It hasn't been that long. There are still a couple of drops left in that perfume bottle you gave me last Christmas."

Meg gazed at the deer. "So, I finally get to meet the infamous Jane Doe!"

Jessica pulled the door closed and stood for a moment looking at the scene in the living room. Nanny Meg, Lexi, Deb Morris, and Jane Doe had all arrived to look after her little girl. Loving angels once again surrounded them.

16

The second week in August, Jessica sat at Amber's bedside. She remembered Dr. Sullivan's prognosis— three months, *maybe* more. She closed her mind against the thought.

A glance at the clock on the mantel put the time at 6:00 a.m., minutes away from sunrise. She pulled the blankets up around Amber's shoulders. Temperatures in Placerville during the month of August reached highs in the eighties, but overnight temps dipped into the sixties.

They had set up a roll away bed next to Amber, but Jessica couldn't bring herself to be even that short distance away from her daughter. She would sleep for short stretches of time, waking frequently to check for the rise and fall of her daughter's chest. Daytime hours were no different. At least until the "mother hens" shooed her away.

She heard the faint sound of a phone alarm coming from the bedroom down the hall. Her sister would soon appear to check on Amber.

Washing her hands at the kitchen sink, Lexi gave Jessica a tired smile. She slipped on a pair of surgical gloves before retrieving her stethoscope and joining her at Amber's bedside.

From the foot of the bed, Jessica watched Lexi take Amber's vital signs. She stared at the port embedded in Amber's chest. They had come full circle since her daughter's first battle with this disease.

Amber woke and smiled weakly at her aunt. She lay quietly as Lexi listened to her heart, lungs, and tummy. "Any pain, honey?"

Amber shook her head. Lexi gave her a thumbs up and retreated to give mother and daughter some alone time.

Jessica came around the bed and sat at her daughter's side. "Hi, baby."

"Hi, Mom."

"Can I do anything for you? Your lips look parched. How about some lip balm?" Jessica reached into the side table for the tube. She gently applied it to Amber's lips. "Want some ice chips?"

Amber shook her head. "Maybe a little ice cream?"

"Butterscotch or vanilla?" A standing joke. In truth, Amber seemed to tolerate the vanilla flavor best.

Jessica spoon fed her daughter the ice cream. One for Amber, one for her. It brought back memories of Amber's childhood when they'd performed the same ritual with hated vegetables.

After a few helpings, Amber leaned her head back against the pillow. They heard Jane Doe's hoofbeats crossing the room, and Jessica rose to take the bowl to the kitchen. She watched her daughter stroke the deer's head and thought about the phenomenal wonders of nature that brought this unlikely pair together.

Jane Doe settled nearby, and Jessica brought a basin of soapy water to the bed table. She removed Amber's hospital gown and her soiled diaper. Carefully, tenderly, she sponged her daughter's pale skin. It was heavily mottled with blue and purple splotches because of her poor circulation.

Bathing her daughter was a labor of love. Jessica locked away her feelings of despair in a box, one she would open under the spray of the showerhead where she could bite down on a washcloth to drown out the sound of her cries.

Amber's spirits lifted when Jessica brought out her knitted socks collection. Three, and counting. Grandma's doing, of course. Instead of knitting caps, Ellen had turned her talents to animal socks. Today's choice was green alligators. On her feet, they appeared to be chomping their way up her legs. Ellen had been busy. She had finished a pair of great white sharks, and how could she quack around without a pair of duck socks? Amber loved them all.

Lexi returned, and together they changed the bedding. Because Amber was experiencing some pain, Lexi administered medication, and Amber was soon resting comfortably again.

Jessica carried the soiled linens to the large hamper provided by the laundry service and wheeled it out onto the front porch where it would be picked up later that morning. The service was a gift from Amanda and the firm. It was a godsend.

Back inside, Jessica poured herself a large mug of hot tea. She brought it to the table and added a squeeze of lemon. The house around them was quiet, and the clink of the spoon sounded loud to her ears. She grabbed a napkin from the holder, carefully folding it around the spoon before setting it aside.

They sipped their drinks in silence until Lexi sighed heavily. Her voice barely carried across the table, "You're not going to like what I'm going to say."

"Then don't say it."

"Sis, you're not eating. You're barely sleeping. I'm worried about you, that's all."

"Convince me you'd do anything different."

Lexi opened her mouth, then closed it.

"Exactly." Jessica's response came out harsher than she meant it to. She softened her voice when she said, "I'm sorry. You're right. I know you're right. It's just that my energy— everything I have— is focused on Amber right now. It has to be."

They heard movement from the back bedroom. Ellen and Meg joined them a short time later. They nodded before going into the living room where they stood for a moment at Amber's bedside. Returning to the kitchen, Ellen poured herself a cup of coffee, and Meg busied herself making breakfast.

Meg slid a plate in front of Jessica—a broccoli and cheese omelet nearly spilling over the sides. She wanted to push it away, instead she silently conceded and picked up the fork.

The chatter around the table was mostly low-pitched small talk relaying anecdotes about the Langston clan. Meg passed around her phone to show off photos of her great grandchildren.

As for Ellen, well, she never seemed to change, except for letting her beautiful hair grow out to its natural silver-gray.

She took out her knitting needles. Her role as a grandmother sat well on her shoulders. Jessica remembered Ellen from all those years past. The Jimmy Choos and the chic fashion sense. She was still stylish, although in a more comfortable way these days. The Jimmy Choos had been replaced with ballet flats.

Jessica nodded toward the yarn in Ellen's hands. "Amber loves those socks you knitted for her. She's wearing the alligators now. They're so cute. I wouldn't mind a set of my own."

"Have something in mind?"

"Surprise me."

Ellen smiled and nodded. "I'd like to hear more about this Better Place Forests. You said Amber found it on the internet?"

Later that morning, Jessica took her laptop out to the patio. She knew there had to be families out there experiencing what she was going through. Maybe she'd come across a discussion group.

During her search, she found a website for the *Children's Neuroblastoma Cancer Foundation* in Bloomington, Illinois. On an impulse, she pulled her phone out of her back pocket and punched in the number. She was expecting to speak to a receptionist or hear a recording.

Instead, Pam Townsend, the foundation's president, answered.

Jessica was taken aback.

"Hello, this is Pam Townsend. Is anyone there? Can I help you?"

"Hello. I'm sorry, I wasn't expecting the president of the foundation to answer the phone. I promise, I'm not usually at a loss for words. This is Jessica Langston. My little girl— uh, not so little—my daughter is thirteen. Amber. Her name is Amber. She has neuroblastoma, and she's in the end stages of her . . ." The words trailed off. She felt helpless to bring them back.

"Jessica, I'm so sorry. How can I help?"

"I'm not being coherent, I know. I'm sorry."

"You're experiencing what no parent should ever have to go through. Periods of lucidity are rare. Tell me about Amber. That's a beautiful name."

Pam's voice was a soothing balm to her nerves. Jessica felt her tension ease. Her words then came to her more easily. She began to tell stories about Amber's baby years and how her little girl skipped the terrible two's only to rear back with the incorrigible three's. She relayed how her daughter's bully in preschool turned into her BFF and other great memories from years past.

Pam never interrupted her.

When she finally ran out of words, Jessica was a little hoarse and near tears.

"When was Amber diagnosed?" Pam's voice was soft.

The words didn't come as easily this time. "She was four. She suddenly complained about a stomachache that wouldn't go away. The pediatrician found a mass. That's when our nightmare began." Her voice trailed off again.

Only a beat passed before Pam said gently, "Amber is thirteen now?"

"Yes, she had eight years of remission. Amber had kicked cancer's butt. She was so sick and so brave. Now, it's started all over again. Only this time, there's no winning the war. This time *I'm* the one who has to be brave, and I just don't know if I have it in me."

"You have it in you Jessica, I promise. At the bleakest times in our life, we find our greatest strength. I wonder if I might suggest something to you. A psychologist works closely with our foundation. She is so awesome, and she's keenly attuned to what our angel families go through. Her name is Helen Vandermeer. Her practice is in Sacramento. That's in Northern California."

"Yes, I know. I live in Sacramento."

"That's perfect, then. I'll contact Helen and ask her if it's all right to share her email with you. When, and if, you're ready for it, you'll have her contact information. Our foundation holds yearly parent-and-caregiver education conferences. She has been a featured speaker at our conferences. Those videos are posted on our website. When you feel up to it, I urge you check out her video and our other speakers as well."

"I will, I promise." She knew Pam was a kindred spirit and thought this might the beginning of a long friendship with this admirable woman.

While her conversation had helped her feel less isolated, she didn't think anything could prepare her for the loss of her daughter. Filled with despair, she wondered how she would get through it.

At lunchtime Amber pushed Jessica's hand away when she was spoon feeding yogurt to her. "Come on honey, just one more spoonful. For me?"

"How about you do something else for *me*? Mom, you're not eating, and that stresses me out. I'm worried about you."

"You're worried about me?"

"Yes," Amber replied. "You've lost weight. And that makeup isn't doing much to hide the dark circles under your eyes. The covers on that roll away aren't mussed because you don't sleep on it. I know you'd do anything for me, so please—"

"Name it."

"Please take care of yourself. I need to know you're going to be okay."

Jessica put her hand over Amber's, giving it a gentle squeeze. "I promise you I'll take better care of myself."

Amber pulled her hand back and held up her fingers. "Pinky swears?"

Jessica complied. The dimples flashed briefly, but they belied the earnestness in her daughter's gaze. Before Amber closed her eyes to sleep, Jessica held her palm up to her daughter's cheek and whispered, "I love you."

* * *

True to her word, over the next few days, Jessica ate and slept better and began short, daily walks. She noticed the sunshine and exercise brought some color back to her cheeks and the dark circles under her eyes started to fade. The outdoors also brought back the smattering of freckles, but the dreaded scourge was worth it because it brought her daughter peace of mind.

A surprise package appeared on the doorstep later that week. Inside was a two-way radio set. It appeared suspiciously like the one the ranger carried on his belt. No one would own up to calling him, but she suspected it was Lexi's doing. The radio solved the problem with spotty cell phone reception in the forest, and Jessica was grateful.

A couple of days later, Jessica perched on a large boulder not far from the cabin. Despite the radio, she couldn't bring herself to be further than a short sprint from Amber's side. The sun broke through the trees, but it didn't dispel the chill she felt in her bones.

She'd been torturing herself with images of Amber's final moments. That was the reason she came across the foundation; she looked up *Neuroblastoma End of Life*. Although she spoke to Pam about her concerns, she couldn't ask the question that was burning a hole in her heart. She closed her eyes and willed away her thoughts.

"Good morning," Jessica heard.

Her eyes flew open. Only his voice gave him away, as Reese stood silhouetted against the sun.

"Sorry to startle you. Have I caught you at a bad time?"

Jessica shaded her eyes and caught a momentary hint of sadness before he masked it. "Don't apologize. I wasn't expecting company out here, that's all. I'm glad to have the chance to thank you for the radios. That *was* from you, right?"

He leaned against the boulder, waving his hand dismissively. "Figured they'd come in handy. They were just gathering dust in the storage room."

That box had not been sitting on a shelf collecting dust. The price tag had been carefully scraped away. She let him think she believed the fib and thanked him again.

"You're welcome, Jess. Amber's been on my mind, and I've been meaning to stop by, but I don't want to intrude. I hope you know that. Is it all right to ask how she's doing? If you can't talk about it, I'll understand. But I'm a good listener."

Jessica didn't meet his gaze as she tucked her hair behind her ears. She didn't want to burden him. Then she realized he *was* burdened. He was full-on invested in her little girl. When she finally looked up, his eyes told her that he was hurting, too.

"Reese, I don't think it will be long now. We met with her doctor last night on Zoom. We talked about Amber and what happens from here. The not knowing has been tearing me apart. But I was equally convinced the knowing would do the same."

"God Jess, I'm sorry."

Jessica turned away, struggling to hold it together.

She took a shaky breath and tried to put her fears into words. "The scans showed lesions on her brain. That could mean she'll experience seizures. Thankfully there are drugs to manage that. The other day I was noticing that all the towels in the cabin had been changed out for dark brown ones. Lexi's doing. I thought it was for health reasons until her doctor mentioned the possibility of nausea. And blood."

Jessica felt herself start to tremble. "Worse still, there might come a time when she won't be able to eat or drink. I'll have to make the decision whether to put her on artificial means to feed her and hydrate her."

"Just when I thought there was no way I could bring myself to deprive her of nutrients, I learned about the possible side effects of those remedies: blockages, a sense of feeling trapped. A sense of drowning. How can I possibly make the . . ." Jessica choked on the words. She covered her head with both arms, trying to catch her breath. She was shivering uncontrollably now.

"I'm here, Jess. Let me help you. I can't offer much else, but I'm here for you."

She slipped from the boulder and into the comfort of his embrace.

* * *

The week that followed brought the anguish of watching Amber slip in and out of consciousness. Jessica made a call to Daniel early that Friday morning, and he was on the next flight out.

When he arrived that evening, he dropped his bags inside
the door and rushed to Amber's bedside. As if sensing her
grandfather's presence, Amber rallied, and Daniel spent
some precious time with his beloved granddaughter until
the seizures appeared with a vengeance.

Daniel helped Lexi administer the drugs that brought
them under control. There were many soiled brown towels
over the next few days, thankfully not from blood but from
everyday normal use.

Jessica profoundly believed that Danny stepped in and
had a word with God. Although their daughter was taking
minimal amounts of food and water, Jessica never had to
make the decision about artificial nutrition.

Amber slipped completely into unconsciousness over the
weekend. Her breathing slowed, and by Sunday there were
long pauses between her breaths. In the early morning hours
of Monday, August 13, Lexi grasped Jessica's hand across the
bed and whispered, "It's time."

Lexi rose and went to wake the others.

Jessica watched from her daughter's bedside as Meg
approached and touched a trembling hand to Amber's cheek.
"Goodbye, my darling girl."

Lexi was next. "You are loved. You'll be so missed."

Daniel and Ellen held hands as they approached. Fighting
tears, her grandmother whispered, "My precious Amber, you
brought such light to this world and so much joy to our lives. I'm
going to miss you so much, but you'll always be in my heart."

Daniel stood for long moments with his head bowed,
not speaking. Jessica knew him as a man who measured his
words carefully. Never more so than now.

He cleared his throat and reached for Amber's hand. "I've
told you so many stories about your dad. But did I ever tell

you that at Christmas time, when he was a little boy, his whole body shimmied with anticipation of opening the gifts under the tree? And I know—I *know* he's there, and he's shaking with anticipation of the moment you step through those gates. The thought of that is going to help your grandpa get through this unbearable pain. Go with our love." Daniel kissed her forehead before taking Ellen's hand again. It was hard to tell who was holding up whom when they made their way out of the cabin and onto the back patio.

Alone in the cabin with Amber, Jessica lowered the handrail on the hospital bed and climbed in next to her daughter. Her breathing was so shallow that Jessica feared she'd slipped away. She put her hand on Amber's chest. It rose and fell almost imperceptibly.

Jessica fussed with her daughter's hair, smoothing it back from her face and tucking it behind her ear. It was a gesture performed many times over the years as she woke her sleepyhead child.

"My precious baby . . . They tell me you can hear me. There's so much I want to say to you. But I know you're exhausted from this fight. Just know that I love you. I love you so much. And I'm going to be okay. It might take a little time, but I promise you I'm going to be all right."

The words were barely out when Amber took a last shuddering breath and stilled. Jessica let out a wailing cry and pulled her into her arms. The others must have heard, but they didn't intrude.

Only Jane Doe broke the silence. She rose and stood at Amber's bedside, her head down. She remained in that position for several minutes, then snorted and curled her front leg into her body before sliding down onto the floor. A moment later, she rose again and made her way out of the cabin. Jessica bid her a silent goodbye. She knew this was likely the last time she'd see her daughter's little friend.

Jessica rested her cheek against Amber's head. She closed her eyes and let the reel of her daughter's short life play through her mind, starting with the moment the doctor placed her baby girl on her belly.

Her arms were numb when Daniel's voice penetrated the fog of her consciousness. "Jess . . ." His hands gently guided her out of the bed. Her legs collapsed under her when she finally stood. Daniel lifted her in his arms and crossed to the couch where he set her down and sat beside her. He took her hand and held it tightly.

Jessica was reminded of that day, years before, when he comforted her in much the same way. The day he lost his only son.

They sat quietly while activity swirled around them. Jessica never took her eyes off Amber as the medical equipment was cleared away and loving hands gently stripped the soiled garments. She heard their voices, but nothing registered until the word *coroner* pierced the fog of her mind. Horror filled her at the thought of an autopsy, and her whole body went stiff.

Daniel must have read her thoughts because he tightened his hold. "Jess, it's not what you think. Dr. Sullivan's been notified, and she'll sign the necessary paperwork. Notification of the coroner is routine. Nothing more than record keeping. That's all, I promise."

Jessica relaxed a little. "They're coming for her?"

"Yes." He glanced at his watch. "Yes, about an hour from now."

Jessica got to her feet. "I have to get her ready. She's not ready."

He rose and went out on the front porch to await the transport while Jessica saw to Amber.

Lexi helped her change out the bedding, while Meg gathered water and soap, and Ellen brought out a fresh nightgown and the knitted duck socks. Jessica nodded her approval, and Ellen set the items nearby, then lent a hand in helping prepare her granddaughter.

Jessica held it together by reminding herself this was her last gift to her daughter. Still, she could not hold back her tears when she slipped Ellen's socks onto Amber's feet. When they finished preparing her, Jessica sat at her side, holding her hand until the attendants arrived.

They were so gentle when they loaded Amber onto the gurney. Jessica kissed her forehead one final time before she pulled the sheet up to her daughter's chin. She couldn't bear the thought of covering Amber's face. The older of the two attendants nodded that he understood.

Jessica walked alongside the gurney and watched as Amber was loaded into the back of the van. She stood there long after it disappeared from sight.

* * *

Jessica sought refuge in Amber's room. She lay on her daughter's bed where her scent still lingered.

Sometime later, she heard the knob turn on the door. She didn't open her eyes, but recognized Ellen's favorite perfume, Estee Lauder's *Beautiful*.

She felt Ellen's hand touch her cheek briefly. "I've put a cup of chamomile tea and an apple Danish here on the nightstand. Try to eat a little. Okay?"

The door closed behind her, and the room grew dark again. She must have nodded off because she woke to see Lexi standing in the doorway, backlit by the faint glow of the nightlight in the hallway.

When Lexi approached the bed, Jessica stirred herself enough to put up a hand to stop her. "Don't. Please, just don't. I can't bear the thought of a lecture. Not now."

Without a word, Lexi slid onto the bed and wrapped her arms around her.

17

Three days after they came for Amber and two days after she sent everyone home, Jessica sat at the kitchen table with a plastic container of lasagna in front of her. She pushed it away.

She looked around the cabin. Like Amber's bedroom, all traces of illness and death had disappeared. Nothing remained to remind her of the last few months except her memories.

It would be two weeks before her daughter's ashes could be claimed. Matt had taken on the job of arranging everything in accordance with Amber's wishes. Jessica's relief was palpable when he made the offer.

She rose from the table and put the untouched lasagna back in the fridge. Maybe her appetite would return by dinner time.

She planned to leave in the morning. Her suitcase was packed and on the dresser top. She looked down at herself, debating a shower and change of clothes. Then decided, *why bother*?

Jessica crossed to Amber's room and stood just outside the door. Despite her resolve, she had to force herself to cross the threshold. She could well imagine Amber scolding her to get on with it. She squared her shoulders and marched to the closet, pushing the sliding door aside with determination.

She found the large plastic bag at the top of the closet in the farthest corner. It was opaque, so its contents weren't visible. The minute she held it in her hands, though, she knew. The Fluffle family.

Moments later, she sat on Amber's bed clutching the teddies to her chest. They were the worse for wear, their much-loved bodies now limp. They had lost most of their stuffing and bore little resemblance to themselves. Much like herself, she thought.

Somewhere along the way, Amber had added clothing. A knitted scarf for the missus. Mittens for Junior. And a red vest for pappa. She noticed a bulge underneath the vest and peeled it back to reveal a neatly folded piece of paper tucked into an inside pocket.

A drawing maybe? A note to Mr. Fluffle? Both were things Amber liked doing as a child. She wondered how long it had been tucked away in that cubbyhole. She unfolded the note and immediately recognized her daughter's neat penmanship. Not written by a child's hand at all.

Tears sprang to her eyes as she smoothed out the folds and started reading,

Hi Mom,

It's me, Amber.

As I'm sitting here writing this note, I'm picturing you sitting on the bed . . . and crying. If it's still morning, I'll bet you didn't touch your breakfast. If it's afternoon, I'll bet you didn't eat your lunch,

Cut it out.
That's an order!

I believe baby angels are awarded to mothers by lottery. If that's true, then I hit the jackpot! You were there for me. Always. You made me fearless as I faced the monster that hid under my bed, and the scarier one that grew inside me.

Do you know I'm in awe of you? Remember all the things I said I wanted to be when I grew up? I think it started with wanting to be a fairy when I was three. Followed closely by superhero at six. A fighter pilot at eight after Roger made me watch that old Top Gun movie like a gazillion times! I bet you didn't know I'd finally decided on the law. Yep, this apple didn't fall far from the tree.

Sorry if this is beginning to read like a greeting card. But I want you to know that you've been the best mother a kid could ask for. My friend. My confidant, My compass.

I love you. Take care of yourself cuz I'll be watching. Daddy, too.

Jessica pressed the note to her heart. She swiped at her tears and offered up a promise, "I *will* be all right. Just give me a beat. Okay?"

Later that night, the suitcases sat by the front door. Only her overnight bag remained. That would wait till morning.

Jessica poured a glass of iced tea and set it on the counter. She scooped a helping of lasagna onto her plate and stuck it in the microwave.

She promised Amber so many things over the years, and never broke a promise to her daughter. This meal was a start. As she microwaved the leftovers, her phone rang.

"Hey you, said Lexi. Just calling to see how you're doing."

"I'm doing okay. I've got everything packed, and I'll be heading out in the morning. Oh, hey, someone's knocking."

"Okay, we can talk tomorrow."

She went over to the door and peered through the peephole. Reese was standing on her doorstep.

Jessica opened the door, surprised to see jeans and a bulky knit sweater. She rarely saw him out of uniform.

"Reese. Hello."

"Hope I'm not catching you at a bad time?"

"Come in. I'm just putting together some dinner. Are you hungry? Please say yes. I've got a fridge full of leftovers. You'll be doing me a favor."

"Put like that, sure." He settled himself at the table while she got out another place setting.

Reese took a final bite of the lasagna and sat back. "So, you're headed home?"

"I'm leaving in the morning. It will be a couple of weeks before Amber's . . ."

Reese's hand closed over hers. "I'm sorry."

"No! I'm sorry. I can't fall apart at every mention of her name. The last thing I want is to scare people away from talking about Amber. Our shared memories are the only things that will keep her from disappearing."

Gathering their plates, Jessica took them to the sink. "So, yes. I'm heading back down the hill tomorrow. It's going to be a couple of weeks before the memorial in Sacramento. Her uncle Matt is making the arrangements. We'll be setting a date for it later in the week. The forest memorial will likely take place within a day or two of the Sacramento gathering."

Reese nodded. "Matt said he'd be in touch about the dates. Jessica, I wanted to talk to you about the forest memorial."

"What about it?"

"It's a private, family gathering. I'm not sure I fit that bill."

"Oh, Reese. Matt told me that Amber was adamant about you being there. You and Nanny Meg top the list. I'm totally on board with it. We all are."

Reese nodded and swallowed hard.

Jessica turned back to the sink, intending to wash the dishes by hand. She didn't want to leave anything in the dishwasher.

Reese came up behind her. "Let me help you with that."

"Okay. How about I wash, and you dry?"

When everything was put away, they moved onto the patio. Jessica curled up on the swing. Reese pulled the patio chair close and sat with his legs stretched out in front of him.

Sunset had come and gone. The night air was cool. They sat companionably for several moments listening to the sounds of nature's night shift, the chirping of the crickets joined occasionally by the hoot of an owl.

Jessica tipped her head back. "Do they ever just shut up?"

"Who's that?"

"The crickets."

"Interesting fact, it's the male crickets making all the racket. It's their way of calling their lady friends and warning off fellow lotharios."

"How is it you know so much about . . . so much?"

"My engagement with inquisitive minds. Especially young minds. Your daughter's, for instance."

"Don't I know it. So, what was she curious about?"

"The usual. What do I do on a typical day. Have I ever arrested anybody? Have I ever shot anybody? Have I ever caught anyone doing *it* in the woods."

Jessica choked on a laugh. "What?!"

"Yep, I get that last one a lot."

"So, have you? Come across naked tourists?"

"The closest I came was a couple making out in a meadow. Luckily, they were fully clothed."

"Luckily?"

"They were canoodling dangerously close to a poison oak bush."

"Oh, Reese. Canoodling?" God, she needed this tonight.

Reese smiled, then grew serious again. "I'm wondering if I might run something by you. If you can put your lawyer hat on for a sec?"

"Sure. How can I help?"

"I'm a volunteer for the Northern Sierra Big Brother program. I'm mentoring a sixteen-year-old. His name is Gabriel—Gabe Corbett."

"A forest ranger Big Brother? That's one lucky kid. Where does the lawyering come in? He's not in some kind of trouble, is he?"

"No, nothing like that. He's been asking me about emancipation. It's not a full-blown thing yet. Just something he's looking into."

"How solid would you say Gabe's home life is? Is there trouble in the family, abuse of any kind?"

"No physical or verbal abuse. It's more in the form of complete indifference."

"There's more to emancipation than just filing the petition. Even with parental consent, Gabe is going to have to show proof that he's able to live on his own. If he has no relative to live with or someone to act as guardian, he'll have to provide proof of a job with pay sufficient to support himself, including enough to cover rent. He'll also still have to go to school. Knowing all this, if he still wants to petition for emancipation, I'd be happy to talk to him."

"Gabe works part-time for a car mechanic downtown. The shop has an apartment of sorts above the shop. The owner's willing to fix it up and let him live in it rent free. Like I said, it's all preliminary right now."

"Well, at least he'll have an idea of what to expect. My offer stands if he decides to go ahead with it."

Reese glanced at his watch and winced. "I'd better be heading out. I've got an early morning ahead of me."

Jessica nodded. Halfway across the cabin she stopped and turned back to the kitchen. "Wait! How about some leftovers? I wasn't kidding, you'd really be doing me a favor. I'd hate to see all this food go to waste."

"Oh, I don't know. Are you sure you don't want to take it with you?"

"No, there's way more stuff here than I'll ever be able to eat. Please. You have a kitchen in the station, right? The containers are disposable."

Jessica filled a grocery bag and walked Reese out. He hefted the bag onto the hood of the Rover and turned to face her. His arms opened. An invitation. Jessica didn't hesitate, she stepped into the embrace and buried her face against his chest.

"Better?"

She pulled back to look up into his eyes. "Much. Thanks for the distraction, I needed it. I feel like my world's been spinning out of control. It helped ground me."

"Glad to help. Goodnight, Jess."

* * *

Jessica found herself at odds in the days leading up to Amber's memorial. She cleaned her condo top to bottom, but not Amber's room. She caught up on her emails and cracked open a book by one of her favorite authors. She set it aside when she found herself reading the same sentence multiple times.

Desperate to fill her time, she called Amanda.

"Jessica, hello. How are you holding up? You've been on my mind, and I'm sorry I haven't been in touch. I didn't want to intrude."

"That's all right. I understand. To be honest, I'm calling because I need to keep busy. I'm not ready to come back to the office, but I'd appreciate some work thrown my way."

Silence on the other end, then rustling paper. "This request couldn't have come at a better time. I'm working a thorny frozen embryo case. We're representing the husband. The couple are divorced. They did sign an agreement at the time the embryos were frozen. The wife has sole authority over their disposition. She wants them destroyed. As you know, normally, that would be that, but cancer has made him infertile. Like I said—thorny. I could use a second set of eyes on the brief."

"Happy to help. Send it over."

That brief and others Amanda sent her way helped fill the time. She had so much to thank Amanda for.

* * *

A few weeks later, Jessica entered the reception hall for Amber's Sacramento service and couldn't believe her eyes. Beside her, Lexi gave a soft whistle as they stood near the door.

Row upon row of chairs sat to either side of a long aisle. Tables lined the walls on either side of the room, each overflowing with all manner of flower arrangements in every color of the rainbow.

Dominating the front of the room was a stage. Below that, an easel held a large picture of Amber. It was one of Jessica's favorites, taken just the year before. Her smile was huge, and her dimples flashed deep. Both hands were raised in a thumbs up.

Jessica remembered that day well. Amber had just slapped her report card onto the kitchen counter. Straight A's. With a little help from Roger, her BFF, she even aced algebra.

On a table beside Amber's portrait sat a brass urn. Jessica touched her fingertips to the smooth surface and whispered, "Your Uncle Matt did good, baby girl."

The rest of the table was taken up by an enormous arrangement. Jessica counted more than a dozen varieties of flowers. She was about to move on when the object sitting in front of the arrangement caught her attention.

A hardcover book titled *Then Came Heaven* sat on the table. What appeared to be a paper sculpture adorned the cover. It depicted a girl in a field of bright red poppies with her arms raised above her head. A fawn stood watching from under a tree in full leaf. Leaning closer, she realized the figures were carved from the pages of a book. Jessica caught her breath.

Beside her, Lexi's voice was thick as she whispered, "Oh, wow. Who is this from?"

Jessica lifted the card tented beside the book and read the inscription aloud, "We hope this brings back fond memories of the joy Amber found in life. You are in our thoughts and prayers, Samantha Evans, a.k.a. Bella, the spirited daughter. And Russ Ward, a.k.a. Hux."

Someone must have flipped a switch because at that moment photos of Amber lit up the two screens set up on either side of the stage. They were on a continuous loop and depicted her life from earliest childhood.

Matt joined them. "I just got a text from Samantha. She wanted to make sure the flowers were lush and *munificent*. Her words, not mine. And that the book sculpture had arrived on time and intact. I replied all was good and texted a picture back. She asked me to tell you her thoughts and prayers are with you."

The memorial turned out to be a true celebration of life. The most somber clothing Jessica spotted was Reese's dark gray slacks that went well with his crisp white shirt and a pink and white polka dot bowtie. Amber's classmates wore the school colors, and the male associates from her firm all wore Hawaiian shirts. She couldn't believe her eyes when her boss, Amanda, appeared in pedal pushers and her bowling league shirt, and of course she had paired her ensemble with her signature Manolo Blahniks.

Matt took his place behind the lectern. He relayed stories of happy times, of which there were many. He even gave Amber credit for talking her aunt into letting him join the family. He ended by walking over to Amber's picture and tapping it with his knuckle. "When you close your eyes and think of her, this is what you see, am I right? She chose this picture for tonight for just that reason. It's how she wants you to remember her."

Kevin came next, and Jessica saw her daughter through the eyes of an eight-year-old. Their bond, their antics, and a five-year-age difference had only brought them closer. Kevin brought down the house when he retold their conversation about Amber saying she would be looking down on him from heaven but promised to close her eyes when he used the bathroom.

Matt was about to conclude the ceremony when Roger stood and made his way forward. He said something to Matt then turned to the lectern.

"I'm not much of a public speaker, but I know Amber would call me a wuss for not sharing what's in my heart."

He cleared his throat before going on. "Our friendship started off pretty rocky. I was kind of a bully when I was a kid. We attended the same preschool and Amber was kind of my favorite target. She had this long ponytail that just begged to be pulled. And I gave her the nickname Red because I knew she hated being teased about her freckles. I got a talking to, and after that I didn't pull her ponytail anymore. And I stopped calling her 'Red.' I called her poop-butt instead."

"I'm glad you find this amusing. You might understand why I was surprised when I was invited to her birthday party when she was four. As part of the festivities, the boys got to make swords and the girls made wands. But Amber was never one to follow the rules. She insisted on making a sword. Then she challenged me to a sword fight. Imagine how I felt when she fought me to a draw three times! We became the best of friends after that."

"Anyway, I want to thank you for letting me share my memories of my best friend."

Jessica watched Roger swipe at his tears as he returned to his seat. Her heart hurt for him.

Matt concluded by announcing that Hailey, Amber's cousin, would end the memorial with the song "Wind Beneath My Wings."

Before starting, Hailey glanced toward Jessica. "I'm singing this song at Amber's request. A message from her to you, Aunt Jess." She sang it a cappella, and she did her cousin proud.

Jessica's emotions swirled with a mixture of contentment and gratitude. She was grateful to Matt and Hailey and to all those who made Amber's send-off so special.

Afterward she stood in the lobby and thanked the departing guests. Her heart felt lighter when she returned to the main hall, intending to put the space back in order. She was tired, but it was a good tired.

But when she entered the hall, it was nearly cleared. The whole family had pitched in. Reese, too. There was little left to be done. The men loaded the last of the chairs on a roll-around platform and carried the flower arrangements outside to the back of Matt's truck.

The forest memorial was scheduled for two o'clock the next day, so Lexi and Matt planned to stop by the local hospital in the morning to donate the flowers.

After Matt finished putting up the screens and the audio-visual equipment, he handed Jessica the CD he made of the pictures. She grabbed his shoulders and stood on tiptoe to kiss his cheek.

Jessica accepted Reese's offer to drive her home. His Rover was roomy enough to hold Amber's picture and easel.

When they arrived at her townhome, he helped carry everything inside. Afterward, he stood in the archway leading to the living room, hands jammed into his pockets. "I'd best be heading out. Got a drive ahead of me."

"You'll be all right? The couch makes into a bed if you don't feel up to driving."

He glanced over at the couch, then back at her.

He sighed and said, "Thanks, but I've got a head honcho meeting first thing in the morning."

She nodded and swallowed hard. "I'll see you tomorrow then. We're planning on arriving at two, the reserved time. Allie asked that we not arrive early because they'll be using the time to prepare for the ceremony."

"Okay, thanks for the heads-up."

Jessica watched his car drive away with regret. When it disappeared around the corner, she softly closed the door and leaned against it, wondering how she would get through the long night ahead.

* * *

Reese and Nanny Meg joined the family and other mourners in the visitor center of the Western Sierra Forest just before two the next afternoon. As befitted the outdoor terrain, they were dressed casually.

Allie and five other forest guides led them outside. The staff sported Better Place Forests branded t-shirts.

A long rectangular table sat in a gathering area nearby. It held two bronze pails with lids and a trowel they provided to combine Amber's ashes with the soil from under the tree.

One of the young guides stepped up to Jessica. "Would you like me to bring Amber's ashes to the memorial table? When everyone's arrived, we'll all gather there to prepare the containers to be placed under her tree."

Jessica hesitated briefly. He smiled understandingly. The dimple in his left cheek won her over. She handed him the urn. "Everyone is here."

Jessica watched as he mixed Amber's ashes with the soil. She remembered Allie explaining the process. They would neutralize her ashes by combining it with native soil from under the tree, something done to protect and nourish the forest.

As she watched, the process took on a greater meaning. Her daughter was nurturing the earth.

The guide finished and handed Jessica the trowel, inviting everyone to help mix the ashes. Jessica noticed Reese held back when his turn came. She knew he was thinking of this as a rite meant for the family. She squeezed his arm reassuringly. He nodded and stepped up to the memorial table.

Afterward, Allie and the other stewards led the way through the forest pathway to Amber's tree. This was the first time most of the group had the opportunity to see the tree and its locale within the forest. There were murmurs of delight when they passed the pearly everlasting sign.

Jessica was pleased to see the staff had set everything up before their arrival. There was a watering can, a trowel, the wildflowers they would sprinkle at the base of the tree, and a binder Allie helped prepare for the simple program Amber chose.

Allie and the rest of the staff moved back and remained silent as everyone gathered near the tree.

Matt handed out the programs so that everyone could follow along before moving to the head of the small group. He cleared his throat and began.

"When Amber asked me to deliver the eulogy for this memorial, I was both honored and a little nervous until her Aunt Lexi pointed out that Amber had everything planned to the last detail, and it was likely she had already written the eulogy. While she didn't write my speech, she did add her two cents worth." He opened the binder and removed a bookmark, holding it up for everyone to see. It reads, *Keep it short and sweet!*

I'll start by reading this piece which Amber wrote. It perfectly epitomizes her views on death.

I have returned to the river of creation, the place, if there is such a thing, from where I emerged. I was an entity unknown, a slice of granite, a dash of sky, a mix of oil and water and I have returned to my original form. I am not gone, not dead, I am transformed in the way we all eventually are. Know that I will always be with you. When you feel that wind touch your cheek, you will know it's me floating by with my father by my side. He has waited all these years to hold me in his arms. And I am so grateful to finally feel his love firsthand.

Jessica choked back a sob as tears streamed down her face. She understood the message. Amber would always be with her. But believing it didn't lessen the struggle to let go. Ellen and Daniel moved to either side of her and clasped her hands. They gave her strength.

Matt took a moment to compose himself before continuing.

"Over the last few days, I've been hearing many shared memories. Amber was in a class of her own."

"Smart. She beat me at trivia games every single time, and I had a lot of years on her."

"Kind. She hated bullies, always went to bat for the underdog. Curious. *Why* was her favorite word."

"I liked her question about facial hair the best—'Why can't girls grow beards?' When I asked if she wanted to grow one, she said yes, so that she could join the circus."

"Maybe this last word describes her best: Loving. I remember her at five, holding her baby cousin. She had a real knack for soothing his colic." Matt's knuckles were white where he gripped the binder.

Left unsaid was that her daughter would never get the chance to be a mother. Jessica swayed on her feet. Daniel put his arm around her shoulders to steady her.

"I'm going to end with these words. 'Amber, our world is a little better for having had you in our lives.' And you will be dearly missed."

Matt moved back, and Hailey stepped up. She sang "Amazing Grace." The song was hauntingly beautiful, and there were no dry eyes after the last note.

Allie came forward with the vessel of mixed ashes. As she did this, Nathan and his father began the violin and flute duet of "Londonderry Air."

Jessica felt her father-in-law's shock when his whole body tensed. His voice shook as he whispered, "Danny Boy."

She leaned over and explained, "Amber shared this one thing with me. She asked me to relay her exact words—*This one's for you, Grandpa.*"

When the music ended, Allie spread Amber's ashes under the tree, encouraging everyone to participate. Afterward, she poured wildflower seeds into the hands of all the attendees and encouraged them to sprinkle them around the base and in the surrounding meadow.

"We will be sending you home with the same seeds to plant in your own gardens or in other special places Amber loved."

Kevin's gift to his cousin was the release of butterflies. He carefully slit the tape on the sides of the container and lifted out the ribbon covered box inside. He opened the lid and quickly raised it high into the air. A couple of dozen butterflies flew out.

Jessica held her hand up to shield her eyes from the sun and one landed on the tip of her finger. For a long moment, it didn't move.

She gently flicked her finger to encourage it to take flight, but the butterfly still didn't move. Hope filled the hollow space in her heart, and her lips curved into a smile for the first time that day.

18

Jessica returned to work the week after the forest memorial. She told herself keeping busy would help. She convinced herself, and Amanda, that she was ready. Sometimes she even believed it.

Over the course of the next two months, her caseload ate away at her free time. She pushed herself relentlessly. In the past, she would have relied on her paralegal for research. Now she took that upon herself. Most nights she found herself in the office till seven, and weekends were the same.

Despite her best efforts, she couldn't escape her silent, empty house altogether.

She ate because she knew Lexi would force-feed her otherwise. She managed to get some sleep because she drove herself to exhaustion. When family and friends asked how she was doing, she had a ready reply, "I'm coping all right. Keeping busy helps."

October flowed seamlessly into November while Jessica kept up her grueling pace. She gave no thought to Thanksgiving, now just a couple of weeks away.

She took a rare Saturday off when she woke to the sound of wind and rain pelting the windows of her bedroom. Later, she sat at the kitchen table with a piece of toast and a boiled egg. Her laptop sat open, but drudge work for a case wasn't her priority that morning.

She was trolling the internet, searching for the latest clinical trials and treatments showing promise for Neuroblastoma. The handbook on Pam's foundation website had a section outlining ways to help families fighting for their children's lives. One suggestion caught her attention—help find research treatment options. That was something she could sink her teeth into. It was her stock in trade.

Whenever she could carve out some time, she did research and posted her findings on the foundation's Facebook page. Pam lauded her efforts.

Jessica posted her latest findings and shut down her computer with a heavy sigh. She cleaned up her dishes and broke out the vacuum cleaner. After going over the first floor she dragged it upstairs, then paused outside Amber's bedroom. With renewed determination, she turned the knob and pushed into the room.

Instantly, the wind went out of her sails. The bed beckoned, and Jessica stretched out on top of the covers. She lay there for a long time as memories overwhelmed her. Finally, she rose and set about straightening things up. She wasn't ready to do much beyond that, but it was progress.

She was doing all right until she found one of Amber's old discarded, canvas totes under the bed. Dragging it out, she plopped it onto the bed, then flipped it over, spilling the contents.

Movie ticket stubs—one for *Coco*, another for *Wonder Woman*. Two tubes of cherry lip balm, one worn down to the nubbin, the other most of the way there. She lifted it to her nose. It still had the faint smell of cherries. She dug through a mound of old receipts and found a gum wrapper carefully folded in on itself.

Jessica sat staring down at it in her hand. She thought about how Amber used to love to pop her gum, and how it had annoyed her to no end. Now, she'd give anything to hear it just once.

Unfolding the wrapper, she brought it half-way to her lips before catching herself. She could imagine her daughter's hoot of laughter. She closed her eyes, trying to bring the image of Amber's dimples to mind. Her breath hitched in her throat when she saw only lines of worry. That was the moment she knew she needed help.

Dropping everything, she hurried to her bedroom and grabbed her phone from the charger. Before she could change her mind, she pressed the number for Helen Vandermeer, the psychologist Pam had recommended. She left a message on the office recording and breathed easier for the first time in months.

Later that evening, Jessica rummaged around in the fridge trying to figure out if she had enough ingredients for dinner or whether she'd have to order take-out again. A cheese sand-wich or a toasted cheese sandwich were her choices. She was still undecided when Lexi showed up at her door.

She had a pizza box in one hand and a handful of DVDs in the other. "Okay, I gave you some time. I gave you your space. Now I'm here for an intervention."

"It's Saturday. How did you manage a day off?"

"How I manage most primo days off. I lied. I told Mallory I had a hot date night with Matt. She took my shift, but only because I promised to spill all the *glory* details."

Half an hour later, their bellies full, they sprawled on the couch and watched Tom Hanks cavort in the sea with a mermaid. When Jessica crossed to the TV and ejected the

DVD, she ran her hand fondly over the case. "You know *Splash* was a real favorite of Amber's, right?"

"Nope. That's your favorite Tom Hanks movie. She just indulged you. Her favorite was *Big*. Want to watch it?"

Jessica surprised herself, "Yeah. Let's."

At the end of the movie, they watched the credits roll and relaxed, both too sluggish to move.

"Lexi, I called to set up an appointment with a psychologist. I know I'm not fooling anybody. I know I need help."

"So, what convinced you? The dark circles under your eyes or the ugly hair?"

* * *

Helen Vandermeer's office took up the bottom half of a long and narrow Victorian in midtown. A chiropractor's office was up top.

When Jessica stepped inside, the receptionist was on the phone. Her nameplate read Darla Gayton. Darla appeared to be in her mid-sixties and had blue eyes that fairly snapped with energy. They gazed out at Jessica from an almost wrinkle-free face. She smiled and gestured for Jessica to have a seat.

The psychologist's office was inviting. Despite being converted, the house still had the charm of the original dwelling. Sheer curtains let the light flow through the large bay window.

Jessica's attention was drawn back to Darla when she hung up the receiver. "Dr. Vandermeer is just finishing up some notes. She won't be much longer. Can I offer you a refreshment? We've got tea, or coffee if you'd prefer."

"I'm fine. Thanks." Jessica picked up a *People* magazine from the side table and barely glanced at the cover when Helen opened the door to her office.

"Jessica. Hello. Please come in."

Jessica had researched Helen on the internet, of course, but she was even more striking in person. She had chestnut hair that fell in waves to her shoulders. Jessica guessed her age at mid to late-thirties. She was attractive and chic, dressed simply in wide-leg heather grey pants paired with a white silk long-sleeved blouse. Her most striking feature was her eyes. Her large deep-brown eyes conveyed intelligence and compassion.

Jessica felt a deep calm come over her. Pam's recommendation aside, she was in the right hands. She was certain of that.

Helen gestured for Jessica to have a seat on the large cream-colored Chesterfield sofa. It nearly dwarfed the room but was comfortable and inviting at the same time. A handsome high-backed armchair was across from the sofa.

Helen sat in the armchair with her crossed hands on her lap. "Hello, Jessica. Pam said you might be contacting me. She told me a little bit about Amber. I'd like to hear from you about your daughter and your relationship with her. I'd also like to know how you're doing."

Where should I start? Jessica wondered. At the beginning, she supposed. "It was just the two of us. Amber's father was killed in the Iraq war before she was born. I realized I was on my own raising her. I was scared, mostly afraid I wasn't ready to be a mother."

"That's a common feeling, even for new mothers with a supporting partner."

"Then when I held her in my arms it changed everything." She told Helen all she could about her wonderful life with her daughter. Talking about their life together brought back so many memories. She thought it would hurt and was surprised to find it didn't. She realized the happy times far outweighed the bad.

"You know, I was dreading this meeting. I guess it's why I put it off for so long. But it feels so good to talk about Amber. I miss that. Everyone around me avoids talking about her."

"That's often the case. It comes from the fear of adding to your grief. It might help to understand that people around you are on tenterhooks, and they'll take their que from you. If you bring Amber up, they'll know it's all right to share their memories."

"You're right. I'll try to remember that." A chenille throw lay on the arm of the sofa. Jessica ran her fingers over the fuzzy, fluffy fabric, and went on, "Everyone always said Amber was an old soul. From a very young age, she knew her mind. She picked her own clothes, her Halloween costumes, even her own hairstyles. Unless they were too outrageous, I indulged her. Spoiled? Maybe just a little. But I never wanted to clip her wings."

"It sounds as if Amber was a remarkable young girl."

"She was. You asked about my relationship with her. We were best friends. We completed each other's thoughts. I can't tell you how many times I'd be thinking about something, and it was as if she'd reached up and grabbed it right out of my head."

"You read all the time about the child who looks up to you and trusts the decisions you make for them, who suddenly hits their teens and become distant and defiant. That never happened. Don't get me wrong, it wasn't always sunshine and roses. When I yelled at her that I wished she'd grow up and have a daughter just like her, it wasn't really an angry come-back. I didn't share that bit of information with *her*, of course."

Jessica paused and looked out at the side yard patio, memories flooding her mind. Helen didn't interrupt her thoughts.

After several moments, Jessica closed her eyes and refocused. She ran her fingers through the fringe on the throw to soothe her jumbled emotions.

"You asked how I'm doing. The circles under my eyes probably say it all. I'm not sleeping well. I've returned to work and set a punishing pace for myself. I do eat, but only to keep up the energy needed for my punishing pace. Pam suggested I check out the foundation handbook for parents of children with neuroblastoma. You're acquainted with it, I'm sure. But there's also a section about the angel families."

"Yes, I'm familiar with it. It's a wonderful resource."

"One particular section caught my attention. The one about helping research treatment options for families. So, that's what I've been doing. I know I'm helping families desperate for information. Every time I read about clinical trials showing promise, I wonder if letting her go was the right thing to do. The miracle cure might have been right around the corner."

"Jessica, it's so easy to get lost in all the *what if's*. It can torture you. Sometimes we have to ask ourselves what's helping us and what's hurting us. You said Amber was mature for her age and was very clear about what she wanted. When you think about that, and what your goals were together, what do you come back to? *What do you come back to?*"

Jessica hung her head, and tears came. "It was the right decision."

"Try to remember what you just admitted to yourself the next time those feeling of guilt intrude. It was a choice your daughter was adamant about. You were simply honoring her wishes."

* * *

The days leading up to Thanksgiving were a little easier for Jessica although certainly still difficult. Her session with Helen the week before had set her on the right course. She wasn't all the way there yet, but she knew she made the right decision to seek help.

Jessica sat on a bench outside the west portico of the state capitol building. November was usually a cold and rainy month, but the city was enjoying unseasonably warm weather. She was here to meet Gabriel for the first time, and she wanted this first time to be away from the stuffiness of the office. It broke her heart that the business of a dissolution of a family would come this close to the holiday season.

A noisy altercation and honking between two drivers drew her attention. Spotting Reese and Gabriel heading her way, she set aside the folder in her hands and stood up for a brief hug for Reese and a firm handshake from Gabriel.

Jessica was surprised how much they looked like father and son. The same dark hair, nearly the same height and build, the military-style haircut. She wasn't sure what she had expected. A gawky young kid, maybe. Certainly not the young man who stood before her. Reese had a big smile on his face. Gabriel was much more reserved. A serious young man. She liked that.

"Thank you for meeting with me, Ms. Langston," he said.

They sat on the bench a little apart from Reese. She had briefed him about the petition when he called.

Jessica opened the folder. "Reese informed me your parents are going to give their permission for your emancipation."

"Yes, ma'am."

"That will make the issue of a judge signing off on your petition much easier. In some cases, a judge will award emancipation without requiring a court appearance. But you'll want to be prepared, just in case."

Gabriel's face lit up. "It would be great if I don't have to go to court."

"Yes, but there's no guarantee of that. Now, I want to go over some of the requirements of emancipation. I know Reese has talked with you about this, but you'll want to keep it fresh in your mind in case the judge asks if you understand the action you're taking."

"If the petition goes through, it means you can do some things without your parents' permission. You can get medical treatment. You can apply for a work permit, or sign up for school, and you can live where you want. But school *is* a requirement. Even though you won't be under your parent's control, you can't marry without their permission."

A faint blush colored his cheeks. "That's okay, I'm not looking to get married anytime soon."

"You'll need to provide proof of your ability to support yourself and have a place to live. I understand you're employed by Mr. Richard Johnson, of Johnson's Auto in Placerville and he's providing living quarters. Is that correct?"

"Yes, ma'am."

"Good. But understand this. Emancipation can be canceled at any time. Obviously, breaking the law is number one on the list. Lying to the court is another."

"That's not a problem."

"Glad to hear it. I've given you the basics, but there are very detailed requirements associated with taking this step. I've included the website for an emancipation manual put out by the Legal Services for Children. It's seventy-seven pages, so

I saved you the cost of printing it out." She handed the file to Gabriel whose hands shook ever so slightly when he took it.

"Thank you, Ms. Langston. How much do I owe you?"

"Well, I've not eaten lunch, so a hot dog from that stand across the way would be welcome."

Gabriel's shoulders relaxed. "The works?"

"No onions. But before you do that, I wanted to let you know that I've included the name and number of a family law facilitator in Placerville. This facilitator is an attorney who'll help you prepare your court documents. There's no charge for his services, and he can help you complete the forms to request a waiver of the fee for filing your petition. One last thing. This attorney is only a facilitator. He won't appear in court with you."

Gabriel appeared visibly upset over that. "I'll be alone in front of the judge?"

"As I said, I don't believe it will come to that." When he still looked worried, she added on impulse, "I'll tell you what, if a court appearance is required, I'll make the time to appear with you."

"Thanks, Ms. Langston. Thanks so much!" Gabriel reached out and hugged her. She was touched by his gesture and knew she had made the right decision.

"You're welcome, Gabriel. Now how about that hot dog?"

They watched Gabriel hurry toward the stand. "You did good, counselor," Reese said.

* * *

Jessica had nodded off in her recliner one evening in mid-February when she was startled awake by the ring of her phone. It was Reese. The hellacious day she had in and out of court was reflected in the weary pitch of her voice. "Reese. Hello."

"You sound exhausted. Rough day?"

"Yeah, not one of my best."

"It was the same the last time we spoke. And the time before that."

"Sorry."

"Well, I've got some news that will cheer you up. The judge signed off on the emancipation petition. No court appearance. Gabe is over the moon."

"Oh, I'm so glad. That does make me feel good. Thanks for letting me know."

"You bet. I was wondering if I could take you out to dinner this Saturday night to celebrate?"

She didn't answer right away. She was tired, and sorting through her own thoughts took some effort. And she didn't want to encourage something she wasn't ready for. "Reese, it's not that I wouldn't like to take you up on that. I have strong feelings for you. You know I do. But I'm so broken right now. I'm still trying to piece myself back together. I'm seeing a psychologist. I've not told many people that. It's helping, but it's slow going. I honestly don't know when I'll be ready to move forward."

"It's good to hear you're getting help. As for you and me, well, I'm a patient man. That's especially true when it comes to something worth waiting for."

Sessions with Helen continued, and Jessica could see she was making progress. Though she no longer slept in Amber's bed, spring cleaning had come and gone, and her daughter's room remained untouched.

Helen asked her if Amber's things brought her comfort. They did. After all this time, they still did.

Then Helen brought out the big guns. What would Amber say if she were still here? Jessica didn't have to give *that* a second thought.

Helen asked if Amber had a favorite charity she might consider donating her things to. Jessica found one for American vets that accepted donations of clothing and accessories. Amber would have approved of that. Jessica even had a stack of storage boxes leaning against the wall of her daughter's bedroom. They were empty, but that was progress, wasn't it?

The biggest hurdle to move beyond was the pain of loss. Helen explained it would change, that she'd feel less and less miserable each day. She assured her it was okay to let those feelings go, that it didn't amount to a betrayal of Amber.

Taking a page from Helen's playbook, whenever she felt herself sinking into that darkness, she would ask herself what Amber would say if she saw her like that.

* * *

The June heat in the valley made her anxious to escape to Placerville. Amanda gave her permission to use the cabin as often as she liked. Jessica suspected she'd taken it off the market for just that reason. She even had her own key.

On her way through town, she stopped for goodies to fill the picnic basket sitting in the backseat. She planned to have a good sit down at Amber's tree the next day. She checked in with Allie, and no memorials were scheduled.

Close to noon the next day, she headed out, maneuvering through relatively light traffic on the drive to Pollock Pines, which was fifteen minutes up the highway. Her spirits always

lightened when she was on her way for a visit to Amber's
final resting place. Not buried, not interred or entombed, but
resting . . . it helped to think of her daughter in those terms.

Jessica parked her car and headed into the visitor's center.
She spotted Allie walking out from the office area.

"Jessica, hello! It's a gorgeous day for a visit."

Jessica smiled and nodded, "It is!"

She walked the trail slowly, enjoying the beauty and peace-
ful tranquility of nature at its best. In this cocoon the forest
offered, she could pretend, for a moment, that this was just a
hike. An outing like they'd experienced many times over the
years. Lost in those memories, she extended her hand, fully
expecting Amber to grasp it. She imagined Amber's laugh.

The echo faded as she neared her daughter's tree.

She spread out the blanket she carried under her arm and
sat near Amber's memorial marker. Pulling the sleeve of her
sweater over her fingers, she wiped the surface of the marker.
She read again the words that brought her comfort, *Amber
Langston . . . my spirit roams free, healthy and whole at last.*

Jessica ran her fingers over the inscription. "I haven't
visited as often as I would like. The firm has been throwing
a lot my way. I promise I'll take the time to get away and come
visit my favorite girl more often."

Reaching into the picnic basket, Jessica pulled out a
chicken drumstick. She waved it in the air between bites.
"So, how are the visits with Nathan going? Yes, he calls now
and then. Even admitted he comes up here on occasion. He's
special, that one."

She ate while she talked about the happenings in the world
of the living, thinking the words when her mouth was full. She
paused at one point after taking a long drink of her tea.

Wiping her mouth, she pointed the thermos at the sky, "See, I'm eating and keeping hydrated. Gained a little weight, too. I told you Helen was making progress. Speaking of which, I've got boxes, so I can pack up some of your things for the American Veteran's Charity. And I'm planning on calling for a collection real soon. Honest."

An hour passed before Jessica rose and brushed off the seat of her pants. "Well, I think I'd best be going, my gluteus maximus is starting to go numb. I'll be coming back more soon; work schedule be damned." She kissed two fingers and pressed them to Amber's marker. "Love you. Miss you."

Jessica shook out the blanket and was about to fold it up when she looked up and spotted a deer, no more than forty feet away. Jane Doe. There was no mistaking the chewed-up ear. Jane Doe pawed at the ground then moved aside, revealing her fawn. The young deer nudged her mother's neck, then turned to look at Jessica.

The fawn came forward slowly, pausing several times. She stopped an arm's length away. The air around Jessica felt heavy, charged somehow. The hair rose on the back of her neck. The deer stood very still, never taking its eyes off her. Jessica reached out with trembling fingers, palm up.

The deer pressed her cheek against her hand. The memories flooded back. Amber's cheek pressed against her palm, seeking comfort. It couldn't be real. She must be dreaming. She would wake up at any moment from this beautiful dream.

But she felt the fawn's breath and the warmth of her fur. They stood still for a long time. The deer finally raised her head but didn't move away.

Jessica barely took a breath. She kept perfectly still; afraid she would startle her and break the wondrous spell.

Finally, Jane Doe let out a snort. The fawn looked toward her mother, but didn't move.

Deep inside her, in that raw, hurting place, Jessica knew this was real. "It's okay. I'll be all right now, Amber. I promise . . ."

EPILOGUE

Boxes were everywhere. Jessica looked around in utter frustration. First order of business, hire an assistant.

Where was her sister? She was close by more than an hour ago, and it was nearly noon. Not that she would be much help. Lexi had trouble organizing her sock drawer.

Jessica spotted the box she'd been hunting down. A quick slice of the cutter and she lifted out the hand-forged sign: a scale of justice and below that, *Jessica Langston, Family Law.*

Her own practice. Wow. In Placerville. A dream come true. Jessica ran her finger over the engraving. She still found it hard to believe, but here was proof.

Her phone rang just as the bell above the door let out a clamorous, jarring sound. Getting rid of that bell was at the top of her to-do list. She fished the phone out from under crumpled newspaper scattered on the top of her desk and brought it to her ear.

Lexi was breathless on the other end of the line. "Sorry, had to stop for gas. I'll be there in ten."

Jessica barely got the gist of the conversation as she turned and saw Reese standing in the doorway. Her heart fluttered, and she said, "Reese."

Lexi's *woo-hoo* snapped her back to the phone call.

"Uh, you know what, Sis? I'm feeling a little hungry. Think I'll stop by that burger joint and pick up some fries. I'll be another half-hour at least."

A smile played at the corners of Reese's mouth as her phone slipped from her hand and clattered to the desk. He held her gaze and asked, "Did I catch you at a bad time?"

"No, your timing is perfect."

ACKNOWLEDGMENTS

While one might think that an author writes alone, the truth is that we make the journey with an entire crew at our side.

I would like to thank my family and friends for their support and encouragement along the way. I especially want to acknowledge my dear friend Margie Cassie, gone too soon. You are missed.

Randy Peyser, of Author One Stop, who got me the book deal. And my incredible book coach, Lana McAra. Thank you for picking me up when I fell and for getting me across the finish line. I couldn't have done it without you.

I want to thank the staff at SelectBooks for believing in my story. I also want to express my gratitude to my editor, Nancy Sugihara, for all the late nights and for helping me polish my craft. And another big thanks to my book designer, Janice Benight for the gorgeous book cover. It's as if my character walked out of my head and stepped onto the cover!

While writing *Amber's Way*, I had the good fortune to make many wonderful connections and wish to give a special thanks to:

Patricia Tallungan, President and Founder of the Children's Neuroblastoma Cancer Foundation, Bloomingdale, Illinois. A true champion of helping families find hope in the darkest hours of their lives.

Dr. Mark Ranalli, Nationwide Children's Hospital, Columbus, Ohio. For taking the time out of your busy schedule to explain the MIBG treatment.

Dr. Hillary Van Horn-Gatlin, Clinical Psychologist Kaiser Permanente Hospital Sacramento, CA. Thank you for suggesting the role-play. It gave me the opportunity to speak in Jessica's voice and made the story authentic.

Mr. Sandy Gibson, Co-Founder and Chief Innovation Officer, Better Place Forests. Thank you for your consent to feature one of the company's conservation memorial forests in my book. And another big thanks to Gillian Nye, Allison Callaway, Libby Friede, Jessica Nobriga and Alicia Heber for sharing your expertise about the process. Your dedication and enthusiasm came through in every conversation. A special note: All information is factually depicted in my story with the exception of the Western Sierra Forest, which is set to open in 2023.

El Dorado County Search and Rescue is an amazing group of volunteers whose mission is to save lives and reduce human suffering. My gratitude goes to Kathy Albrecht and Deputy Scott Bare for giving so generously of their time and for sharing Pip's remarkable story.

And lastly, my heartfelt thanks to my daughters Kimberly and Stefanie, my biggest cheerleaders.

All errors are my own.

ABOUT THE AUTHOR

Photo by J.C. Penney Portraits
Roseville Galleria, Roseville, CA

GLORIA GALLOWAY is a member of the Authors Guild and the Sacramento chapter of the California Writer's Club. She has enjoyed storytelling since childhood. She grew up in Sacramento, California, within driving distance of the beautiful Sierra Nevada mountains, which provided inspiration for writing *Amber's Way*.

She is a strong advocate for the Children's Neuroblastoma Cancer Foundation and the volunteers who work for the Eldorado County Search and Rescue Council (ESARC).

Gloria enjoys traveling and spending time at home with family and friends. She is often found curled up with a book next to her rescued cat, Summer.

Meg Hunter Photography, Auburn, California

Pip

Retired K-9 dog with more than 13 years of dedicated service to El Dorado County, California Search and Rescue and the California Rescue Dog Association (CARDA).Pip is still on the trail, but simply enjoying the view these days.

Children's Neuroblastoma
Cancer Foundation

A percentage of the book sales for *Amber's Way*
will be donated to the
Children's Neuroblastoma Cancer Foundation

360 W. Schick Rd. Suite 23, Unit 211
Bloomingdale, IL 60108
info@cncfhope.org
1-(630)380-4058